A HARD BARGAIN

"All right," Morgan said thinly. "You go back to Santa Fé. We'll go on, and we'll take the traps."

"What guarantee have I got that I'd ever see you again?"

"My word."

Ryker snorted digustedly. "Would you take mine?"

Morgan was silent a moment, digesting that. Then he grinned slowly and balefully. "I guess that leaves you one thing."

"What?"

"Come or not, like it or not, take my word or not, I'm heading north . . . and I'm takin' the outfit."

Ryker took a step backward and in the same swift motion elbowed aside his bearskin coat to draw one of the Ketland-McCormicks. Morgan followed him in a single long lunge, swinging his five-foot rifle up in a vicious arc. It whipped against Ryker's neck as he pulled the pistol. . . .

THE CAVAN BREED
LES SAVAGE, JR.

LEISURE BOOKS   NEW YORK CITY

50¢

THE CAVAN BREED

Chapter One

Don Tomás Biscara was waiting for her. The room was dark, and she could barely see him in the high-backed inquisitional chair. He made her think of a spider in its web. Teresa Cavan stopped just within the door, not wanting to go farther. She was barefoot, wearing only the *camisa* and coarse wool skirt of the *campesina*. They did little to hide the ripe curves of her nineteen-year-old body. She saw Biscara's eyes rest on the lace at the neck of the *camisa*, pulled taut by the bold swell of her breasts.

"Qué bonita," he said. "How beautiful." His voice was a cat's purr. He beckoned with a slim swordsman's hand. "Closer."

She did not move. His smile faded. In Santa Fé of 1837 a *campesina* did not decline the order of a man like *Don* Tomás Biscara.

"Have you no ears?" he asked.

Teresa's mother pushed her from behind. She took a pair of stumbling steps into the room, stopped again. There was no shyness in her expression, no fear. Her face was too boldly formed to be delicate. It was tawny-fleshed with high cheek bones, framed by a tumbling mass of fire-red hair. Her eyes caught reflection from a distant window, looking green as jade. Their heavy lids gave them a smoldering insolence.

"You have been here two weeks now," the *don* said. "I

thought to give you time to get over the death of your husband and child." She did not answer. He moistened his lips. "The Navajos will be punished. The governor sent out dragoons to find the men responsible." Still she did not speak. Irritation made his voice rusty. "Your mother has been faithful here. She tells me you are a hard worker, quick to learn . . . and willing."

"I will work."

"Ah . . . ?" he said. His piercing black eyes swung for a moment to the woman standing behind her. Teresa's mother, Dolores Cavan, in the same kind of flimsy *camisa* and a grimy wool skirt, not yet forty, but already gnarled and stooped and half blind with the age that swiftly overtook so many women in this barren land. *Don* Tomás Biscara said to her: "You may go now."

Dolores Cavan caught her daughter's arm with callused fingers. "He is your *patrón* now. Remember that. Your *patrón*." She turned and disappeared in the darkness of the hall behind Teresa.

Don Tomás Biscara's lean brown hands, holding the carved arm of his chair, were all cord and sinew. Teresa had known hands like that once, so expert at playing a mandolin or holding a sword or finding the secret places of a woman's body.

"Cavan," he said. "An Irish name."

"My father was Irish."

"But you were married to Pepe Rascón."

Her eyes went blank. Rascón. The very name rekindled a memory of hate and misery she wanted to bury and forget. "I've taken back my father's name," she said.

He shrugged. "As you wish." He smiled sardonically. "An Irish father, a Mexican mother. An exotic combination."

She did not answer. He made an impatient sound and

rose, lithe as a panther, every inch the *hidalgo,* the aristocrat. His hair was jet-black, queued behind his neck. He wore a blue velvet jacket, *calzones* that fitted tight to the leg and were adorned with silver buttons on the outer seams from hip to calf. His boots were of cordovan, soft as silk, their thin soles making a brittle clatter against the hard dirt floor as he walked to the cabinet at the end of the room.

"You are beautiful. We will admit that." He poured wine into a pair of silver goblets. "The work in the fields is hard. Would you rather be a servant in the house?"

"Yes."

"It can be arranged." He brought a drink to her. He tilted his own goblet, looking over its rim at her body. It sent a dull throb of anger through her. From the first, she had known how it would be. She had hoped against hope that it would be different. She had told herself that in the protection of Santa Fé, the capital of New Mexico, with the man whose family had been *patrónes* of her people so long, it should be different. A *patrón* was like a father to his *peónes;* he watched over them and protected them and supported them in their sickness and old age.

"You do not drink," he said. She looked at the glass, without speaking. The shadows moved smokily in the hollows at his temples and beneath his sharp cheek bones, coupled with his pointed black goatee, they rendered his face distinctly satanic. He smiled maliciously and waved at a chair. "Be seated, then. Perhaps I can open your heart with a song."

She watched his face for mockery. Was this a game? Or was he so habituated to this prelude that he had to execute it to the point of absurdity? Reluctantly she moved to one of the stiff chairs, lowering herself into it. Near it, against the wall, was one of the *colchónes* that lay about the room. These were mattresses, rolled up and covered with bright Navajo blankets during the day. In this barren and isolated frontier, even the houses of the rich had no bedrooms, and few chairs or tables. The finest people were accustomed to sleeping on the floors at night, rolling up their mattresses during the day to sit on. He got his mandolin from the corner, seated himself cross-legged on the mattress before her, and began his song:

> *Teresa, tu eres hermosa*
> *Como los rayos del sol . . .*

This was the way it was done. The tradition of courtship set by a million young *caballeros* back through the years, sitting on their hams and playing their mandolins and singing one thing and thinking another. It deepened her anger that he should take her acquiescence so for granted—licking his chops and mocking her with a ritual that could have meaning only to the daughters of the rich. Yet this was an accepted custom of the land. He was one of the most powerful men in New Mexico, offering her his protection, his patronage, his hearth and his bounty, in return for something that a hundred others of her class and her background had given him without question.

She had been married and knew what it was to bed with a man and knew no fear of the act itself. And yet his suave cultivated voice and his smooth hands and his lickerish anticipation only intensified the rebellion in her. It was a rebellion that went way back—so far back she didn't know when it had started. But somehow this was a culmination. It came like a decision she had made, yet could not remember making. It was simply knowledge, a certainty, a sharp focusing of all the pain and the tears and the subjection of the years behind her.

With a discordant twang, he set the mandolin down. "Do

my verses bore you?" Black eyes shimmering with anger, he rose, not waiting for her answer now. With one practiced movement he slid the Navajo blanket off the *colchón* and unrolled it. "Perhaps I made a mistake," he said thinly. "I was according you the courtesy of a gentlewoman. A *moza de labranza* is courted differently."

She did not move. She saw the anger fill his face and knew a sudden impulse to flee, but she could not even give him the pleasure of seeing her run. She was gripped by an adamant refusal to yield to him in the slightest way. He stood above the mattress, lean cheeks flushed, waiting for her to come to him. When she did not move, he took one step to her and grabbed her arm. She rose to his strong pull, and, when she was against him, she hit him across the face with the goblet.

"*¡Chingada!*" With this oath of pain he stumbled blindly backward, falling heavily to the floor. The blood and wine dripped from his face onto the cement-hard adobe of the floor.

Teresa stood transfixed for that instant. The anger and the rebellion were drained from her momentarily by the enormity of what she had done.

He turned his contorted face up to her. There was a vicious anger in his eyes, but there was surprise, too. She realized this had probably never happened to him before, with one of her class. She had violated a tradition. It was the last thing he had expected. With a curse he started to rise.

The spell was broken, and she turned, this time unable to block her simple animal impulse for escape. Before she could reach the door, it was pulled open by García, one of the numberless servants of the household. He blocked the way, and Teresa wheeled around and ran for the other door out. But Biscara was on his feet, near this door, and it took him but

11

three stumbling steps to reach it. She stopped, six feet away, panting and flushed.

Biscara wiped blood from his face, transferring his rage to García. "Do you dare intrude at a time like this? I'll have you flogged."

The man cringed like a sycophant. "But *patrón* . . . I did not know . . . there is a personage . . . *Señor* Kelly Morgan . . . he wishes an audience. . . ."

Biscara gulped, nodded, disappeared down the hall, calling for Igualo. In a panic, Teresa darted for the door he had left open, but she saw that he was only a few feet away, and another man was coming from the opposite end of the hall. He was bigger than García, a Taos Indian, thick-chested and ape-armed, his loose cotton *taparrabo* flapping around hairy calves.

Biscara smiled maliciously at her. His voice was nasal, vicious. "It is a pity we could not continue, *mi* Teresa, but there are many ways to break a horse that will not be ridden."

Igualo and García entered the room. In the last instant she tried to evade them, but García moved, quick as a ferret, cutting her off, and Igualo swung in from behind, snaring an arm. While she was still writhing in their grasp, she heard the scrape and rattle of spurs in the hall leading from the parlor. Like a frightening apparition, a huge man appeared in the door.

She did not think she had ever seen one so tall. She recognized him as one of the Yankee trappers who frequented Taos and Santa Fé when they were not in the mountains. He had to stoop as he stepped through the door to keep his coonskin cap from being knocked off. From under the cap a veritable golden mane of hair spilled out. He wore an antelope blanket for a shirt, its four tails held at the waist by a broad black belt, and his elkhide britches were slick and blackened with the grease of a thousand meals. The spurs were great cartwheels with jingle bobs on the rowels that tinkled and rattled at his slightest movement. He had blue eyes, the color of ice in shadow, and there was a satyr's arch to his tufted eyebrows that lent his whole face a devilish look. He saw Teresa, and then moved his glance to the blood still oozing from Biscara's cheek. His chuckle was malicious.

"Looks like you picked one outen a varmint's cave."

Biscara was white with outrage. "*Señor* Morgan, could you not have the manners to wait in the *sala?*"

Morgan's grin died. "I got tired waitin'," he said. "My party's ready to go. If you still want a stake, it's time we made the deal."

Controlling his anger with obvious effort, Biscara spoke to García: "Take her out!"

She began to fight again, as they dragged her toward the rear door, but both men were field workers, and she was helpless in their grasp.

"*Tu borrachones,*" she panted. "*¡Hijos de la gran puta . . . bueys, rumberos, pendejos!*"

She heard the American chuckle again. "Curses like a muleskinner. You got a real chili pepper, Biscara."

Then they were in the long dark hall, with its adobe walls, whitewashed with *yeso* and light filtering through the spindle door at the end. The grapevine had already informed the household of what was to happen. They were gathered in the patio, a score of barefoot, sun-browned servants, muttering among themselves and calling questions to Igualo and García. Then Teresa's mother broke through the press, catching at Igualo's arm.

"Please, Igualo, I give you something. I have saved three *pesos* for a candle to burn before *La Conquistadora. . . .*"

He shook his head, pushing her away. "It is the word of the

master, old woman. We can do nothing."

She followed them like a whipped dog, wringing her hands, muttering prayers to her patron saint. Teresa could see the fear in her mother's face; but she could see the resignation, too. Beaten by this land, broken on the wheel of its primitive ways and its ceaseless labor, aged and feeble before her time, left with no strength to rebel or fight back. It only made Teresa struggle more frantically. But they finally got her into one of the stables at the rear of the patio.

They lashed Teresa's wrists high to the crossbar at the mouth of an empty stall. Her heart was pounding from the struggle, and she sobbed for breath. She saw García get a horsewhip from its peg on the wall. Igualo bunched her skirt at her hips and gave a sharp tug. The skirt and undergarment jerked painfully across her hips, then was ripped down about feet, and left there.

"Forgive me, *señorita*," Igualo said.

The whip swished through the air, cracking across her posteriors. The pain ran like fire, and she stiffened, all her weight swinging against her lashed wrists, biting her lips to keep from crying out.

"A thousand pardons, *señorita*. I am sorry it could not be across your back."

The lash fell again, echoing through the stable with a sharp crack. This time Teresa could not help her stifled cry. She could hear her mother pleading with the guards, begging Igualo to stop. She could feel the blood now, running down the globes of her buttocks.

"With an aching heart, *señorita*."

The crack of the whip came again, the pain branding her flesh with another bleeding welt. The cry was torn from her. The wailing. Then it was a new sound, a husky outcry of voices from outside, someone's shout, like the clap of thunder rising above all the others. Dizzy with the pain, she turned her head. First, she saw that great yellow head, towering above the shawls of the women and the black heads of the men. Then one of the guards at the door was flung aside so hard that he tripped and fell full length in the straw. And the American was in the stable, like an angry god in his wrath.

"What the hell's fixin' here?"

Both Igualo and García were gaping at him in surprise. Before they could answer, *Don* Biscara elbowed his way through the mob, right on Kelly Morgan's heels. His face was pale, and his eyes blazed.

"*Señor,* you have no right to interfere. This is no business of yours."

"A woman bein' whipped is any man's business," Morgan said. "Cut her down."

Biscara drew himself to his full height. There was a white ridge about his compressed lips. "You will leave at once, or I will turn you over to the governor."

For answer, Morgan slipped twelve inches of Bowie knife from its brass-studded sheath at his belt and took two long steps that placed him beside Teresa. Before any of them could move, he had slashed the rawhide binding her wrists. She sagged against him, almost falling. As from a distance she heard Biscara's voice.

"You are a fool, Morgan. I give you one last chance. Release her and leave here."

"On your promise that you won't touch her again."

"She belongs to me. I will treat her as I choose."

"The hell you will."

"You have made your choice, then," Biscara said. "Igualo, disarm this man and take him to the Palace."

A dozen other *peónes* had pushed into the stable. Still holding Teresa with one hand, Morgan swung to face them.

They did not move for a moment. He made a frightening figure, towering a foot above the tallest of them, his knife glistening wickedly in one trap-scarred hand.

"Igualo," Biscara called.

With a grunt, the Taos Indian responded, swinging his whip back and lashing at the trapper's hand, but Morgan swung his knife up, and steel parted leather like hot butter. Igualo gaped incredulously at the two feet of his whip dropping to the floor. But the others had begun to pull their *sacas de tripas*—the wickedly curved gets-the-guts knife of the Mexican peasant.

Before they could surge against Kelly Morgan, he dropped Teresa and lunged at Biscara. The *don* tried to jump back, but Morgan caught his arm, almost tearing him off his feet as he swung the man around. Holding the man that way, with Biscara's arm twisted cruelly between their two bodies, Morgan placed his knife blade against the man's throat. It stopped the surge of the other men.

"Clear the way now," Morgan told them in his cow-pen Spanish.

Sullenly the men parted, leaving a path into the patio. Morgan looked at Teresa. She had pulled her torn skirt back over her lower body, holding it together at one side.

Biscara's voice left him in a strained, wheezing bleat. "Teresa, if you go, your life will be forfeit."

She knew he meant it. He was powerful enough in the province to have it done. Yet she knew how it would be if she stayed. She had made her choice, back in that room, when she had hit Biscara. She moved to the trapper's side.

It was like marching down a gauntlet. The servants stood on every side, knives in their hands, watching for some break, looking up at Biscara's face for some indication. But he was powerless. He walked like a man on eggshells, with that knife pressed to his Adam's apple. They came to the *zaguán*—the great door in the wall through which passed the carts and coaches and riders. Morgan told Igualo to open it.

The bar was lifted from its sockets, and the heavy gate, groaning and protesting, was swung open.

Dolores Cavan was wringing her hands again and pleading with her daughter. "Teresa, do not do this thing. It is better that you stay. He is your *patrón*. He will be your protector, the food for your belly, the roof over your head. . . ."

Teresa looked helplessly at her mother. Holding her skirt together, she followed Morgan out. East of them, down San Francisco Street, lay the main portion of Santa Fé, a tawny huddle of flat-roofed mud buildings. At the hitch rack beside the *zaguán* stood a roan horse.

"Step aboard," Morgan said.

She took the reins off the hitch rack. The half wild horse shied and reared. She pulled him down, toed its wooden stirrup, and swung into the saddle, almost losing her skirt in the process and wincing with pain as her backside touched the leather.

"*Señor,*" Biscara said, "you will regret this. I will have every dragoon in the province on your trail in ten minutes."

Without answering, Morgan swung him around suddenly, releasing him. The action slammed Biscara back into the men massed in the open gate, checking their anticipated rush for an instant. In that instant Morgan ran for his horse, vaulting up over its rump, and slamming to a seat directly behind the saddle. His arms were around Teresa's waist, and he raked the horse with his huge spurs, deafening Teresa with his roar.

"Now, you spotted bastard . . . light a shuck!"

Chapter Two

At breakneck speed the horse raced down San Francisco Street toward the sun-drenched plaza. The stringy bulge of Kelly Morgan's biceps pressed so hard against Teresa's ribs that it hurt, but they held her tightly in the saddle.

"The governor's in that Palace on the square, ain't he?" Morgan asked. She stiffened a little as she realized he meant to take her there. Her complete lack of response made him add, almost as a question: "He'll protect you, sure?"

"He will give me back to Biscara," she said in English.

Her tone was metallic. He took the reins from her hands, pulling the horse out of its mad gallop. "He won't do that. Not after what Biscara was doin'."

"Biscara will have another story. He is a powerful man. The governor will believe him."

The abysmal emptiness of her voice convinced him. He stared at the reins till the horse came to a complete stop by the mouth of Burro Alley. They both looked back and saw a dozen horsemen galloping from the *zaguán* of Biscara's house.

"You got any people in town?" Morgan asked.

"My people are with *Don* Biscara."

"Somebody that'll protect you?"

"Not here. Only a cousin in Taos."

He swore softly to himself, but there was no backing out now. He wheeled the horse and headed it at a gallop into Galisteo Street. They passed blank walls of houses sleeping in the sun, creaking two-wheeled *carretas* with Indian drivers. Then they were across the Alameda and sliding down into the bottoms of the Santa Fé River. Splashing into the water to hide his trail, Morgan turned east toward the mountains.

In a few minutes, with the horse roaring and laboring beneath them, they reached the Camino del Cañon, following the river toward Taos. They passed snowy fields of marguerites that had popped up after a summer rain, the gray bayonets of aloe sawed at the horse, and he almost pitched his riders, shying at a roadrunner that darted from a clump of beargrass bushes. Then it was the first broken, rising country, where piñons grew dense and scrubby. The trapper looped and backtracked, creating a dozen false trails. He followed the river into a cañon that led them deeply between the jaws of the mountains. At last, Morgan pulled to a halt on a ridge, with the horse coughing and wheezing.

Beneath them, like the surface of an undulant sea, the tops of pines and spruce and piñons billowed away toward the west. There was no sign of pursuit. The tension of flight began to slip away from Teresa. For the first time the bizarre element of all this made its impression. In the space of a few short minutes her whole world had changed completely. She had been snatched from the comfort and familiarity of surroundings that had been her life and had been plunged into the unknown with a perfect stranger. But she had known the implications of the step she had taken—she had known exactly what she was choosing when she opposed Biscara. It was not in her to go back now. She took a long, deep breath, rising in the saddle and pulling her torn skirt together. The stripes across her buttocks continued to give her a dull, aching pain.

Her father's razor strap had never hurt her as much as those few strokes with a horsewhip.

"Where to now, *señor?*"

Morgan started the horse squirming down through the timber. "I guess we shook 'em off." Then he grinned ruefully, and it etched a million tiny lines into his weather-roughened young cheeks. "It all happened so fast I still don't know which way I'm aimed," he said. "I guess the Morgans always was suckers for red-headed women. We got a camp northward. We'll decide what to do there."

As they rose through the Sangre de Cristos, she found her mind returning to the last half hour, to *Don* Biscara, to the choice she had made. Had it really been a decision, there in the room? Or was it merely the logical turning point in a road that began so many years ago? That began, perhaps, with her father—Johnny Cavan, green-eyed, red-headed, rakehell, gambler, adventurer. In 1812 his world wanderings found him in Santa Fé, then the capital of a province still under the colonial rule of Spain. His colorful personality and his flair for making friends won him a place in the circle of grandees, one of whom was *Don* Celso Biscara, the father of *Don* Tomás. So on one of his visits to the Biscara house Cavan saw Dolores. She was but a *moza de la hacienda,* a slave of the powerful family, but she was beautiful. With blarney and flowery promises, Cavan won Dolores, as well as a place in the Biscara trading post at El Pasó del Norte, then the gateway between Mexico and the northern country.

In 1818, at El Pasó, Teresa was born, a second child of the union. Through those early years, the seeds of degeneration planted in Johnny Cavan began to flower. The heat, the primitive native life, a tendency toward dissolution—all had begun to make their marks, and the added frustration of a failing business added its corrosion. Teresa's childhood memories were of a sodden drunk, sleeping through the day, tomcatting all night. Teresa was his favorite, and it became the custom for her to take his mind off the pangs of endless hangovers with a game of cards. She had supple fingers and a remarkable memory. As a matter of course he was soon teaching her how to memorize all the cards in the deck, no matter how they fell, how to mark the key cards, and follow the markings though a shuffle, how a center dealer worked and how to make a belly stripper and how to distract an opponent with misdirection while you dealt from the bottom.

It was a land where women bloomed early. At fourteen Teresa had the breasts and hips that would not have graced a girl in another clime for several more years. At fourteen the commander of the presidio began watching her, as she passed, and the idlers in front of the *cantina* made sly remarks. Wheezing, mustached Pepe Rascón, a rival trader who had taken advantage of Johnny Cavan's indolence to ease much of his business away, seemed always to be at the Cavan house, when Teresa's father was away, bringing little gifts of food or clothing, sitting in the corner and watching Teresa and smiling and nodding and talking with her mother. She thought of him only as a friend of the family that summer.

It was a time of intolerable heat. Night brought little relief. With the smells of the baked earth still filling the air, and the mud town beaten into a soundless hush, it was a frequent thing to seek the solace of the river. One night, unable to beat the suffocating heat of their little mud *jacal*, she had left her pallet and had gone to the banks of the Río Grande. Naked, in the shallows, trying to wash off the grime and sweat, she had heard the song.

> **Where the River Shannon meets the sea,**
> **A colleen waits and cries for me . . .**

He might have passed by, for she knew the house he was heading for, farther up the river, but his eye had caught sight of the heap of her *camisa,* shining like a snow-patch on the bank. Her heart began to pound wildly as she crouched in the willows. She wanted to run. She seemed frozen. Then she heard the husky laugh, and the wild crackling of the willows.

She rose to flee, and the moonlight ran like silver over her wet body. A gusty sound came out of him. She felt his hand catch her arm. Maybe he was too drunk to know who she was. Struggling, sobbing hysterically, she wanted to believe it, ever afterward she had wanted to believe it. She tore free and ran; she slipped and fell in the muck, and got up again. She would never know when he dropped behind. In nightmares for years afterward she always ran forever through the night with the slime dripping off her naked body and the pound of his feet descending upon her till its cannon-roar jarred her awake, trembling and crying and soaked with sweat.

The church had been her haven that night—a time of trembling and sobbing and hysterics under the protection of a bewildered priest. She was afraid to return home for days. When she did, Johnny Cavan showed no sign of remembering, but she could no longer play cards with him. Her fingers trembled, a cold sweat broke out on her face, and she wanted to run again.

That torture had ended, six months later, when he disappeared. Some thought his drunken nocturnal wanderings had brought him under an Apache's scalp knife in the desert. Dolores Cavan knew better. He had been a wanderer when he had first met her; a man like that could not stay in one place for long.

For Teresa, the scar healed slowly, but youth and vitality and a return to the peaceful patterns of life finally buried the marks. Three years later a handsome young lieutenant joined the garrison at El Pasó, fresh from the Colegio Militar in Mexico City. Juan Esquivel, a polished scion of one of the finest families, a young *hidalgo galante* and dashing enough to turn the head of every girl in turn. Who could refuse his attentions if he chose to bestow them upon one of the most beautiful? It was where Teresa got her first taste for jewelry. A fabulous *gauchepourri* brooch from Santa Fé, a pair of solid silver bracelets set with *cabochon* emeralds, tinkling and clashing barbarically with the slightest turn of her wrist.

"Teresita, I never believed in fate before. Now I must. Why else should I be sent north? It was destiny that I should find you, that I should take you back to Mexico City, that we should be together forever. . . ."

He had given her the betrothal ring that night. She remembered the almost unsupportable joy it had brought, the love, the first faith and belief she had known since that terrible night on the river two years before. Was that how it happened? Too immersed in her happiness and her new-found faith to mistrust Juan any longer, to maintain the defenses with which she had held him off before. Was first passion always like that—the kissing, the crying, the bittersweet struggle, understanding what was happening, yet not understanding, knowing it should not be, yet not really knowing, trying to stop it, yet desiring that it should not stop? The right and wrong of it, the joy and the hurt, all running together in a sort of giddy transport till there was no will left in you, and you were drowned in the thunderous pound of pulse and heart, till the whole world seemed to tremble and shake and fall to pieces?

Those following weeks were something to remember. Her life was changed. She had been told that such a thing was wrong. Yet how could it be wrong, with the betrothal ring on her finger, with love in their hearts? He explained, and she believed. Love was the important thing. Juan had many fine words, as convincing while she was under his spell as had been the words of the priest who had taught her it was wrong. And when the words weren't quite convincing enough, there were his kisses again, his passionate protestations, his questing hands that she could not deny. They were to keep the engagement a secret till his orders came for a return to Mexico City. Then, triumphantly, he would take her with him.

The orders came. She woke that morning to find him gone. That same week the nausea came, and she had to tell her mother. They waited together, Teresa and her mother, for word that he was returning to her. The word came via the annual *conducta* returning from trading in Mexico City, not directly to Teresa, really, just an item in the general group, of how the handsome young Lieutenant Esquivel, lately stationed at El Pasó, had married into the rich Molina family from Vera Cruz. A fine match. It would facilitate his rise in the army.

Chapter Three

It was black night by the time Teresa Cavan and the yellow-haired Kelly Morgan reached the trappers' camp. It stood in a glade surrounded by endless miles of dense timber. There were a dozen horses, snorting and fretting on a rope line, and then a pair of fires with a heap of gear banked up on one side—saddles and blankets and guns and the inevitable *aparejos* of the trapping party—the x-shaped Mexican pack saddles that were filled with food and traps and supplies now and would return laden with the harvest of swart beaver pelts.

Around the fire were three men and an Indian squaw. Teresa recognized the one to the right of the fire, standing up. He was John Ryker, a Texas trader who had operated through El Pasó and who these last two years had moved up to Santa Fé. He was a solid, bear-like figure in his blackjack boots and corduroy trousers, dark with grease. He wore a knee-length coat made from the pelt of a cinnamon bear, and firelight glinted on the brass butt caps of two immense Ketland-McCormick pistols nakedly thrust through his belt.

"You didn't tell us you were a-goin' after a squaw," he said.

Morgan slid off the beaten, hipshot roan. He made no move to help Teresa dismount. "Ain't my woman," he said. "Biscara was havin' the holy hell whipped outen her. I couldn't see it."

Ryker glared at him. "You mean you put the kibosh on the deal over a little greaser slut like this . . . ?"

"Slack off," Morgan told him. "Biscara wouldn't make no deal."

"You're crazy," Ryker said. "The last time I saw him, he was willing to go in with us. He'd guarantee our duties would be cut in half if we'd take the hides to Saint Louis with our furs."

"He's afraid to ship his hides out, with this trouble around Taos."

"What trouble?"

Morgan shook his shaggy head. "How do I know? Somethin' about the Pueblo uprisin'."

Another of the trappers moved from the fire. He was a giant of a man with an unruly mass of hair as red as Teresa's and a hoary red beard that curled and spread all over his chest, filthy with grease, matted with dirt and burrs. "All this palaver . . . with the lady ain't even off her horse yet." He stopped at the horse, smiling up at Teresa, and held a hand out to help her down. "Cimarrón Saunders, honey, with apologies fer these varmints fergettin' their manners."

She regarded Saunders a moment from uptilted, heavy-lidded eyes. Then she accepted his hand and let him help her off the horse, holding her skirt tightly with one hand. Ryker was regarding her with black, angry eyes.

"So you got mad!" Ryker said to Morgan.

"Wouldn't you be, seein 'em beatin' a girl bare-assed with a horsewhip?"

"So you charge in there like a bull in a china shop, busting up everything that gets in your way, all over a little slut that don't mean no more to you than pinto beans."

"Now, hold off, Ryker. . . ."

"You just pulled the whole damned province down on our

26

heads, that's all. Biscara's one of the most powerful men in Santa Fé. He'll have every dragoon in the Palace out after you."

"Ain't that a sack o' shit," Morgan said.

"We won't be able to show our noses within a hundred miles of Santa Fé."

"Fearsome."

"There won't be a foot o' mountains we can trap in from Colter's Hell down to Chihuahua!"

"Plumb sergiverous."

"All because some damn' fool kid lost his head over a. . . ."

"Damn it, shut up!" Morgan shouted. He towered above Ryker.

Ryker's eyes glittered, and the blood ran into his face, staining his leathery cheeks like dye. For a moment the tension shimmered between the two men like a living thing. Then Ryker's weight settled back on his heels. "This's the last time I'll put up with your temper, Morgan. I've got too much at stake to risk it on a man with a hair-trigger like you." Sullen as a bear, he turned and shambled back to the fire.

Morgan watched him a moment, face bleak and raw. Then he seemed to become aware of Teresa. He looked at her. His anger fled as swiftly as it had come. He grinned broadly. "Git over to the fire. Black Blanket'll take care of you."

She walked ahead of them toward the fire. Its flickering light played across the stir and ripple of her buttocks, so tantalizingly outlined by the torn wool skirt. When she looked back, she saw that both Morgan and Saunders were watching. Morgan had seen it before, without anything covering it.

Black Blanket was Ryker's Arapaho squaw, a tubby, buckskin-faced woman with hide wrappings to her knees and an elkhide dress glittering with beads and quills and dripping long fringe. She nosed around in the timber till she found some black root, chewed it to a pulp, and then, beyond the light of the fire, applied it like a poultice to Teresa's buttocks. It burned like salt, drew like fire, and then settled down to a low throbbing that soon seemed to cover Teresa's whole backside. The squaw loaned her one of her own buckskin skirts to wear over the poultice, and then went back to cooking.

Teresa learned that the fourth man in the trapping party was Turkey Thompson, a tall, unbelievably skinny man with an Adam's apple that bobbed like a cork on a string every time he looked at her. He had shot the buck they ate; they had venison steaks and crumbly pemmican and a cup of precious, bitter coffee apiece. Kelly Morgan took off his shoulder belt before sitting down. It was laden with the incredible assortment of tools so typical of the mountain man—an awl with a deer-horn handle, a worm for cleaning his rifle, a squat bullet mold with buckskin-wrapped handles to protect the fingers when running balls, an antelope-horn phial containing the beaver medicine for baiting traps, a cow horn scraped transparent to reveal the black DuPont gunpowder inside, a tiger-tail bullet pouch, and finally a buckskin bag for flint and steel and tinder. Laying this heap of gear beside him, Morgan lowered himself cross-legged into the dirt, speared a steak off its spit with his Bowie knife, and began to cut off huge bites.

Teresa felt that Ryker was nominally their leader, but Kelly Morgan exerted an indefinable domination over them that swung the command subtly to him. He looked to be in his early twenties, the youngest of the band, yet his size and the marks left by a violent life made him appear older. He towered over the other men by a full head and emanated a vivid, earthy vitality that crept against her whenever she looked at him.

It angered her that she should feel any attraction toward him. He was a part of her rebellion. Hurt, alone, helpless, she had brought out what meager gallantry lay in such an elemental man, but it would soon wear off, and he would be as quick to take what her ripe body offered as had been Biscara, or Johnny Cavan, or Juan Esquivel.

Morgan ate like an animal, swiftly, ravenously, stuffing his mouth till the juice ran out the corners and stained his blond beard stubble. When he was through, he wiped his greasy hands on his long hair, cleaned his Bowie knife against his pants, and began scraping with the blade at his cheeks, shaving himself.

Ryker had been watching Teresa all through the meal, and finally said: "You speak English?"

She licked her fingers. "My father was Irish."

He raised black brows, surprised at her fluency. "Then you might as well pay for your keep. How about telling us what you know of this uprising Biscara spoke about?"

"More a revolution," she said.

Ryker leaned toward her. "They been talking like that for years in Santa Fé. You sure it isn't just another rumor?"

She saw that they were all watching her closely. This was a new rôle for her. Never had men asked her opinion on such things. Yet she knew as much about the politics of the country as most men. In El Pasó, her father's set had included most of the saloon politicians and petty officials of the town. A thousand nights she had been kept awake on her pallet in the back room by their drunken, boastful discussions over a game of monte in the front. As petty and spurious as these men were, they knew much of what went on in the outer world, for El Pasó was the hub of many trails, and it had built in Teresa a hungry longing for any knowledge of that outside world. It had led her to the camps of the countless traders that passed through El Pasó, where she added to her knowledge of the countries and the cities she had never seen. She had a retentive memory and often astounded her parents with what she had learned.

It seemed that all her life the country had been in a state of upheaval. Mexico and New Mexico at the time of Teresa's birth had been colonial provinces under Spain. But in 1822 they had revolted against the Spanish Crown, declaring themselves a Republic. Ever since then there had been revolution, and rumors of revolution.

"I don't think this is just another rumor," she said. "This northern department's been seething for years. It won't go much longer without an explosion. New Mexico's too far away from the center of government. Mexico City hasn't got much control over what goes on up here."

Ryker leaned toward her. "Just what does go on?"

"Anything you want to name. Those in power at the capital can do almost what they please. Santa Fé's riddled with graft and corruption. Nothing's being done about the Indian problem. Every year hundreds of ranchers are killed by the Apaches. The people are sick of it. I think there will be a real battle for power soon."

Turkey Thompson sucked the marrow out of a bone as he listened. When she was finished, he said: "Last I heard the governor was tryin' to blame it all on the customs inspector at Taos . . . Nicolas Amado, or somethin'."

Teresa glanced sharply at him. "Who?"

"Amado."

"A friend of yours?" Ryker asked.

She tried to sound indifferent. "I thought he said Sonado."

Morgan had finished shaving; he slid his Bowie into its brass-studded case, stood up, stretched like a cat, let out a resounding belch. "I seen enough revolutions. Let's stick to our traplines." He circled the fire and came directly to Teresa. He bent over and reached out a hand. She pulled back sharply, eyes smoldering. She saw surprise cross his face. Then he straightened up. "You got a hate on for every man in creation?" he asked. He wheeled and stalked away.

She turned and saw the heap of blankets and robes beside her, and realized he had merely meant to spread one for her. He circled the fire, kicked open his saddle blanket, sat in it, lay flat, rolled up in it, and was snoring huskily, all in the space of two minutes. Black Blanket made Ryker's bed, spreading out a carpet of springy pine needles, covering a buffalo saddle at its head with a blanket for the pillow. Ryker gave Cimarrón Saunders first watch.

Before rolling in, Ryker pulled the two Ketland-McCormick pistols from his belt, laying one carefully on each side of his pillows, within reach of his hands. Then he lay down. Pulling the robe over him caused him to roll a shoulder aside for a moment, putting his back to Teresa. She flipped her own robe open across the ground, covering one of the pistols. When she dragged the robe away from Ryker, the pistol came with it. She left it there, and got a saddle blanket for the top cover.

The camp settled down. Some of Teresa's tension abated. She grew drowsy. Finally one thought only remained. *You got a hate on for every man in creation?* Maybe she did. Hate and anger and rebellion seemed so inextricably bound up with every man she had known. What else could a woman feel for a man who had lied to her and seduced her and left her with a child? This was taking her back once more, to the dark memories. She could feel again the sense of betrayal that had crept through her like a sickness the day she had heard that Lieutenant Juan Esquivel had been married in Mexico City. She could feel again the misery, the apathy, the abysmal indifference to life itself that had filled her during those days following, when she sat in the dark little *jacal* at El Pasó, not eating, not sleeping, not talking.

After that, during the months of adjustment, Pepe Rascón was a perpetual caller at their home. With Johnny Cavan gone, this aging man had become the biggest trader in El Pasó. The arrangement was made between him and Teresa's mother before Teresa knew of it. Pepe took them to his house, a sprawling *hacienda* of countless rooms. He opened his storerooms to them and revealed handsome dresses—taffetas and silks and laces. Dolores Cavan's eyes grew wide and greedy. That night, in their miserable mud *jacal*, she had told her daughter: "A woman would live like a queen in a home like that. Sleeping till ten, awakened by an Indian maid, served with chocolate and cakes before you get out of bed, even. And look how he would dress you. How many of us get a chance like this, Teresa? It is not as though he would be a real husband to you. He is obviously too old for that. More a father. A father of great kindness and benevolence, giving your son a name and you a home."

A few months before it would have been abhorrent to her, but she had grown old and wise in those few months. She had learned how little a woman of this land could expect from life. To get this much was unheard of. She was surprised at how calmly she made the decision. After the soaring ecstasy with Juan, it was strange that one could so coolly decide to take a man, but ecstasy had betrayed her. And now her baby would have a father. That was the most important thing.

So they were married, carrying candles through the dimness of the chapel, reciting their vows. That very day Dolores Cavan took the rest of her brood on the trail to Santa Fé; she had tried in vain to support the children by working in town and was now returning to the rest of her people at the Biscara *hacienda,* and Teresa moved with Pepe to the great house on the edge of El Pasó.

The baby came closer. They slept in separate rooms, and the Pima Indian housekeeper brought Teresa chocolate and cakes and told her the things a mother should know and acted as doctor and midwife when the baby came. It was a boy, christened Pepe Gregorio Jayan Ignacio Miguel de Rascón y Cavan.

Then that evening, three weeks after he was born, while she was nursing him in her room, Pepe had tramped heavily through the door, scowling and pulling at his mustache. He circled the baby.

"He is still so red. Are you sure he is not sick?"

"Nexpa says he is perfect."

Pepe pouted, then sat down on the bed, and began to take his shoes off. She frowned at him, not quite understanding. He belched, smelling strongly of chili. "You can put him aside for a few minutes, then. It is time for me to nurse you now."

She could not believe it. He was too old. Her mother had said so. He was obviously too old. Yet here he was undressing, wheezing, his neck turning red and swollen. When she finally understood, she thought she couldn't breathe and thought she couldn't submit. Then the baby gurgled in her arms, and she looked down at his pink little face, his helpless little hands. This was his only haven. Pepe's name and Pepe's home were all she could give him. Without it what would he be, doomed to picking his life out of the gutter or to the endless labor of servitude in the household of some *rico?* For his sake, she had made a bargain. If this was its fulfillment, she must make her payment. Leaving the baby resting, she knelt down before her husband.

How could the same thing be so different? How could it be such blind ecstasy one time and such hateful repugnance the next? When it was over, he sat on the edge of the bed for a moment, and then began dressing again.

"Tomorrow you will clean the house," he said. "I also wish some trade goods transferred from the storehouse to those carts in the corrals. They must be loaded when the drivers arrive."

She lay down with her eyes closed, holding her sickness in her till she heard him stamp out of the room. Then she rolled over and buried her face in the pillow and bit her lip till the blood ran to keep from crying.

The house and the trading post were an establishment that would ordinarily have occupied the time and labor of a dozen servants. Yet there was only the Pima housekeeper, Nexpa, and a pair of sullen stablemen to keep the animals and help load the carts. The satin and the taffeta stayed in the storerooms or went in the creaking *carretas* to Santa Fé, where the *gente fina* paid handsome prices for such things. The rest of it, for Teresa, was the constant hours of labor, helping Nexpa in the house—the cleaning and washing and cooking, the weaving of coats and pants and homespun shirts, the ministering like a slave to the ceaseless, petty demands of a surly old miser who begrudged her the food she put in her mouth.

The only thing that sustained her was the baby. He had become the core of her life. He was the only thing in her world that had given affection unstintingly, the only thing she could call her own. It gave her the strength for the endless drudgery that seemed to be—most of the time—all that Pepe had brought her here for. If it hadn't been for the grotesque ritual of the bedchamber, she might have borne it, but it became regular as the winding of a clock, the tramp of his feet outside her door, the sight of his red face, the gouty wheezing. Finally she could stand it no longer. One night, as he took down his pants and sat down on the edge of the bed, she refused to go down on her knees, instead crawling up against the wall and pulling the covers about her.

"I'm sick," she said. "Have you no feelings? How can you enjoy it? I give you nothing. You could get the same thing from those women down by the river."

The purple veins in his nose swelled till she thought they would burst. With a grunting sound, he grabbed her arm, pulling her down to the floor. She fought back. It was a rebellion that had been building up in her for months now. She cursed him and clawed him like a cat, tearing free. Before she could get out of the way, he hit her. It sent her sprawling onto the floor. He followed her and tangled his gnarled hand in her hair and pulled her to her knees and hit her again. He kept hitting her, one side and then the other, till her body sagged against him like a sack of sand. Then he released her, and she slid to the floor, barely conscious.

Naked, hairy as an ape, he walked barefooted around the bed to the cradle. He put his hand over the baby's mouth, cutting off its squalls, so he could be heard. "Now," he said, "perhaps you know why I married you. I wanted a son, and a woman. I guess I am too old to have a son the regular way, even though I can still perform the function. But I have a son anyway, don't I? If you do not want to be my wife, I will take my son and leave you."

"No. . . ." It left her in a pitiful sob. She tried to sit up. He looked blurred to her, across the room, and her head was still roaring from the blows. She could not stand to lose the child. She knew that.

Pepe took his hand off the baby's mouth, and it went into a paroxysm of coughing. Teresa crawled to the cradle on her hands and knees and took the child in her arms and pressed his cheek against hers, trying to soothe him. The beating and the fear of losing her baby had left her without any resistance. She made no sound when Pepe spoke.

"Now," he said, "*you* will be my wife . . . ?"

This ugly picture faded from Teresa's mind as she heard the stirring across the fire. She opened her eyes to see that Cimarrón Saunders was coming back from the horse lines. He stopped by the fire.

She pulled the corner of her robe off Ryker's Ketland-McCormick. The brass furniture of the big pistol glittered dully in the backlight of the fire.

Saunders's eyes moved slowly from the weapon to her sullen face. Finally, through the unruly bramble of his red beard, she saw his lips peel back in a grin—a mixture of grudging admiration and sly malice. He chuckled softly and turned to walk back into the darkness.

Chapter Four

 Don Fernández de Taos lay some seventy-five miles north of Santa Fé. It was an ancient village of tawny mud houses surrounded by a huge adobe wall, sprawled on a plateau at the very base of the Sangre de Cristo Mountains. Coming from the south, through the Río Grande Cañon, it was like climbing into the land of the gods. The air was so clear it hurt the lungs and the colors so pure they were hard to believe. Every year or so the houses were replastered with a mixture of sand, mud, and straw. The straw gave them a golden hue in a bright sun, and at mid-morning, from a distance, the buildings looked like so many glittering doubloons cast carelessly at the foot of the frowning red mountains.

This was how it appeared to Teresa as she rode with the trappers into the old town. They came out of the mountains on the old Pecuris Trail with budded willow brush screening their flanks and wild plum bushes banked white as snow along the gurgling irrigation ditches. They had given Teresa a pinto with a buffalo saddle. She rode like a man, the long antelope skirt given her by Ryker's squaw hiding her legs.

They rode through the gate of the adobe-walled town and down one of the crooked streets to the plaza. It was more of an Indian town than was Santa Fé. Indians were everywhere, squatting against the blank golden walls, standing like mahogany statues in the gates, the barbaric colors of their blankets blazing in the hot sunlight.

As the riders neared the plaza, Teresa heard the sound like the roar of an angry sea crashing and breaking against a rocky coast. Within sight of the treeless square, the sound gained identity, becoming shouts, the voices of a crowd. The square seemed filled with people, standing in the strong shadows beneath the *portales* fronting the buildings or massed in dense bunches across the open ground. It seemed to her that the bulk of them were Pueblo Indians, their primitive faces bronze and enigmatic beneath the blue *bandas* crossing their foreheads and tied about their jet-black hair. One of their number was standing on a load of wood in a *carreta,* engaged in an oration.

Ryker pulled his horse to a stop at the edge of the plaza, glancing at Teresa. "It looks ugly," he said. "Can you find out what's happening?"

Teresa kneed her horse to the fringe of the crowd, asking one of the Mexicans there: *"Hola. ¿Qué es de su vida?"*

"El alcalde es en la cárcel," he said. "The mayor is in jail. The government claims that the corruption in the customs department was traced to *Don* Melgares. Some dragoons are coming from Santa Fé to take him back there."

Teresa told Ryker. His black brows pulled together, and he surveyed the crowded square, shaking his leonine head. "Maybe we better camp outside till it quiets down," he said.

Morgan answered disgustedly. "Hell, it may take days. If they riot, they might wreck Barton's post, and we'd never get our traps. I say we get what we come after, right now."

Reminding Teresa of a dog with his hackles up, he touched his roan with the great cartwheel spurs. Sullenly, looking up at the blond giant with glittering eyes, the crowd gave way. Ryker glanced at Cimarrón Saunders. The red-bearded man grinned broadly, kicking his big pinto after Morgan. Reluctantly the others followed. Teresa could feel the hostility of the crowd like a pressure against her as she rode between their ranks. They reached the opposite side of the square. The buildings here were fronted with the usual *portales*—a roof extending out from the wall and supported by peeled cedar posts—making a shady arcade that ran along the edge of the square. On one of the poles was nailed the crudely printed sign: **Barton's Trading Post.** The party pulled to a halt here. Morgan and Ryker dismounted and went inside. Teresa swung off the horse to ease stiff legs. The welts itched dully. They were healing. She rubbed her hands up and down on her buttocks.

Cimarrón Saunders stepped down beside her. The leering grin was on his bearded face, the sly shimmer in his eyes. "You don't look so big, without Ryker's gun," he said.

She did not look at him. "I don't need a gun now," she said. "Can't you see their faces? *Don't* you know what would happen if an *americano* so much as touched one of their women?"

His eyes fled from her, circling the crowd. As his grin faded, the carnal lips disappeared into the fiery thicket of his dirty beard. The orator was still shouting from the top of the cart. Next to the cart, on the ground, was a man unique to this crowd of peasants and Indians—a man dressed in the handsome blue velvet jacket and silver embroidered pants of a *rico*. His glazed sombrero of yellow vicuña skin cast the upper half of his face in deep shadow. Perhaps it had once been a strong face; now the thick meat of jowls gave the jaw a slack look, and the brilliant black eyes seemed faded and veiled by the folded, veined lids of dissolution.

Teresa had seen this man in Santa Fé and knew him to be

Don Augustin Gómez, one of the few men in the land who had fought his way up from the poverty-ridden household of a peasant into the large landholdings and political power of a *rico*. There was a lull in the oration. Gómez was watching the speaker craftily. He spoke in a tone that did not carry to the bulk of the crowd, but Teresa was near enough to hear.

"And the military, Villapando," Gómez said. "What have they done about the military?"

The Pueblo glanced down at him, looking surprised. Then he raised his arms and began the exhortation again. "An act was passed in Eighteen Twenty-Six for three troops of cavalry at Santa Fé. How many do we find there? Not a full troop in the whole province. The Apaches and the Navajos go on murdering and robbing at will."

Again the angry sea roared, as the crowd shouted its answer. When the yelling began to die down, Gómez moved closer to the cart, calling softly to the orator: "And the Expulsion Law?"

Villapando raised his arms again. "In Eighteen Twenty-Eight a law was passed to expel the *gachupínes* . . . all the native-born Spaniards in your country. How is it that a *gachupín* like *Don* Biscara is allowed to remain? How much do you suppose Governor Carbajal has accepted from *Don* Biscara to let him stay?"

As Gómez went on needling the Pueblo Indian into more outbursts, Teresa saw another man move toward the cart. With a shock of surprise, she realized it was Nicolas Amado.

Amado was not a tall man. It was his massive head with its mane of black hair that gave him the illusion of great size. He had the oblique, thin-lidded eyes of an Oriental tyrant. The splayed nostrils and deep bridge of his nose lent a primitive brutality to his face. No matter how often he shaved, a blue shadow would always stain his blunt jaw, like a hint of treacherous undercurrents in the man. He wore a serape, head thrust through its center hole. The flutter of his slender hands, pulling the deep folds about his body, held a sense of suave, feminine cruelty.

Amado was a man of obscure origins. Somehow the legend had arisen that he was the illegitimate son of a Spanish grandee. Yet he bore the name of one of the poorest families in Albuquerque. He had come north from that town a few years before with the avowed purpose of making his fortune in Santa Fé, the capital of this northern department. He had no concern, no money, no sponsorship. Yet he had soon wormed his way into political circles, rising swiftly through the hierarchy of petty officialdom till he had been appointed customs inspector for the whole Río Arriba.

As he drifted through the mob toward the cart, his shadow followed him. This was Inocente, a wizened little ferret of a man dressed in the soiled rawhide *chivarras* and cotton *pantalones bombachos* of the peasant. A horse had kicked him in the head when he was a child, leaving him hopelessly addled. He leered and giggled as he shuffled along behind Amado, winking at the Indians as though he held some sly secret.

From his vantage point on the cart, Villapando was still haranguing the crowd. With Gómez's crafty needling, he was proving to be a spellbinder, a demagogue. Teresa knew that many of his accusations against Governor Carbajal were of dubious validity, yet there was a burning sincerity, a dedication to the man that was lifting the crowd into a frenzy. The wild excitement on their sweating, avid faces had all the makings of a riot. Such an outbreak might well mark the beginnings of the revolt that had been building for so many years in these northern towns.

Teresa knew that Gómez had a political axe to grind. The

department of New Mexico was traditionally divided into two parts. Everything north of Santa Fé was the Río Arriba—the Upper River—and everything south of the capital was Río Abajo—the Lower River. Because of his peasant origin, Gómez had always been looked down upon by the *gente fina*, the aristocrats. Thus, in the politics of the capital, Gómez and his Río Arriba had always been relegated to the humiliating position of a country cousin by the Biscaras and the *gente fina* of Río Abajo. Could it be that Gómez saw in this embryo of revolution a chance to gain the recognition he had always coveted?

Teresa knew that in actuality her cousin in Taos was not capable of protecting her from *Don* Biscara. She had only let the trappers bring her here as a last resort, because there was no place else to flee. But if these men were plotting an uprising that would result in Biscara's exile, and she could somehow ally herself with them . . . . The possibilities of it kindled an excitement in her that Villapando's wild harangue had failed to touch. She started edging toward the fringe of the crowd. The trappers were too intent on the speaker's wild display to notice. In a last swift lunge she ducked into the crowd. She pushed through the mass of sweating, yelling men; few of them even noticed her in their excitement. Buffeted by their shifting bodies, surrounded by their earthy stench of sweat and chili and tobacco, she finally saw the cart ahead of her. Standing by one of the head-high, solid wheels, Amado caught sight of her.

His eyes went blank and wide with surprise. Then a broad smile came to his lips. They were thick, carnal lips, pinched down to tight corners—made for the lechery and slyness and guile she knew so well. He called her name and pushed toward her through the crowd. The folds of his serape fell away from his outstretched arms, and for a moment she thought he would embrace her. A foot short he stopped, hesitating.

"I do not know if I have the courage," he said. "The last time I saw a man take you in his arms, he died."

Her eyes went dark with the memory. She forced herself to smile and hold out a hand. "Then let us greet each other like *compadres*."

He laughed, taking her hand. "And how do I find you here, *compadre*?"

She told him of Biscara. Her face grew bleak as she spoke. "I am through being used by men, Nicolas. They have done all they are going to do to me. Somehow I will change it. I don't know how, but somehow I will."

"You have come to the right man, *mi chiquita*. You and I together. . . ."

"Not that way, either, Nicolas."

He sighed, rolling his eyes heavenward. "Why must you be so unreasonable, Teresa?"

She broke in on him. "Why are you here? If the governor found out you were involved in something like this. . . ."

He shrugged. "My customs report did not suit Governor Carbajal. I told him I was merely making *diligencia*. A *peso* in this hand, a *peso* in that. How does it compare with the *diligencia* Carbajal makes? For every *peso* that seeks the proper haven in my pocket, a thousand fall into the governor's coffers. Yet who pays, when the order comes from Mexico City to unmask the culprit, the real thieves, the real grafters? *Por supuesto,* no. It is the little ones like me and Mayor Melgares. Do I want to rot for years in those Mexico City dungeons? *Á fe mía*, no. Before they come to get me, I escape." A pawky grin pinched the tips of his lips, and he made a dramatic gesture with one hand. *"Vale más estar tomado por valiente que serlo."*

It was a favorite saying of his—it is better to be thought

brave than really to be so—and was so typical of him and of her past experiences with him that she had to smile. She had sought him out with some vague idea of getting his help. Now she realized more clearly what she had to do. If she meant to ally herself with these people, she must take her place in their ranks. But they would have no use for a woman. They would suspect and mistrust one who came from a family that had been in *Don* Biscara's service for generations. Her only link with them—her only chance to identify herself with them— was Amado.

"Do you think this is the beginning of a revolt?" she asked.

His frown dug deep, vertical furrows between his black brows. "Gómez is up to something."

"And you?"

He shook his head. "The difference between a political prisoner and a revolutionary is usually a noose around the neck."

"But what if the revolt succeeds? They'll execute Governor Carbajal and all who stand with him."

"But I am not with him."

"You are either with him, or against him."

She saw that shook his confidence. He frowned again, saying: "How can it succeed? A bunch of unarmed Indians, a handful of disaffected politicians?"

"You know it's more than that."

His eyes narrowed, and he pursed his lips. She could almost see the wheels of a complex mind at work. He knew the background of these intricate politics far better than she— knew that this explosion had been building for years. Governor Carbajal had only a couple of hundred regular troops in Santa Fé, and half of those would desert. A hundred dragoons against thousands of aroused rebels.

"Gómez wouldn't be in this if it were just another Indian

uprising," Teresa said. "There'll be Mexicans involved. They'll need a leader, Nicolas. A man like you. Governor Carbajal wouldn't have made an example of you if you hadn't been important. You could be more than a customs inspector, under a new government."

She knew his vanity, his ego, and was using it. She saw the zealous gleam varnish his eyes, blotting out the doubts, the reservations. He looked around the crowd with a new expression on his face. Gómez was prompting the Pueblo orator.

"And the outsiders, Villapando, the outsiders in our government?"

The Pueblo glanced blankly at Gómez, then turned back to the crowd, taking his cue. "Governor Carbajal comes from five hundred leagues away. How can he understand our problems?"

It was a recapitulation of all the complaints and wrongs, the cruelties and misrule under which the people had suffered for decades. As Teresa watched *Don* Gómez slyly prompting Villapando, the picture became clearer. Gómez, with his peasant origins, should have been more sympathetic to the needs of the people. Yet his large holdings and his desire to be recognized by the aristocrats blinded him to the moral issues involved. He was obviously bent on power, and would use any means to get it. The Pueblos, on the other hand, were thinking only in terms of justice. These sedentary village Indians had been here before the Spaniards, had never amalgamated with their conquerors, and were patently sincere in their wish to throw off the yoke of misrule. And for once the Mexicans stood with them. In the crowd were many *pobres*—small, poverty-ridden Mexican farmers and ranchers who made up the peasant class of the country. They were descended from the original Spanish settlers and were as proud of their pure blood as were the aristocrats. But they, perhaps more than the Indians, had suffered under these aristocrats and were as sincere as the Pueblos in their desire to get rid of the corruption in Santa Fé.

The orator was in a frenzy now, and it was driving the mob wild. Their shouts boomed and roared deafeningly about Teresa. She knew this was the crucial moment, sensed it was the point Gómez had been whipping them up to with his insidious needling of the Pueblo orator. She clutched Amado's elbow.

"Now is the time. Let it come from you. They'll remember the man who started them to freedom. Tell them we must free Mayor Melgares."

Amado was whirled up in the excitement. There was no more room left in his own frenzy for doubt. In a wild voice he screamed to be heard above the tumult. "It is time to strike! We must free Melgares!"

Gómez had turned his face to Villapando, mouth open to shout. The sudden anger stamped into his seamed face convinced Teresa that he had meant to yell the same thing. But now Amado had taken it from him. The faces of the crowd swung toward Amado, then the shout left them in a frightening roar.

"Amado is right. The time has come. Free Melgares, free Melgares . . . !"

Like a bright blade of sound slashing through all this diffuse din, Teresa heard the brazen blast of a bugle. It made her wheel toward the source, and she saw a file of blue-coated soldiers galloping down the main street and into the plaza.

Amado saw them, and fear ran in a flutter of muscle through his face. "The dragoons sent to get Melgares," he said.

The mob had already begun to surge across the plaza toward the jail. The troops galloped against their front ranks, beating at heads with the flats of their sabers, knocking men off their feet with the lunging shoulders of their horses. Their leader, a young lieutenant, rode his frothing horse into the middle of the cleared space, barking a command. Six of his chosen men dismounted, slipping from under the saddle leathers their *escopetas*—the short smoothbore muskets of the dragoon. Then the lieutenant stood in his stirrups, yelling at the top of his voice to be heard.

"One minute to scatter, or I will order you fired upon!"

It was a clever military maneuver. A man on horseback exercised a subtle domination over those on foot. The lieutenant had kept enough men in the saddle to retain that domination, yet had added to it with the threat of those loaded guns. The front ranks of the crowd began to press back; some of the men on the fringe began to drift into the streets leading away from the square. Few of the Indians had come prepared for an out-and-out battle with regulars. Most of them had no guns, were armed only with their knives or lances.

The lieutenant rode back and forth behind his riflemen, a fine, proud figure on his spirited black horse. He was a vividly handsome young man, rapier-slim in his blue coat with its red cuffs and collar. His black hair was queued beneath the round-crowned Andalusian hat, and under his jacket his torso was encased in a cuirass of double-folded deerskin. Teresa had seen him in Santa Fé. He was Lieutenant Hilario Pérez, recently transferred from the Escuadrón de Vera Cruz in Mexico City.

Teresa saw that Gómez was moving swiftly through the crowd, saying something to a man here, a man there. Each one he spoke to began to shove his way toward the mouth of one of the streets opening into the square. And Teresa saw that each was a Mexican—not a Pueblo Indian—and was dressed in the spurred wing boots and rawhide *chivarras* of the cattleman. These were probably Gómez's *vaqueros,* with their horses hitched somewhere off the plaza. She saw pistols thrust in the belts of some and knew there would be carbines and *escopetas* on their animals.

"Gómez is up to something," she said. "We've got to give him a chance."

"How?" Amado asked hotly. "Our minute is almost up."

"Lieutenant Pérez can't make good his threat, and he knows it," Teresa said. "Once his men fire, they'll be no better off than we."

Amado's eyes began to glow as he saw her logic. He turned to Villapando again, shouting above the babble: "How can the troops fire? One volley and their guns will be empty!"

Villapando began to exhort the crowd again, echoing Amado. The drift toward the streets began to stop; the men began to pack up again. Lieutenant Pérez raised his saber.

"I warn you. If you do not scatter, my men will fire."

"The minute is up," Villapando taunted. "Why do you not shoot?"

Pérez rode his prancing, shimmering horse down the line of his riflemen. His dark young cheeks looked down with frustration. Villapando shouted at the Indians again. The lieutenant pulled his lathered horse to a halt, stood in the stirrups, pointed his sword at Villapando.

"Corporal, shoot that man on the cart!"

A gun cracked. The ball missed Villapando and buried itself in the adobe wall at his back. He ducked and dropped off the cart. At the same time, from the mouths of other streets and from the roofs of half a dozen buildings around the plaza, other guns began to fire. Teresa knew that it was the *vaqueros* Gómez had drawn from the crowd. Three of the dismounted dragoons were hit, stumbling and sprawling on the ground.

"Charge them!" Villapando screamed. "Get their guns!"

The mob surged forward. The three remaining dragoons on the ground fired in panic. A pair of Pueblo Indians were hit, but the rest of the mob engulfed the dragoons on foot.

Teresa dodged into the mouth of an alley to keep from being knocked down and trampled. She looked over the dark sea of heads in the plaza to see the mounted dragoons hacking about them with their sabers. Another burst of fire from the rooftops spilled a pair of them from their saddles. It panicked Lieutenant Pérez's horse, and the beast plunged headlong through the mob. Scattering men right and left, it galloped directly into the alley where Teresa had taken refuge.

The horse ran past Teresa with the lieutenant sawing savagely on the reins. Ten feet beyond her he got the animal stopped. But when he tried to wheel it in the narrow alley, the frenzied animal reared and spilled him from the saddle.

Shaking his head dazedly, he rolled over and gained his feet. He had lost his saber but was drawing a big Spanish pistol. As he got it out, one of Gómez's *vaqueros* appeared at the end of the alley, gun leveled.

Pérez took a snap shot before the man could fire. The *vaquero* was hit in the belly and sprawled on his face. The sound of the shot was lost in another burst of gunfire from the rooftops.

Pérez wheeled and ran toward the plaza. In the dark shadows he must have mistaken Teresa for a man. He struck savagely at her with the gun barrel as he ran by. She had to plaster herself against the wall to escape the blow. It had all happened in a few seconds, and Pérez gained the mouth of the alley before any of the crowd reached it.

Teresa knew she was the only one who had seen him fire. To the rest of the mob it must have appeared that he emerged from the alley with a loaded gun. He struck with his gun again as the first Indian reached him. Pérez wheeled and ducked under a *portal*. This arcade running down the front of the building had been deserted by the surge of the mob into the plaza. Others in the mob tried to dart between the posts and stop him, but he struck their arms down with the gun, eluding them.

Teresa saw that he was heading for the jail and began to run after him, under the *portal*. She saw Amado in the crowd and called to him. The mob, struggling with the remaining dragoons, had left a portion on one side of the square open. Pérez appeared from beneath the *portal*, ran headlong across the mouth of a street, and reached the front of the jail. He put his back against the door, chest heaving, face covered with dirt and blood.

Villapando was already fighting his way to the edge nearest the jail, turning the mob's attention that way with his shouting. But the sight of Pérez, standing against the door with his pistol, stopped the surge toward the mud building.

"The first man within ten feet of this door will get a ball through his head."

No single man wanted to be a martyr; they had been responding to the authority of a uniform all their lives. The *vaqueros* on the rooftops had discharged their guns and would have to reload. And there was something so frighteningly indomitable about that single man facing them alone that it gave pause to the most avid rebel among them.

Villapando thrust himself into the forefront. In his fierce eyes shone admiration for such foolhardy courage. "Declare for us, Lieutenant," he shouted, "and we will spare you."

"I declare for God, for Santa Anna, and for the Republic. Now clear this plaza or suffer the consequences."

The pure audacity of it held them a moment longer. Teresa reached Amado, pressed him through the crowd toward the front ranks. She hissed in his ear: "There is no ball in his gun. We are the only ones who know it."

He turned to stare blankly at her. "How can you be sure?"

She kept prodding him through the pack of men. "I saw him shoot a man in the alley."

Amado's face shone with sweat. "*Pues* . . . he may have reloaded."

He didn't have time. I saw. This is your chance. Think what a hero it would make you."

"Are . . . are you sure?"

"Have I ever lied to you before?" she said. For a moment he hesitated. She saw fear on his face, doubt, hesitation. She leaned closer. "It takes greatness to snatch such opportunities as this, Nicolas."

She saw the vivid eyes begin to shine. With a deep breath he shoved aside the few men in front of him and stepped into the open. Villapando, thirty feet away, looked at him in surprise. The whole crowd seemed to grow quiet, awaiting this new development. She saw Amado stop, his face growing pale. But the focus of their whole attention was upon him now. If he quailed, he would be branded forevermore.

The lieutenant aimed the brass-bound pistol at his chest. "You have two paces more, Amado."

Teresa saw Amado's lip twitch. His voice sounded strained. "This is a thing of the people, Lieutenant. You might as well try to stop the sun from rising. If my death will prove that, it is in a good cause."

In the hot, yellow sun of late afternoon a hush had settled over the crowd. Amado held out his hand for the gun.

Pérez jerked the weapon back, meaning to strike with it. Amado let one of his arms fly into the air, as if he had knocked the gun up. The lieutenant tried to club him with the gun, but Amado blocked the blow and hit him in the stomach. Pérez gasped and doubled over. Amado wrenched the gun from his nerveless fingers and struck him over the head with it.

An instant later a shout rose from a hundred throats. The crowd surged forward, trampling the lieutenant, battering at the door with their own bodies. Then they were pulled away by those behind, leaving an open space for the dozen men who came in with a log. Three times they had to strike before the iron hinges were torn from their sockets. Then the mob poured in and pushed Mayor Melgares from the depths of a dark cell.

A small, frightened, blinking man in a dusty alpaca suit he was lifted onto their shoulders. Another man was lifted up, to sit beside him, Nicolas Amado, while Villapando and Gómez stood on the ground below, looking up.

Teresa looked up, too, standing with her back pressed against a building, while Amado and Melgares were carried around the square, the heroes of the hour, and the wild shouts rang triumphantly down the crooked streets of the ancient town.

"*¡Viva* Melgares! *¡Viva la revolución! ¡Viva* Amado!"

Chapter Five

 Kelly Morgan had been born in Nashville, sometime in 1813, one of a family of twelve spawned in a two-room dogtrot cabin by a drunken keeler who died in the Red Stick War fighting with Jackson. Morgan grew up to believe that the only god was Andy Jackson, the only salvation was a Jake Hawken rifle, and the only hell was a place where they didn't serve enough Kentucky red-top to get drunk on.

When Morgan was sixteen, a Nashville rake seduced his sister and got her big with child, and Morgan hunted the man and cut off his ears and put the HT brand on his cheek. The jury held that the rake was not technically a horse thief, and, therefore Morgan had no right to usurp the authority of the law by marking the man's face in such an outrageous fashion. The sentence was a year and a day, despite his youth. Morgan had served the day when four of his brothers bolted a log chain to the bars of the jail window, hooked it to a team of mules, and pulled the wall out of the building, thus rendering Morgan automatically GTT. In those days, Gone To Texas was a common appellation attached to the men who fled west to escape the law, a hanging, or a nagging wife. In most cases it could be taken literally. Texas, still under Mexican rule, was becoming a haven for more and more of the growing tide of emigration—both of the lawful and the unlawful—that was moving west.

In Austin young Kelly Morgan met Jim Bowie and learned how to use his knife, perhaps too well. A frontier restlessness would have pushed Morgan on if the revolution hadn't started. He was with Sam Houston when things were finally settled at San Jacinto. Six months after the battle, Morgan killed a man with his Bowie in an Austin brawl. He might have gotten off on self-defense, but a man with an unfinished jail sentence in Nashville couldn't afford to take a chance. So it was west once more, with a party of trappers bound for the great shining mountains.

This was the man who stood with the party of trappers in front of Barton's Trading Post, watching the triumphant Indians carry Amado and the mayor around the square. During the battle, the mob choking the square had prevented the trappers from escaping. Barton had advised them to load their guns and pull their horses in under the *portal,* prepared to make a stand should the Indians turn on them.

"They'll begin to break up in a minute," he said. "Soon's you see it clear, take that street north toward the gate. Any of 'em make a pass at you, jist keep ridin' like hell."

Cimarrón Saunders and Turkey Thompson began to load the buckskin sacks of Miles Standish traps they'd gotten from Barton onto the pack horses. Ryker stood by one of the posts supporting the overhang, his immense Ketland-McCormicks in his hands.

"I wonder where she got to?" Morgan said.

"Forget her," Ryker growled.

Morgan only half heard him. The marching, chanting, shouting mob had shifted away from the front of the jail. Through a scattering of Pueblos that remained he saw the blue-uniformed man sprawled on the ground in front of the jail door, and crouching beside him was Teresa Cavan.

Ryker led his skittish saddle horse out from beneath the

portal. He stuffed one of his Ketland-McCormicks into his belt, grabbed the saddle horn with his free hand, and stepped aboard. "I'll lead out," he said.

Morgan dragged his quivering, excited roan into the open. "You go ahead. I'll meet you outside the wall."

Ryker saw where he was looking. "Damn you, Kelly, we can't stop for that girl. . . ."

Without answering, Morgan led his roan across the plaza. The few Pueblos around the jail spread away from his towering figure, watching him suspiciously. They stirred and muttered among themselves, and Morgan caught the gleam of a knife blade. The girl looked up, saw him coming, saw the gathering tension among the Indians.

"Leave him alone," she called in Spanish. "He is not your enemy."

A Mexican woman came fearfully from one of the houses next to the jail, carrying a clay bowl filled with water and some rags. Morgan put his rifle against the wall, hitched his roan to a post, and helped Teresa drag the half-conscious lieutenant to a sitting position against the wall. Then Teresa washed the blood and dirt from his face with a wet rag. Her lips were soft and slack, and her eyes were dark with compassion. The lieutenant moaned and opened his eyes.

"*Pobrecito*," she said. "You'll be all right now. I don't think there is anything serious."

A half dozen buckskinned *vaqueros* crossed the square, herding seven dragoons before them. One of the soldiers held a wounded arm and two others showed blood on the front of their coats, but the rest were just badly battered. They were driven into the gaping door of the jail, and one of the *vaqueros* stopped above the lieutenant, waving a pistol at him.

"He is to be imprisoned, also, *señorita,* by the order of *Don* Gómez."

Shakily Pérez got to his feet. He bowed stiffly to Teresa. "My thanks, *señorita*."

He marched into the jail like a drill sergeant on the parade ground.

Morgan grimaced down at Teresa. "You'll be all right here, with your cousin?"

"Of course. I told you."

"What if *Don* Biscara comes?"

Her eyes grew tempestuous. "He'll never find me."

"Maybe you better tag along with us."

The storm had gone from her green eyes. She smiled at him. It was a dazzling sight, with the vivid lips curving off the perfect small white teeth. "This is quite a change from Santa Fé. As I remember, you were rather sorry you'd rescued me."

He grinned abashedly. "It wasn't that. I jist didn't know what to do with you."

"And now you do?"

All the humor left his face. His eyes grew dark and heavy-lidded. "Yes, miss," he breathed. "I sure do."

She was a sight to see. The way her body dipped and curved and flared fairly took a man's breath. Her flesh was like gold, with a glowing, satiny life all its own. Her breasts, bulging so impudently against the *camisa,* made a man think of ripe apples, they were that round. Like a flood of heat the intense desire for her swept through him. It was the plain carnal desire of an elemental man, but it seemed to cut through him more cruelly than ever before. She saw the flush seep into his gaunt cheeks, and she moved back, with the smile gone.

"You'd better go now."

"Yeah." He moistened his lips. "I'd better go."

He picked up his rifle, unhitched his roan. Up on the horse, he looked ten feet tall. "You'll be here come winter?"

Her lips grew petulant. "I don't know. I suppose."

He stared at her a moment longer. Then he reined the skittish roan around and pricked it with his cartwheels, and the horse went at a dead gallop across the square and down the crooked street. He didn't slow it down till he was outside the walls because the want of her still burned in him like fire, and, if he'd stayed a moment longer, he would have made a damned fool of himself over a woman and ended up with a clout on the head or a knife in the ribs for his trouble.

Riding north along the Taos Trail, he met a party of Indians coming from San Geronimo, the Pueblo village three miles from Taos. All of them carried buffalo lances for war clubs and had naked knives stuck in their waistbands. There was something sinister about the way they went by, hardly looking up at him, their bare feet slapping against the earth in a muffled, unremitting drumbeat.

A half mile from Taos he found the trappers. They had pulled the horses into a field beside the trail and were all dismounted except the squaw, sitting like a chubby brown doll on her split-eared buffalo pony. Morgan checked his roan, and it fiddle-footed like a dancer beneath him.

"Let's light a shuck."

"Ryker says we go back to Santa Fé," Turkey Thompson said.

Ryker scowled up at Morgan. He pointed at another party of Pueblos in war paint, approaching them on the trail. "This has the makings of a full-scale revolution. I've got to protect my interests in Santa Fé."

"What about our interests?" Morgan said.

"They're involved. There's no telling what attitude a new government would take about trapping."

Morgan swung off his horse. There were gaunt hollows under his bleak cheek bones, and his mouth was tight as a jump trap. "And while we're down there protectin' our interests, we'll get paid?"

Ryker scowled. "With what?"

"That's what I mean," Morgan said. "Go back now and we lose a whole season. I didn't come a thousand miles to sit around Santa Fé all winter and starve to death."

"We've got to go back. You know the feeling against foreign trappers in this country. If I don't keep my contacts in Santa Fé, we wouldn't be able to sell the furs we got."

"We'll take 'em to Saint Looey, then."

"We couldn't even get them out of the country. You'd have a squadron of dragoons down your neck."

Ryker was thinking like a trader now, a businessman, with no sympathy for the trapper's position, and in protecting himself he was violating the contract he had signed with Morgan. He had agreed to finance the expedition and supply all the equipment for seventy percent of the profits, while the trappers divided the thirty percent remaining. Morgan hadn't come all the way from Texas on the strength of that contract, traveling for months through an Indian-infested wilderness without a cent of pay, to be left holding the trap sack because Ryker got cold feet.

"All right," he said thinly. "You go back to Santa Fé. We'll go on, and we'll take the traps."

"What guarantee have I got that I'd ever see you again?"

"My word."

Ryker snorted disgustedly. "Would you take mine?"

Morgan was silent a moment, digesting that. Then he grinned slowly and balefully. "I guess that leaves you one thing."

"What?"

"Come or not, like it or not, take my word or not, I'm heading north . . . and I'm takin' the outfit."

Ryker took a step backward and in the same swift motion elbowed aside his bearskin coat to draw one of the Ketland-McCormicks. Morgan followed him in a single long lunge, swinging his five-foot rifle up in a vicious arc. It whipped against Ryker's neck as he pulled the pistol. Ryker's eyes rolled up, and his face went slack and pale with the shock. He fell heavily to one side, dropping the gun, and struck the ground as limp as a drunk.

Morgan kicked the pistol away from the man and whirled on the others. Neither Saunders nor Turkey Thompson had made a move. The squaw dropped off her buffalo pony with a broken sound and went to her knees beside Ryker. Morgan stooped to yank the second pistol from Ryker's belt. He dropped it beside the other Ketland-McCormick and with the butt of his rifle deliberately smashed the flints in both pistols. Ryker groaned and rolled over, face squinted up in pain. Morgan proceeded to load his rifle.

"Who's goin' with me?" he asked.

Turkey's Adam's apple bobbed like a cork in his neck. He looked at Ryker, at Cimarrón. Then he gulped. "You're right, Kelly. He ain't got no right to go back on his contract."

Saunders scratched his jaw absently through the mat of his fiery beard. "You're a couple of damn' fools. These Pueblos take it in their heads to include the Yankees, you'll be a target for every Indian from here to the Picketwire."

"We'll take that chance."

With the help of the squaw, Ryker sat up. His broad, brutal face had a putty color, and he breathed in stentorian gusts. "It's highway robbery, Kelly. I'll have you posted in Santa Fé. Set foot inside any town in a thousand miles and they'll clap you in jail."

Without answering, Morgan swung onto his horse. Turkey hesitated, then got on his spotted horse. Ryker made a grating sound, saying to Saunders: "Stop them, damn you!"

Before Saunders could react, Morgan swung his loaded rifle to cover the man. "Git 'em on the road," he told Turkey. As the groaning, snorting line of pack animals walked out into the trail, Morgan said: "I'll be back come winter. You'll git your split."

He followed the pack train northward on the trail, keeping his horse turned and his rifle covering them. When they were out of range, Morgan joined Turkey Thompson. The skinny trapper looked at the curing grass, gold as wheat on the slopes.

"Early winter," he said.

"Beaver'll be prime," Morgan said.

In a while they came in sight of San Geronimo, the Indian pueblo. Like terraced citadels the two communal buildings faced each other across the placid mirror of Taos Creek. Before they reached it, Morgan heard a horse behind and saw Cimarrón Saunders riding to catch up. He pulled his broad-chested pinto down to a walk beside them.

"Ryker started jumpin' down my craw after you left. I guess you was right about him."

"Maybe Ryker sent you to keep an eye on us," Morgan said.

Saunders leaned toward Morgan, eyes like gimlets. "This is your first season in the mountains, son. You got a few things to learn. To a free trapper, there's one thing lower than a varmint."

"What's that?"

"A spy, son, a spy workin' for a booshway like Ryker."

Morgan regarded him for a moment. "All right," he said. "Let's ride."

They skirted the Indian town and left it behind them in the shimmering of late afternoon. They headed north with the red mountains pressing in all about them. Only once, with the dying sun staining the sky like blood, did Morgan look behind him.

"You thinkin' about that gal?" Turkey asked.

Morgan's grin squinted his eyes almost shut in his face. "Ain't that a sack o' hell?" he said.

Chapter Six

The morning after Mayor Melgares was freed, the insurgents marched southward. From their villages along the Río Grande—from Taos and San Juan and Cuyamangue and Nambe and a dozen others—came the Pueblo Indians. From the ranches in the mountains and the towns in the valleys came the Mexicans.

Teresa was with them. At Taos she had met her cousin, Lupe Tovar. Lupe's husband, Santos, was a shopkeeper in the Mexican town of Taos, separated by three miles from the Indian pueblo of the same name. Though Santos Tovar was a *pobre,* born in New Mexico, he was of pure Spanish blood, as were most of the Mexican peasants in the Upper River.

Lupe and Teresa rode in a creaking *carreta* behind the rabble, two of dozens of women who made the journey. At Santa Cruz, twenty-five miles north of Santa Fé, the army made their headquarters. Along with the other women Teresa cooked and carried water and collected equipment and melted lead and molded it into half-ounce balls for the flintlocks of the men.

The Indians were camped in the fields outside of town, but the plaza had been designated as headquarters. The sleepy little village had never beheld such frantic activity. Its ancient mission cast the shadows of huge buttressed corner towers over a mob that filled the square and the streets twenty-four hours a day.

On the evening of the first day they had arrived, Teresa stood in that square with hundreds of others and heard *Don* Gómez read the declaration he had helped prepare, the sententious phrases rolling from him in a deep, resonant voice.

Viva God and the nation, and the faith of Jesus Christ; for the principal points that we defend are the following:

First. To be with God and the nation.

Second. To defend our country till we spill every drop of blood in order to obtain the victory we have in view.

Third. Not to admit the departmental plan.

Fourth. Not to admit any tax.

Fifth. Not to admit the disorder desired by those who are attempting to procure it. God and the nation.

Encampment: Santa Cruz de la Cañada, August 3, 1837.

After the ceremony, Teresa and Lupe went outside the town to see the war dances. The campfires were a thousand falling stars blooming on the dark fields, and in each camp the Pueblos from the various villages were dancing. The firelight flickered on their shining, sweaty, painted bodies, and their weird dancing ran out into the night like the ululation of animals in pain.

The two women stood for a while on the fringes of the crowd. Lupe was a fat, moon-faced woman, harried with the burden of eight children and a lazy husband. She pulled her shawl about her shoulders, shivering in the warm August night.

"It makes me have fear, Teresa. There are things we should not see. I have lived in Taos all my life and never have

I seen them bring their war dances out of the *kivas*. Let's go back to town."

Teresa followed her cousin back to the square. She was beginning to see more clearly what she had become involved with, and knew a reflection of Lupe's dark apprehension. Although these Indians had been defending their villages for hundreds of years against the nomad Apaches and Comanches, they were not essentially a war-like people. While the nomads had fought the Spaniards through the centuries, the enmities, the bitterness, the hatred of a foreign conqueror had simmered and boiled. In using those enmities Gómez had started something that might prove more dangerous than he had dreamed. Already the character of the insurgent army was changing. The Pueblos vastly outnumbered the Mexican peasants. What had started as a political reaction might well turn into an uncontrolled Indian uprising.

With these dark premonitions stirring within her, Teresa made her way through the crowd. A young mother paused, soothing a crying baby in her arms. For a moment everything else was blotted from Teresa's mind by the poignant memory of her own loss. It had never left, really. Even when it was not in her conscious mind, it lay deeply within her, a hopeless misery, underlying everything she did or thought. That was what men had done, too.

Pine-knot torches blazed in the plaza, casting an eerie light over the mob of Mexicans and Indians milling back and forth. Some of the women had set up *puestos* near the church where they sold coffee and tortillas and other food. Lupe stopped to talk with friends at one of the coffee stands. Teresa grew bored with the chatter. She drifted around the plaza toward the headquarters building, housed in a store across from the church. Although Villapando was still the nominal head of the rabble, Nicolas Amado was rapidly assuming the mantle of leadership. His act in facing Lieutenant Pérez's presumably loaded gun had elevated him to the position of a hero. The mob had elected him military commander, and he was given Pérez's saber and coat and a pair of tawdry epaulets from some ex-soldier's war chest.

The store was crowded with newly appointed officers and couriers and givers of unwanted advice. Amado was ensconced behind a makeshift desk piled with official-looking papers and documents that Teresa knew had little to do with the operation of his army. His swarthy, primitive face glowed, and a feverish shine lay like lacquer on the surface of his vivid black eyes. With a ragged goose quill he was signing papers. Teresa stood against the wall, watching him, till he noticed her. He threw back his head and laughed excitedly.

"Did you ever see so much to do, *mi* Teresa? Being a general is like going crazy."

She moved to the desk. "They say you are going to execute Lieutenant Pérez."

Amado put his hand on a paper. "This is the order. It is the will of the Pueblos."

"You have enough power now to countermand it. Pérez is popular with the regulars. They would hate you for killing him."

"I don't need the regulars. I have an army of my own."

"You'll need them if you get in power. You'll need every friend you can get."

Amado struck the table. "Pérez is a chief representative of the tyranny and corruption. An example must be made of him."

"Why? He was only doing his duty."

"Enough. Can't you see how much I've got to do?"

He began shouting orders at a new courier, and the crowd closed around her, shoving her away from the desk.

She moved moodily out of the store. In her mind again was the picture of Lieutenant Pérez, so proud, so vividly handsome, standing with his back against the jail door and facing the mob with an empty gun. They couldn't just kill a man like that in cold blood. It was so brutal, so uselessly cruel. Then she shook her head angrily. Was it because he was so handsome, reminding her so poignantly of Juan? Was she really still clinging to her romantic dreams about the man who had left her with the baby despite her surface attempt to hate him?

The place was full of men indulging in the national pastime of gambling. She saw a monte game and stopped to watch. The thrower was a hawk-nosed young man, his glazed sombrero dripping silver pendants, his blue velvet trousers buttoned down the seams with big silver bosses. He looked like a town idler, the kind of a man who lived off his wits, and perhaps off his skill with cards.

Monte was an ancient Spanish game played with a deck that contained no eights, nines, or tens. Before playing, the money staked by the bank was placed on the ground by the dealer. After the shuffle and cut, the dealer held the pack face down, drew off the two bottom cards, and placed them on the ground face up. That was the bottom lay-out. Then from the top of the deck he drew two more cards, putting them down face up. When all bets were made, the pack was turned over. The card exposed was the gate. If it matched in denomination a card in either bottom or top lay-out, the dealer paid all bets that had been made on that lay-out.

The hawk-faced young man had just finished one deal and was beginning over again. He squatted on his hams, surrounded by a dozen players and onlookers, keeping up a running line of chatter. "Queen and a four on the bottom . . . any more bets on the bottom? I see a *peso* coming up. Is that all you have, my friend? Surely such a handsome *caballero* has more courage. . . ."

The grinning farmer added another silver piece to the heap of jewelry and money lying before the queen of the bottom lay-out. Then the dealer slid the pair of cards off the top of the deck in his hand, laying them face up. The bets were made on them. By the small number of players, Teresa guessed that the game had just started. This would be the come-on, then. As the smooth young man started to turn the deck over in his hands, to expose the gate, she took a guess.

"The blonde queen."

Everyone looked at the exposed gate card, then glanced at Teresa in surprise. She saw that it was the blonde queen, matching the queen already showing in the bottom lay-out. The farmer who had bet began taking in his winnings, laughing excitedly.

"The red-headed one, she brings me luck, Miguel."

Miguel, the monte thrower, smiled lugubriously at Teresa. "We'll see," he said.

He began to deal again. All the things Johnny Cavan had taught her began to return to Teresa now. She knew this would be another come-on. If the deck was marked, it was usually the face cards. The lay-outs were down, top and bottom, and the only face card showing was a jack of swords. With the bets down, the dealer was ready to expose the gate.

"Jack of cups," Teresa said.

The men in the group exclaimed in surprise. She had called it right. The same farmer pulled in his winnings, chortling and calling to the thrower. "You should get a redhead yourself, Miguel."

Still holding the deck, Miguel looked obliquely at Teresa. He was smiling, but there was malice in his shrewd black eyes. "Perhaps the clever *señorita* would like to play."

"I have no money," she said.

The rancher pulled at her arm. "You bet for me. You bring me luck. I split with you." He pulled his blanket roll up beside him, and she sat on it. "I am named Pablo," he told her. "From Chimajo I come. If I keep winning like this, who cares about the war?"

Sweating, eyes shining in the torchlight, the men watched Miguel deal again. The bottom lay-out was a seven and a four. Teresa sensed Miguel's intent now and told Pablo not to bet. Poker-faced, the dealer put down the top lay-out. One of the cards was the blond king. Teresa realized he had pulled a switch. This was still the come-on. She told Pablo to put everything on the king. She saw Miguel's face tighten. But he could do nothing. They were all watching too closely. He had to deal as he had planned. He turned the deck up. The gate was another king.

Pablo jumped to his feet, laughing and shouting in excitement. Sullenly, looking with smoldering eyes at Teresa, Miguel paid off. The noise of the farmer's shouting was drawing more men now. They crowded around, babbling and asking questions. Teresa saw Miguel start to sweat. He was on the spot now. He probably didn't have enough money to bank for another loss. He had to deal to win.

And he did. When both lay-outs were down, there wasn't a face card in the bunch. She kept Pablo from betting. The others followed suit. When Miguel turned the deck up, there wasn't a *peso* on the ground, and the gate card was a seven of swords, matching none of the cards in the lay-out.

The men looked at Teresa in amazement, and one of them asked: "Are you a *bruja?*"

Pablo laughed like a hyena. "If she is a witch, I would like to know them all."

It was a grim moment now. Miguel had to play to lose

sooner or later. If he kept the gate card from matching the lay-out too long, the crowd would grow suspicious and turn against him. Three times he played to win, keeping all the face cards off the ground, and three times Teresa advised Pablo not to bet, and the crowd followed suit. A sullen murmur began to run through them, and some of the men made ugly insinuations. A dull red flush crept into Miguel's face. He had to give them the bait again or quit. And if he quit, the village would not forget.

Teresa watched his eyes and saw him glance briefly at the pack as he shuffled, looking for the pin pricks marking the backs of the face cards. He was giving them the bait, banking on the hope that Teresa had been merely working on lucky guesses and did not really know how the cards were marked. It was all he could do, and, when the top lay-out came up, it held a queen of swords.

"Bet everything," Teresa said.

Pablo looked wide-eyed at her. Then he shoved his whole pile of silver and jewelry to the edge of the queen. A dozen others did likewise. Miguel's face went white with rage. One of the men standing beside him bent down and turned his hand over. The card it exposed was a blonde queen.

With a waspish curse, Miguel got to his feet. He was too enraged to speak. His eyes blazed at Teresa. He yanked a buckskin bag of silver from under his shirt, emptying it onto the ground. He pulled his sombrero off, silver pendants tinkling, and threw it beside the bag. One by one he tore off the silver bosses on his velvet pants and dropped them into the pot.

"That is all," he said in a strangled voice. "The bank is broken."

In his anger, he left the cards on the ground and turned to stalk out through the crowd. The men began to shout for another banker, and one called to Pablo. "How about you, ugly one? You won the most."

Pablo turned to Teresa, face shimmering with sweat. "I never had such luck. You must be San Augustin himself, the patron saint of all gamblers. You deal for me. Fifty-fifty, all the way."

Someone handed her the cards Miguel had left. She shuffled them automatically, sensitive fingers feeling for the pin pricks on their backs that marked the face cards. Her knowledge of this game was the only heritage Johnny Cavan had left her, and he had taught her that under ordinary circumstances a monte thrower didn't need a stacked deck. The percentage was always with the house.

She threw a few hands straight, and it proved out. She won more than she lost, but the crowd was satisfied because they were winning, too. It gave her a sense of power over these men to see the heap of coins growing before her, to see their eyes fixed on her face, her hands—to know that for once their interest in her was not merely the beauty of her body and what it could give them.

There was a movement in the crowd, and Amado pushed his way into view, trailed by his shadow, Inocente, and surrounded by his retinue of officers and sympathizers. He looked around, tired, harried. When he saw Teresa, the irritation left his face, and he began to chuckle.

"They told me of the fabulous *tahúra* impoverishing my army."

"Do you have time for such frivolities?"

"Even a general must relax."

She knew it was more than just relaxation that had drawn him. He was as much addicted to gambling as any of his countrymen, and rumors of a woman dealing the biggest game in the plaza had goaded him till he could bear it no longer. He nodded at the heap of silver and jewelry before her.

"Is that the limit?"

She nodded. Then a thought struck her, a possibility. It was a gamble, but it was really the only way she had of getting to Amado. She still could not bear the thought of the lieutenant's dying. "It is only a few *pesos,*" she said. "A general should gamble for higher stakes."

"What stakes?"

Her green eyes grew veiled. "The life of Lieutenant Pérez?"

A surprised murmur ran through the crowd. Amado's humor fled. "Are you declaring for the Centralists?"

"What does a woman know of politics?" scoffed Pablo.

"What would you gain by killing him?" Teresa asked. "What kind of a general rewards courage with death? Have you no courage yourself that you let the Pueblos enact a useless revenge on one of your own people?"

It made an impression on the Mexicans in the crowd. Some of them were from Taos and had seen Pérez's audacious stand there. They began to call to Amado that she was right, that Pérez should be given at least a sporting chance.

Teresa's coral lips grew petulant. "Perhaps the general fears not only the Pueblos . . . but a woman, too," she said.

She saw the blood creep into his face. He was sensitive enough to feel the mood of the crowd, and he knew the favor he would lose by refusing her challenge now. Teresa saw that he was weakening. While the attention of the crowd was still upon Amado, she began shuffling. Eyes almost closed, she prayed that her fingers would still be agile enough. It was Johnny Cavan's trick. He had called it the slick throw. She used the marks pricked into the backs to place her cards. When she was finished, there was an ace of swords on the top

71

and an ace of cups third from the bottom.

"It takes a brave man to face a loaded gun," she said. "But it takes a great man to forgive an enemy."

It appealed to the Latin romanticism of the crowd, and their shouts for Amado to accept the challenge filled the air. Grumbling, reluctant, he lowered himself onto his saddle. "Very well, Teresa. But have care. A cheat is worse than a spy."

Her only fear now was that he would call for a cut that would defeat her. She held the cards out to him. "Then you deal."

It was a move of desperation. She hoped the gesture would throw him off guard, make him neglect to cut. Surprised, he took the cards, and—prodded by their clamorous insistence—he began to deal without cutting.

The ace of swords came up first on the top layer. Three miscellaneous cards followed. The noise died down, and the crowd pushed in, watching avidly. Amado looked at Teresa. She put a *peso* on the ace.

Amado turned the deck up. The gate was the ace of cups.

The crowd went wild. They danced in each other's arms, and their shouting filled the place. In all the tumult Amado sat on the saddle, studying the gate card. Teresa felt the breath gag in her throat. The ignorant *peónes* would not know how to read the markings. But a man like him. . . .

A new tone entered the shouting. A man thrust his way through the crowd. "General!" he shouted. "Governor Carbajal has left Santa Fé and is marching on us with his army."

Amado dropped the cards and rose. Gathering his cloak around him, forgetting Teresa immediately, he plunged through the mob toward his headquarters, shouting orders. The only man remaining beside Teresa was Pablo, the farmer who had won with her help. He squatted like a bullfrog over his heap of winnings, grinning slyly up at her.

"Fortune smiles upon you, *señorita*. If he had found you were cheating, I think he would have you shot with Lieutenant Pérez."

Chapter Seven

 From spies and scouts Amado learned that Governor Carbajal had camped with his forces at Pojoaque, some eighteen miles north of Santa Fé. The rebel army, over a thousand strong now, marched before dawn on August 8th. They moved through the country south of Santa Cruz—a land of sequestered valleys interfaced with irrigated ditches and bearded with peach orchards.

Nicolas Amado rode at their head on a prancing black barb. Muffled to his chin in the cloak, shivering in a pre-dawn chill, with the sullen mutter and clatter of the marching army all about him, he sought to rekindle the fires of courage and zeal that had consumed him during the frantic excitement of the preceding days. He had always idolized General Lopez de Santa Anna, savior of the people and ruler of all Mexico. Was it always this way with such a great man—these nagging doubts, these insidious fears that came in the dark hours before battle? What was there in himself, Amado wondered, that held him back, that kept him from knowing the heights of blind and unquestioning courage that had sustained Pérez when he had faced the mob with that empty pistol? Was that what made for true greatness in a man? Or were the great tormented as he was by the devils of caution and skepticism constantly whispering in his ears?

His reverie was broken off at the clamor of hoofs before

him. He turned to see Gómez riding up. The man was wrapped to the chin in a handsome serape. His eyes were feverish, red-rimmed, filmed with the vague frustration Amado had seen before in this man when he was tired and his cynical defenses were down.

"Dawn soon," Gómez said. "Any word from the scouts?"

Amado's chin sank into his cloak. "None."

Gómez peered closely at him. "Some of the men are grumbling about Lieutenant Pérez being spared."

"The rest are with me," Amado said. "They recognize a brave man when they see one."

Gómez chuckled. "That Teresa Cavan seems to have a strange power over you. Did you know her before?"

"Yes," Amado said absently. "Before. . . ."

His eyes lost focus, as if staring into some great distance. The question had taken him into the past. His first meeting with Teresa had been a curious affair, almost a predestined thing. So many of the events of his life seemed to have guided him toward that one point in time. There was the matter of the ring. If he had not worn it, he would not have lived to know her. And yet it had been with him since his birth.

Amado would never know the exact date of that birth, or the exact location. He only knew that sometime in the first decade of the 19th Century a squalling baby had been found on the doorstep of the poverty-stricken Amado family near Albuquerque. He was given their name and raised in the squalor of their household as one of them. His Indian blood soon became evident, in the thick lips, the jet-black hair, the coppery skin. Mama Amado said he was Apache; Papa thought he detected a little Comanche. Yet Nicolas refused to accept the evidence. For there was the *rúbrica*. This was the ring with the ancient seal inscribed on its face left with him when he was abandoned. The seal was not known in Mexico, yet such a ring could come only from an honored and ancient Spanish family. This *rúbrica* surrounded Amado with an aura of mystery and romance that he did everything to perpetuate and expand. To himself and all the world he was the illegitimate spawn of some clandestine romance between a mysterious Spanish grandee and an unknown woman of Albuquerque. As soon as he had been old enough to wear it, the *rúbrica* was slipped on his finger, never to come off. It was with him when he and his foster-brother, Inocente, became shepherds for one of the great ranches outside Albuquerque. It was on his hand as they drifted north to Santa Fé, where Amado found a ripe field for his assorted talents. A nimble-witted sycophant, he ingratiated himself into the circle of minor politicians at the capital and was soon appointed to the customs office. His duties often took him to Taos or El Pasó, and it was on one of these tours, barely a month before, that he had met Teresa.

Returning from El Pasó, he and Inocente were on the Chihuahua Trail, thirty leagues south of Albuquerque, when they came up with half a dozen creaking two-wheeled *carretas* loaded high with trade goods. It was the retinue of Pepe Rascón, on his annual trading *conducta* to Santa Fé. Amado had met the old man several times before in El Pasó, but had never seen his young wife.

While Rascón walked beside his lead cart, prodding the sleepy mules with a sotol stalk, the woman rode on a heap of Indian blankets inside, a year-old baby in her arms. Amado bowed gallantly at Rascón's perfunctory introduction. Teresa's green eyes, the curling mass of her red hair, and her succulent ripeness set Amado's whole body tingling, but she merely nodded at him and turned her heavy-lidded eyes back to the child.

Rascón was grateful for the added protection of their company, so they agreed to travel with him the rest of the way to Santa Fé. They camped by the river that night. While the others sat around the fire with their master eating a silent meal, the woman did not join them. She sat against the great solid wheel of one of the carts, her baby in her lap. Rascón made no move to fill a plate for her, so Amado took one over. She accepted it without thanks. For a moment, as she began to eat, she looked across toward her husband. Her eyes were lit by the coals of a smoldering resentment. The whole story was in that one glance. A young woman, yearning for love and romance and youth, chained to a belching old goat like that.

"There is so much sweet wine to be tasted," Amado said. "It is a pity life has withheld the fount from your lips."

She did not look at him. "I have tasted many times. It was not sweet."

Her complete indifference to him struck at his pride. He could not quite fathom her. On the surface she revealed the subjection and resignation seen in so many of these *peón* women. Yet for a moment in her eyes he had seen that flash of spirit, that smoldering rebellion.

In the middle of the night he was awakened by the gobbling cries. The coals of the fire still burned low, and the ruddy light revealed them, coming in out of the night, like the shadows of doom. A dozen riders, a score, a hundred—he never knew. As he rolled out of his blankets, he saw Pepe Rascón and his drivers jumping to their feet. Three feathered shafts struck Rascón at once, two in the belly and one in the chest.

At the same time Amado saw Teresa crawling from beneath the cart under which she had been sleeping, the baby in her arms. Shouting his war chant, an Indian head man out of the darkness wheeled his horse toward the cart. Teresa was just coming to her feet in front of him, and his horse knocked her back against the wagon. The baby was torn from her arms, falling to the ground. The Indian turned his horse, trampling the child under the horse's hoofs. Another rider circled in from the darkness, and they both swung off to grab the screaming Teresa.

Vale más estar tomado por valiente que serlo. Following the dictates of his favorite axiom, Amado did not run toward the battle but tiptoed from his pallet to the edge of camp, and ran away into the darkness. The earth trembled beneath him with the pound of following hoofs. He turned in time to see the horse behind, to see the war club descending. He rolled with the blow, and the fall stunned him. The Indian wheeled back and jumped down, kneeling to scalp him. It was the *rúbrica* that saved Amado.

These Indians were not the peaceful, sedentary Pueblos from the villages along the Río Grande who were later to follow Gómez and Amado in revolt. These were Navajos, hereditary enemies of the Pueblos—nomads and warriors who for centuries had fought the Spaniards. Yet these centuries of conflict had provided enough contact to superimpose the language and some of the customs of the Spaniard upon these Indians. Most of them spoke Spanish; many had Spanish names. During the short periods of peace between the intermittent warfare some of the men frequented the towns along the Río Grande. There one could see *rúbricas* such as this one on the hands of the aristocrats. As the Indian grabbed Amado's hair, the ring must have glittered in the feeble light from the distant fire. The man bent to stare at it, then called to the others.

The head man soon came. The ring made them think Amado was a *hidalgo*—a man from a family rich enough to provide a big ransom. Amado lied, telling them his name was Pino, the name of the most famous family in the department.

They finally agreed to send Inocente with a message. The payment was to be in sheep, more golden than *pesos* to these Navajos, and was to be driven to this spot within three weeks.

The Navajos released Inocente and then overturned the wagons, spilling the goods out. On their horses they loaded the powder and arms, the Pass Brandy, trade kettles, blankets, and what else was valuable to them. To the rest they set fire.

With hands bound behind them, Teresa and Amado were put on horses and driven ahead of the Indians. He would never know how far they went—that night and the next day and the next night in the saddle without rest. Finally they halted and slept all day in the lee of a mesa. In the evening, Amado was awakened by drunken chanting. Some of the younger warriors had broached the Pass Brandy. On empty stomachs it was dynamite.

The camp was soon the scene of a drunken debauch. The young bucks dressed up in gaudy blankets and fancy Spanish shawls, covering themselves with the rings and bracelets, the necklaces and other gewgaws they had found in the carts. They danced wildly around the fire, chanting of their triumph to their gods, reeling drunkenly, laughing and howling in primitive abandon.

Teresa sat a few feet away from Amado. Her hair was matted with dirt and brush, and her face was so caked with dust that it looked like a gray mask. Her body began to stir, from side to side. It took him a while to realize what she was doing. She had found a sharp ledge of rock behind her and was sawing at the rope.

"*Señora,*" he hissed. "Do not antagonize them."

She did not answer. She kept sawing. After an interminable period she gave a jerk, and he saw the frayed rawhide drop from her wrists. Then she let her glance move across the trade goods littered on every side. At last her eyes stopped. The tip of a Toledo dagger, finely damascened, glittered beneath a taffeta dress. Teresa edged over, inch by inch, till she could reach her foot out, hook it around the knife, and draw it to her. She got it in her hand, then swiftly put it behind her.

Amado pleaded. "You would be a fool. Let them use you as they will. It is the only thing that will save our lives. Fight them and they will kill us."

Her lips, compressing, made a thousand tiny cracks in the dust-mask on her face. The head man almost tripped, stumbling through a heap of dresses and blankets. Then he stopped, swaying above her. She looked up at him with wide eyes. The utter hatred in those eyes stopped Amado's breath. The head man was too drunk to see it. With both hands behind her, it seemed she was still bound. The Indian let his air out in a wild gust, grabbed her by the hair, and dragged her toward the trees.

She made no sound. Limp as a rag doll, hands still rigidly behind her, she suffered herself to be dragged like a sack of meal across the tough ground, into the trees, behind a screening thicket of mesquite.

Amado realized that his whole body was soaked with sweat. He could see nothing now save that dark screen of mesquite. There was no sound from there, utterly no sound. All he could hear was the crazy chanting of the other drunken Indians about the fire.

Then she appeared. Like one in a trance she walked to the edge of the timber and stopped there. The Toledo dagger was in her hand, bloody to the hilt. The implications of what she had done filled him with a sick breathlessness. For a moment he could not get beyond it with his comprehension, could only react numbly to the world of horror embodied in her figure swaying there, her zombie eyes staring fixedly into some distant hell. Then the spell faded, and he realized the peril of his own position. When the Indians found the head man, they would murder both of them.

"*Señora.*" It was a bleating whisper. He had to call several times before she reacted. Like one rising from a trance she moved her head. He jerked his bound arms. "Please, there is only a minute."

Finally she moved. She dropped to her hands and knees and crawled in behind him so that her movements would not catch the attention of the Indians when she came out of the darkness into the light. She cut him loose. Together they crawled back into the darkness. The Indians had made a corral by turning their horses into a box cañon and stretching a rope across its mouth. Teresa cut the rope, and they used two pieces for bridles. Each on a horse, they drove the rest of the animals out of the cañon ahead of them. They drove the herd before them as far as they could, till the horses began to scatter and break up. Then they headed for the Río Grande.

Near noon the next day they were met by a party of ranchers Inocente had raised from the villages south of Albuquerque. Under their protection, Amado and Teresa were taken to Santa Fé, where he had left her at *Don* Biscara's.

A friend found him before he reported to the Palace of the Governors, telling him that he was on the list of those ordered under arrest by Governor Carbajal. According to the reports, Amado had been making *diligencias* a little too freely. It was a type of graft indulged in by most of the officials in the corrupt town, and Amado was no guiltier than a dozen others who remained free. But with the threat of revolt growing, the government had to make a show of cleaning out the corruption, and Amado was one of the unfortunates chosen for sacrifice. Knowing the treacherous politics involved, he had fled with Inocente to Taos, hoping to find a haven with the disaffected

Mexicans there. During those hectic days, whenever he remembered Teresa, he had the picture of her—the one he thought he would never forget—standing in the shadows with the Toledo dagger in her hand, bloody to the hilt.

Dawn seeping over the edge of the world brought Amado back to the present. He was with the rabble army again, marching to do battle with the governor who had ruined him. He saw that Gómez had dropped back to join his cavalry on the flank of the marching men. All about Amado the cotton shirts of the ragged host bloomed like great white moths in the first pearly light.

Rabbit brush and ragged Apache plume seemed to leap out of the ground at Amado's feet. Ahead he saw sandy flats and the Pojoaque River. The horizon was turned to a crouched and broken monster by the outlines of Black Mesa. Amado's scouts splashed through the river and reported to him that they had sighted the enemy near the mesa. As far as they could make out, there were only two or three hundred men under Governor Carbajal. Most of them were Indians from the Pueblo of Santo Domingo, still loyal to the government, and there was hardly a full troop of regulars. This was heartening news to Amado, but he sent the scouts forward again without telling anyone else. Then he halted the army and sent for Gómez and Villapando.

The Indian was mounted on a bareback, snorting pinto. He was stripped to the waist, his broad muscular torso smeared with greasy stripes of red and yellow paint. He carried a buffalo lance and had a machete and a pistol in his belt. Amado told them the battle was at hand, without disclosing the actual number of the enemy.

Villapando answered fiercely: "Let us spread our force across the plain and drive the governor against Black Mesa."

"Would you treat an army like a rabble?" Amado asked.

He saw the Indian's eyes flash with anger. "War is a science, my good Villapando. We will divide our forces. Gómez and I will circle the mesa with the cavalry and come upon the enemy from behind. When you hear the *degüello,* you will attack their force in the front."

Something near surprise fluttered through Gómez's jaded eyes, then, watching Amado quizzically, he said: "I must admit that sounds best. I will gather my men. We will be ready to ride in ten minutes."

The heart of the cavalry was composed of about twenty *ricos*—the large landholders who had declared for the revolt with Gómez. These were fierce, hard-riding men, born to the saddle, inured to the hardships of the buffalo hunt and the cruelties of the incessant Indian warfare carried on by the outlying villages. Each of them had brought with him a score or more *vaqueros* from his ranch, superbly mounted and well-armed. Added to this were other Mexican horsebackers from the towns and several hundred Pueblo Indians who had obtained mounts.

As they circled the mesa, Amado sent an oblique glance at Gómez. He knew the man's politics. Gómez, although he had risen from the peasantry, was now a rich landholder and did not have the full confidence of the rabble. That was why he had chosen Villapando as a figurehead, hoping to manipulate things from behind the throne, and so would logically favor the same tactics in battle. It fitted nicely into Amado's own concept.

"When I was with General Santa Anna," Amado said, "it was his custom to hold back a few chosen members, watching from some vantage point where he could direct the fighting and thus insure victory."

Gómez looked him full in the face. A cynical smile touched his lips, and he chuckled huskily. "General, you are a man after my own heart. I was just going to suggest that a man of my years would probably do more harm than good in a charge."

They both laughed in Machiavellian comradeship. It brought a glow of confidence in Amado. This bunch of disaffected landholders was the most cohesive group in the whole heterogeneous rabble. Their support could well be the deciding factor as to the ultimate leadership. If Amado could swing Gómez's favor this way. . . .

"We will move to the flank," Amado said. "When the bugler blows the charge, we will find high ground from which to direct the troops."

As they edged their animals toward the flank of the cantering riders, Amado heard a snicker from his side. It was his foster-brother, like a hump-backed dwarf on his scrawny burro, his cadaverous face twisted into moronic grimace. "In Santa Cruz it is said that the toll of the bell is not for the dead, but to remind us that we, too, may die tomorrow." He giggled.

"Silence, stupid one!" Amado swept his arm up as if for a blow, and Inocente cringed.

The sun was up as they rounded the end of the mesa and saw the enemy spread out before them. Governor Carbajal's scouts had already made contact with the rebel infantry, and the whole government force was faced toward Villapando with their backs toward Amado's cavalry. Amado unsheathed Pérez's saber and raised it dramatically.

"Bugler . . . the *degüello*."

The blast of Santa Anna's infamous no-quarter call beat brazenly against the thin morning air. It was drowned in the wild shout of the mounted men and the squeals of their horses and the sudden thunder of hoofs. Amado reined his horse aside to join Gómez, but Inocente got in his way. Before he could force the scrawny burro out of the way, the first ranks flooded around him. It excited his horse, and the beast bolted. Amado tried to wheel, to turn, but the horse was running away with him. He was hemmed in on all sides by charging cavalry, and their wild rush was carrying him along like a chip on the crest of a wave.

The excitement of the charge was contagious. Amado forgot his efforts to stop his horse, to pull aside, forgot his sly prudence, his old caution. He began to shout with the rest of them, spurring his horse till it was the first in line, holding his saber up like a general should.

He saw figures ahead turning, raising rifles. Far on the left flank, a squad of uniformed regulars appeared, all turning at once under a command. The ragged figures in the center parted before a rush of mounted dragoons, a dozen at most, who halted in file.

Then the firing began. The first volley came from the dragoons, like the crackling of dry sticks. A horse screamed beside Amado and went down, throwing its rider. On the other side a man slid off without a sound.

"Fire!" bawled Amado. "Fire!"

The crash of guns from his own ranks deafened him. It was a terrifying sound, like the earth coming to pieces. It shocked him and filled him with a furious sort of frenzy he did not understand. He saw Carbajal's men falling like wheat before a scythe. The Santo Domingans were distinguished by their *bolsos*—shell-trimmed bands that crossed their chests diagonally. Amado saw them breaking in a mass and scattering all along the line.

The dragoon officer rode back and forth through the ranks, trying to beat them back into the line with the flat of his sword. But it was no use. The stench of blood and powder and the screams of falling horses and wounded men and the sight of their enemy breaking—it all turned Amado's frenzy into exaltation. He had never known it could be like this. He was a god, like Santa Anna, a giant among men, almost upon them now, riding down upon them, standing in his stirrups and screaming like a berserk.

"Run, you *pendejos!* Run, you *cabrónes!* I've come for your heads. I'll have them on my own sword. We'll spit you on our *lanzas* like pigs at the slaughter!"

With shocking abruptness they met the enemy, like the ocean topping a sea wall they struck the broken pieces of the first line, flowing through and over them. Amado saw a dozen Santo Domingo Indians go down beneath charging hoofs. A dragoon loomed up before him, cutting with a saber.

Amado blocked the blow, wheeling his horse to hack at the man. He saw his sword bite into the blue uniform, and the dragoon fell out of the saddle. The battle had broken into little fights all about him now. Most of the arms were single-shot pieces, and all had been discharged. The fighting was hand-to-hand, with every man for himself.

As Amado fought to get his rearing horse under control, he saw a Santo Domingan pull one of Gómez's *ricos* from the saddle, knifing him as he came down. An Indian from Nambe rode in behind the Santo Domingan, running him through with a lance. One of the dismounted dragoons came staggering out of the smoke, reloading a pistol. He saw the Nambe Indian and shot him out of the saddle. An instant later Amado and two others charged into the dragoon, knocking him flat and trampling him.

The remaining dragoons had reformed and were trying to hack a path through the rebels and reach their retreating infantry. They appeared out of the clouds of thinning smoke, hacking right and left with their bloody sabers, a dozen men who had survived only by discipline and desperation. And they were riding directly at Amado.

For the first time he felt fear. The shocking excitement flowed out of him, and he suddenly had nothing but the impulse to run. He put the off rein against his horse's neck with such force that it spun like a top. The violent wheeling motion spilled Amado from the saddle. He hit with stunning force, losing his sword.

Dazedly he rolled over. He saw that a flood of his own cavalry had surrounded the dragoons. In the cloud of dust and powder, he had a dim impression of kicking horses, upraised sabers, falling men. The dragoons were completely overwhelmed.

As Amado gained his feet, however, one of their number broke through. It was their colonel, streaming blood down his face. His charge took him directly at Amado, and he raised his sword to strike as he went by. In the same instant Inocente, on his hairy burro, ran out of the choking dust, charging into the officer's horse and throwing himself bodily at the man. It took the officer out of his saddle, and they hit the ground tangled together. Inocente was first out of the tangle, and he still had his knife. He came to one knee above the man, raising the blade.

"Inocente!" bawled Amado. The half-wit looked around, blinking stupidly. Amado strode toward them. He stooped to pick up the officer's sword. Amado saw now that the man was Colonel Chávez. With the flat of the blade Amado nudged Inocente away from the fallen man. Colonel Chávez sat up, groaning, dazed.

"In the name of peace and justice and the insurrection, you are my prisoner, *señor*," Amado said.

Colonel Chávez wiped blood from his face. His voice was ironic. "It is a pleasure to be taken by a man of such courage, *señor*."

The battle was gone from about Amado now. In the distance, hidden by the settling dust and the shredding hollows of powder smoke, he could still hear the shouting and clashing of sabers, but it was dying down. Gómez appeared from the direction of the mesa, his black horse picking his way daintily through the fallen bodies. He pulled up beside Amado, coughing in the smoke.

"You surprised me, *señor*. I thought you meant to join the general staff."

"Then you mistook me," Amado said. "A leader's place is at the head of his troops."

Gómez frowned at him, suspicion in his dissolute eyes. Then, grudgingly, he began to chuckle. "You are truly a man of destiny, General."

Villapando came at a gallop through the smoke and the carnage, pulling to a halt on his prancing, frothing pinto. He had lost his lance, but a fresh scalp hung on his belt, smearing blood all over his thighs. "The dogs have fled," he panted. "There couldn't have been over a hundred and fifty of them." He peered closely at Amado. "Did you know that?"

"How could I?" Amado said. He nodded at his captive, still sitting dazedly on the ground. "You know Colonel Chávez. He is the senior officer of the presidial companies at Santa Fé."

"Quite a feather in your cap," Villapando said. "If you wish, I will spread the word to your army myself."

Amado felt the muscles of his face grow still at the man's sarcasm. But he ignored it, turning to Gómez. "We cannot stop here. We march to the capital at once."

Chapter Eight

 The Royal City of the Holy Faith of St. Francis of Assisi—a pretentious name for the squalid cluster of flat-roofed adobe buildings sprawled in a valley like a bowl, seven thousand feet above sea level and completely surrounded by three vast mountain ranges. In this summer of 1837, Santa Fé was already an old town. Founded in 1605, it had been the seat of a Spanish province that stretched from the Pacific to the Mississippi, from Mexico to the Canadian Territories—a vast domain inhabited by sixty villages of peaceful Pueblos and ravaged by the endless warfare carried on by the Apaches and Navajos. Through the centuries the streets of the town had been the crooked narrow avenues for high conquest, cavalier adventures, and bloody rebellion.

This was the town reached by the insurgents on August 9, 1837. They camped on the outskirts with the bulk of their forces, and the people of Santa Fé cowered in expectation of a *saqueo*—a plundering of the city. Governor Carbajal had escaped the battle of Black Mesa, accompanied by a handful of trusted friends, but the Indians had followed his trail and captured him at a house south of Santa Fé. They cut off his head and brought it back to the plaza with his lifeless body. For hours the square was filled with yelling, chanting fiends, carrying the head back and forth on their lances, celebrating their first victory over the people of Spanish blood in centuries. Villapando joined the frenzied ritual of triumph, tearing the striped vest and broadcloth dolman off Carbajal's corpse and putting them on his own naked body. Amado and Gómez and the rest of the Mexicans of the insurgent army remained uneasily outside of town. They could not control the Pueblos; they were outnumbered by the Indians and were afraid to interfere with the orgy of revenge for fear the Pueblos would turn on them. Finally, however, as if the barbarous display had satisfied their need of vengeance, the Indians quieted down and drifted back to their camp outside Santa Fé.

It was then that the Mexicans in the rebel army took official possession of the capital. They made a triumphant entry, with Amado and Gómez and his landholders leading on their prancing horses. Lupe and Teresa rode into town in the same cart that had brought them all the way from Taos. It was parked in the plaza while the leaders of the army repaired to the parish church to offer thanks for victory.

A dense crowd seethed back and forth across the ancient plaza. Most of them were already celebrating the victory, drinking heavily, shouting and singing. A dance had begun in front of La Fonda, and the squeaky fiddle music mingled with the other babble.

Lupe's husband elbowed his way through the crowd to the cart. "I've been talking with Alberto Maynez," Santos said. "He manages the inn here. He tells me *Don* Biscara had to flee town to escape the Pueblos, but he has his men out hunting for you. They heard you were with the rebels."

It was like the touch of a cold wind. Despite herself, Teresa looked about in the crowd. She had known the chance she was taking when she defied Biscara. She knew what had happened to other *peónes* who did the same thing. This was a feudal land, living by ancient customs, where the *patrón* could play god without interference. Suddenly, catching sight of a face in the crowd, she stiffened. It was Igualo, Biscara's man-servant. Lupe saw him, too, and made a moaning sound.

"They have come to kill you, I know they have. Take us home, Santos, take us home."

Santos put a hand on the big Spanish pistol in his waist-band, telling Teresa: "You will be safe among us, *chiquita*."

Igualo had caught sight of Teresa now. His glittering eyes were fixed on her face. But he had seen Santos, too, and made no move toward the cart. Then, across the square from Igualo, Teresa saw the narrow, reptile face of García. Lupe clutched Teresa's arm.

"Come back to Taos. You can't stay here."

The fear seeped out of Teresa before the cold core of her old resolve, and she shook her head slowly, eyes still on Igualo. She knew she would not be safe from Biscara in Taos. This had proved it to her. Although Biscara was a *gachupín*—a man of the hated pure Spanish blood—and had fled Santa Fé to escape the vengeance of the Pueblos, he still had pow-erful friends in Río Abajo. It was problematical whether he would be expelled after things had quieted down. It was all or nothing now. In order to retain her safety she had to stay with the revolutionists. As they stood or fell, so she won or lost.

Igualo and García remained in the crowd, making no move toward her, till Amado and Gómez and the other leaders emerged from the parish church, crossing to the Palace of the Governors. A man circulated through the crowd, telling the women that Gómez had asked for some ser-vants to cook and care for the officials who would be residing in the Palace. Teresa eagerly joined the others who were going, knowing that inside the walls she would be safe from Biscara's men.

Santos and Lupe accompanied her across the square. Teresa looked back once, to see Igualo standing against the wall of La Fonda, watching her with those fixed and glittering eyes. Then the black shadow of the *portal* swallowed her, and she was inside the Palace of the Governors.

This ancient structure was probably the most fabulous building north of Mexico City. For over two centuries, it had sprawled like a sullen watchman on the north side of the plaza. Its windows were narrow and secretive slots in adobe walls four feet thick—walls burned by the sun and beaten by the wind till they were as tawny-gray as weathered buckskin. At either end were the two frowning towers, with the military chapel in one, the dungeon in the other. Along the front of the building for over three hundred feet ran the inevitable *portal*—a covered arcade whose roof was supported by time-silvered pine posts planted twelve feet apart. Behind them, in the dim rooms that had been the seat of so many intrigues, were the two curiosities unique to all of New Mexico—the glass in the windows and the festoons of Apache ears strung on the wall. Teresa had heard of these ears, trophies gathered by the governors in retaliation for the myriad scalps taken by the Indians. They were the first thing she saw upon entering the Palace—repugnant, bizarre, somehow symbolizing the end of the whole nightmarish trail that had led her here. Teresa was only one of a dozen forgotten women who crowded curiously about the half open door of the council chamber as the leaders of the revolt gathered to elect their first officers. She knew that Amado had made himself popular by his deeds of the last few days. Yet most of the insurgents were still Pueblos, and he was not one of them. Perhaps this was what swayed Gómez to give his support to Villapando. And when the election was over, Villapando was governor.

After hours of haggling over details, the meeting broke up. Amado was first out. He was tired and haggard-looking, the dust of open country still caked in a silvery film on his broad face. The folded-down tops of his jackboots rustled against his calves, and his spurs jingled in a muted way as he pushed his way through the gawking crowd of women and retainers. This had been a day of defeat for him, and he showed it.

Teresa went after him. "Nicolas, did you make arrangements . . . ?"

He waved irritably. "Don't bother me now. I did what I could. I suggested to Villapando that we needed someone to manage the servants. He didn't say yes or no. I suppose that means you can stay."

He tramped out the door and into the patio at the rear. She stopped by the door. Behind her, she heard a new babble as more men came from the council room. She turned to see Villapando, halted by the door. Beneath the striped vest and dolman his legs were like stanchions of sculpted bronze. It seemed to underline the travesty of these savages in this building. For just a moment, as he stood among the jabbering group, he turned his eyes toward her. Then he swung his broad shoulders and disappeared back into the council chambers. But the look remained, like a tingling pressure against her body. He had taken her all in—her breasts, her belly, her thighs—and it made her feel as naked as the first woman on earth.

As soon as they were established in the Palace, Amado sent for his wife at his ranch at Lemitar, and Gómez brought his wife from Taos. *Doña* Beatriz Gómez arrived first, wheeling into the walled compound behind the Palace in a black coach with the armorial cipher of her house on its dust-spattered doors. From its dusky, plush-seated interior stepped a voluptuous woman in her early twenties. Her *rebozo* was of flame-colored *crêpe de Chine* with a fringe so long it swished at her ankles. As was traditional with the women of

Santa Fé when in public, this vivid shawl was arranged over her head and shoulders and drawn across her face so that only her eyes were visible.

"Your husband is busy in the assembly," Teresa told *Doña* Gómez. "He told me to make you comfortable."

The woman nodded without speaking, and Teresa led the way to the quarters opening off the patio. The officers of the garrison also lived in the huge compound behind the Palace. One of them was lounging at the well—Captain Emilio Uvalde of the militia—a lean, dark-faced man with a reckless smile and brooding lips that gave him a way with women. As they passed, he smiled crookedly at *Doña* Beatriz. The woman met his gaze for just a moment, but Teresa saw her eyes grow wide and bold with a sudden unveiled need. In that single look, Teresa understood some of the frustration she had seen in Gómez.

They entered the rooms Gómez had been using. The woman stepped within the door, glancing around the room. The ceiling was supported by smoke-blackened beams, between which were laid a herringbone pattern of small round sticks, painted alternately red and yellow. The door was carpeted with rough *jerga*, and the whitewash they called *yeso* was peeling off cracked mud walls like a white scum. For a moment Teresa thought the woman would show disdain, or anger. But neither came. She dropped her shawl from her face with a resigned sigh and walked listlessly across the room.

"Your husband says it is the only building in the province with glass windows," Teresa said.

"How nice," *Doña* Beatriz said.

From one of her bags she got a *guaje*, filled with tobacco, a package of *hojas*, and a flint and steel. Skilled as a man, she tapped a measure of tobacco into the cornhusk *hoja*, rolled it, licked it, struck a spark with her flint and steel, and lit the *cigarrillo*. Then she produced a pair of *tenazitas de oro*—the little golden tongs in which these privileged women held their cigarettes to keep the tobacco from staining their fingers. She saw Teresa watching her and offered the tobacco and *hojas*. Teresa accepted with thanks, and in a minute both women were smoking.

"It will not be so bad," Teresa said. "I understand there is to be a *baile* tonight in the plaza to celebrate the new governor."

Doña Beatriz's eyes started to glow, then the light died out. "I will ask my husband," she said.

"He'll be busy. They have been spending every night with that assembly. We could go, anyway."

The woman looked at her in surprise. "What?"

"Why not? Who would stop us?"

Doña Beatriz smiled, a little sadly. "I talked like that once."

There was the military clatter of boots on the hard ground of the patio, and Gómez's sharp voice. "Beatriz, they tell me you are here."

From boredom and listlessness she went into a stiff, almost painful expectancy, like a puppy waiting to greet its master and not knowing whether it would meet anger or humor. She nodded at the door, and Teresa moved to open it.

"Here, *señor*," she said.

Gómez strode in the door. His eyes were red-rimmed with weariness, his face deeply lined. He glanced at Teresa, went to *Doña* Beatriz, took her elbows, kissed her on the forehead. "We quit only for a bite to eat," he said. "You brought my velvet *calzónes*?"

"*Sí, señor.*"

"Extra shirts?"

"*Sí.*"

"Bueno." He glanced around the room. "You are comfortable? Anything you want?"

"Nada."

Gómez moved to one of the *colchónes* and sat down, leaning back against the wall, pinching his nose between thumb and forefinger. "Ah, these meetings. Battles. Nothing but battles. That Villapando is a stupid fool."

Doña Beatriz knelt before him and starting pulling off his boots. "Perhaps a cool, wet cloth for your face? And some wine?"

He nodded, and Teresa stepped to the door, clapping her hands for one of the servants in the patio. She gave the orders to the woman. *Doña* Beatriz was helping Gómez off with his jacket.

"Maybe it would help to relax tonight. Teresa says there is to be a *baile.*"

He shook his head. "Too much work."

"But there will be dancing, and music. . . ."

"I said no."

Doña Beatriz pouted like a sullen child. Gómez had not opened his eyes; he leaned his head back against the wall, rubbing tiredly at his face. The servant came with a basin of water and a bottle of wine.

"Call me if you wish anything," Teresa said.

Doña Beatriz nodded, without looking at her. Teresa left. It was like stepping from a prison. She took a deep breath of the air outside. She knew pity for *Doña* Beatriz, a little contempt. Hers was not the cruelty and pain Teresa had known, but still it was poignantly typical of the subjugation the women of this land endured. The rich one, as a young girl, was subject to the iron-bound discipline of a father. She was held in Turkish seclusion, prevented from meeting all but the sons of the finest families, courted under the watchful eye of her parents or a *duenna*. When the time came for marriage, the parents made the choice and saw to all arrangements. If the girl had not yet met the man who was to be her husband, it was of no consequence. Often bride and groom did not see each other till the day of their wedding. After that she was imprisoned within the thick walls of another house, subject to every whim of another man—growing as docile and beaten and resigned as *Doña* Beatriz under the insidious fetters of custom and tradition. If the man was kind and thoughtful, she was lucky, and her cross was not so heavy. But often he was restless, brought up in a culture where a man was expected to roam, even after marriage. And if he sought sweets at other doors, the wife had little recourse.

The thought of it, the picture *Doña* Beatriz had made, filled Teresa with a fierce resurgence of her old rebellion. She would have the *tenazitas de oro* in which to hold her *cigarrillos* and diamond earrings dripping from her ears like icicles and a Spanish shawl two hundred years old with fringe so long it swished at her ankles. But she would never bow her head.

She was still sitting in the shade of the willow by the servants' quarters when Gómez came from his rooms. He saw her and walked tiredly across the hot patio. A harried look clung furtively to the corner of his squinted eyes—an aging man trying to keep a restless young wife on the leash, and wondering, always wondering. He stopped beside her. The flesh about his lips was tinged with gray.

"You will let the other servants care for *Doña* Beatriz. You are a bad influence on her."

Teresa smiled tauntingly. "Are you afraid of me?"

He did not answer her smile. "I know what you are doing, Teresa. I know what you were doing up in Taos. Amado did not become a general by himself. Do you think his protection will be enough?"

"It would be," she murmured, "if he was governor."

She saw Gómez's eyes flutter with surprise. But it was not a new thought to her. She had seen the way Villapando looked at her, had seen his popularity waning—had caught other warning signals of the increasing precariousness of his position. The possibility of Amado as governor had started as a vague idea—probably long before they reached the Palace, but now it was a definite hope, another opportunity to be grasped in her constant struggle.

"I think you're already fed up with Villapando," she told Gómez. "You chose to speak through him in the beginning because you knew he could draw the Indians to your cause. But you never thought they'd take over so completely. Villapando is sincere, honest, but no politician. He will not make the deal you want with *Don* Biscara."

Again that flutter of surprise. "How did you know?"

"The servants talk. I know most of what goes on in the council chambers. You know we'll need the support of the rich ones in Río Abajo if we're to survive. The Indians and the *peónes* hate *Don* Biscara because he is a *gachupín*. You hate him because he looks down on you. Yet you know he must be cultivated as the only link between your present government and the *ricos* of the Lower River."

His lips compressed, and a sardonic twinkle came to his eyes. "And I thought I was the politician," he said.

"Perhaps you want a reconciliation with the central government, too."

"Of course," he said. He turned, locking his hands behind him, and began to pace agitatedly. "From the beginning I knew we could not break away from Mexico. Texas or the United States would gobble us up immediately. The most we can hope for is to make Mexico City treat us as an equal instead of a slave. Give us a governor from our own people, adequate protection from the Indians, give us some satisfaction for our other complaint. . . ."

"You know you cannot be governor," she said. "The rebels wouldn't overthrow one aristocrat and put another in. They want a man of the people. But you let the wrong man be put in your place. Villapando is too ignorant to be a good governor, too stubborn to let others make him a good governor. What you need is a man who can be molded."

"Amado?" He smiled wryly. "And then you would be safe, wouldn't you? Protected by the superior power in the country."

She smiled. "We would both gain what we want, *Don* Augustin."

He pursed his lips, eyes cynical. "You are like an eagle who means to fly despite its cage, Teresa. You are as deadly as you are beautiful. A man would be a fool to link himself with you."

He turned on his heel and walked toward the Palace. At the door, however, he halted a moment. He looked over his shoulder at her, and there was a puzzled frown on his face. Then he wheeled impatiently and disappeared inside.

At the same time she saw Amado crossing toward her from the barracks. He had seen her talking with Gómez and did not care for it. He stopped before her, scowling, pulling at his chin.

"What are you concocting now, *querida?*"

She smiled bewitchingly. "*Don* Augustin and I were plotting to make you governor."

The vertical grooves dug into his brow. "Don't joke."

"Who's joking? You know what a mess Villapando is making. The Mexicans are disgusted with him. Gómez thought the time ripe for a man of your talents."

His brows rose, and some of the surliness left his face. She had touched his ego again. But such a bold concept took time to adjust to. She knew what an opportunist he was, knew he must have dreamed of someday attaining such a high office. Yet to be presented with the possibility so abruptly was a little frightening.

"Look how quickly you became a general," she prompted. "Isn't this the next logical step?"

His eyes began to glow with the old covetous light. But as always the questions, the doubts, the apprehensions came to harry him. She saw them cloud the light from his eyes.

"How can it be? Try to overthrow Villapando and the Pueblos would turn on us."

"What if we had more Mexicans on our side?" she said. "A real army. Would you declare a counter-revolution and accept the governorship?"

He studied her a long time. Finally a smile pinched his carnal lips at the corner. He began to chuckle softly. "Teresa, *mi vida*, when will you cease to amaze me?"

He looked at her a moment longer, still chuckling. Then he turned and walked thoughtfully to the Palace. She knew what kind of a seed she had planted. In such a sly, Machiavellian mind it would not take long to blossom.

But something had been planted in her mind, too: a growing understanding of the possibilities unfolding before her. All along she had sensed that what had happened with Biscara was merely a culmination, a turning point. Yet the things driving her went deeper than the simple need to escape him. She had sensed it before—she saw it clearly now. In the shape of things to come she saw a chance of freedom, of independence that far transcended any fear of Biscara. These were the needs that went to the root of her and would have driven her whether Biscara threatened or not.

Chapter Nine

 Toward the end of August, Lieutenant Hilario Pérez was brought to Santa Fé from Taos. He was imprisoned in La Garita—the diamond-shaped, somber-towered prison on the hill overlooking Santa Fé. A portion of the dragoons in Santa Fé had declared for the rebels, and the two men who took Lieutenant Pérez through the dark gate of the *garita* had served under him but two weeks before. They were embarrassed by their position and would neither meet his eyes nor speak to him. They showed him to one of the cramped, dirty cells and shut the heavy door on him.

There was nothing to sit on, and he lowered himself to the dirt floor, hungry and exhausted, his clothes grimy and filmed with dust. He was still bitter and confused over the shocking change in his life. He had been born of the *gente fina*, a scion of one of the most aristocratic families in Mexico City; he had received his training at the Colegio Militar, riding with the finest cavalry in the world. He had won the Golden Cross of Honor for service with General Santa Anna in the war with Texas. After the cessation of hostilities, Santa Anna himself had ordered Pérez to Santa Fé, saying that they needed an officer of his caliber to hold the reins on the restless, rebellious troops of the northern department.

It had been a thrilling experience. Used to the pomp and glitter of Mexico City, the violence and glory of the recent war, he had found nothing but a squalid outpost and a ragged garrison of untrained, unequipped men who had no right to be called regulars. To him, the whole revolt had been a farce. He did not know how long he had sat steeped in his bitterness and his disillusionment when he heard bare feet slapping against the earthen floor outside. A chain clanked, the bolt was drawn, and the door opened. He blinked his eyes in the dungeon. He recognized Teresa Cavan.

Sunlight came through the barred window at his back and fell across her in yellow stripes. She wore a black *rebozo* like a hood, its long ends pulled across the front of her body by her arms. She had worn no *enaguas* when he had seen her in Taos; now the flounces of these petticoats, red and blue and yellow, peeped from beneath the hem of her skirt. Her tawny bare feet seemed a primitive paradox to such frilly femininity.

He got hastily to his feet, smoothing his rumpled tunic. He inclined his head gravely, giving her the traditional greeting of the house, for he was a gentleman and would have been courtly in hell.

"Buenos tardes le de Dios, señorita."

"Que Dios se los de buenos a usted," she said, answering with the same grave ceremony. "May God make the afternoons good to you."

He waved her in. "Would that I could celebrate our meeting more graciously. All I can do is thank you for saving my life."

"You must turn the heart of many *señoritas*," she murmured.

He looked into her eyes. They were green, in this light, and they looked as hard as stone. "I would be naïve to think you saved me for that reason," he said.

She moved closer. Her lips, untouched by rouge, were red as coral. They brought back with sensuous impact all the kisses he had ever stolen. "Then we will not be naïve," she said. "It is enough that you are alive and can help us now."

He frowned, suspicious. "How?"

"There is only one man strong enough to bring some order out of this chaos. General Amado has always been a strong Centralist. He was seduced into this revolt on false pretenses. He thought Governor Carbajal would merely be held as hostage till the central government recognized our claims. Now that he has been betrayed, he is planning a counter-revolution. With our squadron of regular dragoons he could overthrow this rabble and restore the city to its rightful hands."

Pérez could not hide his excitement. "There are squadrons in Chihuahua."

She shook her head. "They would take too long to reach. As you know, many of the dragoons here deserted and fled to the mountains or Albuquerque. You are the most popular man in the army, Lieutenant. They would rally to you."

He looked at her in surprise. She was smiling. Her teeth were perfect—small, white, pointed—giving her, in that moment, a strangely savage look.

"Among these dragoons who have declared for the rebels there still must be some friends of yours," she continued. "Who could you trust implicitly?"

"Lieutenant Miguel, Corporal Chávez."

"Good. Your escape will be arranged. Send a courier to Mexico City immediately, informing them that General Amado is working night and day to defeat our enemies. Bring your troops back as soon as possible."

Twenty-three, impressionable, an incurable romantic—Pérez was completely in her hands. Blindly loyal himself, such evidence of loyalty in another was logical to him. He did not seek further motives. She was offering him a chance to escape, to redeem his pride, to turn defeat into victory. What more could a soldier ask? He took her hand. The satiny warmth of it went through him like a shock. *"Señorita,"* he said, "I am your servant."

A shadow crossed her face, and for a moment the soul went out of her eyes. In a barely audible tone, she said, "I hope you will not regret it . . . Hilario."

That night Teresa found Lieutenant Miguel and Corporal Chávez in the barracks behind the Palace. She told them she had seen the order for Pérez's execution on the governor's desk. They were shaken. Although they had declared for the revolution, they were already becoming disillusioned. Pérez's death would make them lose all faith in the insurrectionists. Miguel had been in Pérez's class at the Colegio Militar and could not let his old friend die.

Then they plotted the escape. At eight that night Chávez would go on duty as corporal of the guard at the *garita*. Miguel was to have three horses saddled and ready in one of the alleys under the hill. At fifteen after eight, Teresa was to light a fire at the rear of the Palace. That would give cause for Chávez to send most of his men from the *garita* to help fight the fire. He and Miguel would then overpower the remaining guards, release Pérez, and flee south with him.

At the appointed time, Teresa started the fire in a woodshed. It was separated from the Palace and would not endanger the main structure, but it made a frightening conflagration, filling the whole courtyard with a pall of black smoke. The troops came from the barracks, some in shirt sleeves, others pulling on trousers. The governor and the retinue of Pueblo *caciques* and *alcaldes* rushed from the Palace. By the weird light of the flames Teresa saw dark figures running down the slope from the *garita*. All pitched in to form lines for the bucket brigades.

Teresa stood in the narrow alley between the Palace and the servants' quarters, watching the turmoil through slitted eyes. The courtyard was filled with shouting, coughing figures that shuttled back and forth like shadows before the ruddy backlight of the fire. When the blaze was under control, Teresa saw some of the men moving back from the shouting mob, coughing and wiping soot from their faces. She made out Amado and Gómez and Villapando, grouped together with some of the *caciques*.

A man ran through the crowd toward them, shouting wildly that Lieutenant Pérez had escaped. This caused a new turmoil in the group. Amado and Villapando entered into a violent argument, and then Amado called orders to a dozen of the firefighters, and they followed him at a run toward the stables. The blaze caught a new bundle of faggots and flared up for a moment, illuminating Teresa by the building. Villapando saw her and came over.

Primitive and savage as he was, Teresa had begun to see a certain nobility in this man. He had led the revolt in a sincere belief that he was breaking the chains that had bound the Pueblos for centuries. Now confused, disillusioned, completely unequipped to cope with the complexities and intrigues of government—he was battling with his back to the wall to keep from failing his people. For a moment she regretted her own part in the intrigues against him. Yet she could see no other way out. He stopped a foot from her, a powerful, deep-chested man, emanating the smells of soot and of the earth. Ignorant, illiterate, he still possessed a native shrewdness that lay in the deep crevices at the tips of his eyes, in the searching way he looked at her face. He spoke a crude cow-pen variety of Spanish.

"Perhaps this fire was convenient for Pérez."

"Do you think he set it, Governor?"

"Do not mock me, Teresa. I know what you are. Already you have pitted Amado against me. Without you he was nothing. Together you become more dangerous every day. I will not have it."

She smiled enigmatically. "What will you do?"

"I will separate you," he said. "I will remove your reason to help Amado. You want protection from Biscara. I offer it to you."

It surprised her. "On what terms?"

He moved closer. The fierce expression of his eyes softened. "You will become my wife," he said. "The *cacique* of my pueblo will join us in the ceremony of my people."

Her whole body grew stiff. "I thought you hated me."

"I do." His voice was husky, trembling a little. "But I want you, too. I can't understand that. Only with a woman like you could hate and love go together." He had his hands on her arms now, the hot and callused palms gripping her tightly. This was no Amado with his sly innuendo, no *Don* Biscara with his suave lechery. This was a man close to the animals, shaken by a primitive passion. "You must give me your answer now," he said.

His body was pressing against her, and his face was so close the hot breath seemed to envelop her. And suddenly it was not the face of Villapando, but the face of that Navajo head man back in the desert, bending over her where she lay behind the thicket of mesquite—a contorted face, a gloating face, a face that haunted her nightmares. Her right hand closed, as if about the handle of a Toledo dagger. She twisted free, and her dress tore in his hand as she slid down the wall. She stopped two feet away.

"I will tell you nothing," she said. "Nothing." She saw anger blaze up in his eyes, and he started toward her. She said: "There are a hundred men in the courtyard."

It stopped him. He glanced aside. The mouth of the narrow alley was three feet from his back, with the shouting soldiers still running back and forth across it. His husky breathing abated.

"Very well," he said. "You have made your choice. I am still hunting Biscara. When I find him, he will be exiled. And you will be exiled with him."

Chapter Ten

 Lieutenant Pérez's escape set off a chain reaction, bringing to a head the tension, the seething caldron of intrigue, of plot and counter-plot that had been boiling in the Palace. The morning after Pérez left, thirty-one men were missing from roll call in the barracks. The next morning thirteen more were gone.

Everyone felt that they were joining Pérez around Albuquerque, where he was reported to be gathering an army to retake Santa Fé. Then the rumor arose that the Escuadrón de Vera Cruz was coming from Chihuahua to join Pérez. This spread consternation through the insurgents. The Escuadrón de Vera Cruz was a crack outfit, famed and feared throughout Mexico. The poorly equipped rebels would have little chance against a force of such men combined with the disaffected dragoons flocking to Pérez's standard.

The Pueblo Indians began drifting back toward their villages. Villapando ordered Amado and a troop of the dragoons remaining to keep his army from disintegrating. Amado tried to round up the deserters, but it was like trying to plug a hundred holes in a dam with but one thumb. The rebels camped on the outskirts had numbered in the thousands before Pérez's escape; within a few days they were counted in the hundreds.

The days were filled with frantic meetings in the council chamber. Villapando rarely slept—Gómez got drunker and drunker—Amado filled the Palace with the clank of his restless spurs.

Against Gómez's orders, Teresa had been attending *Doña* Beatriz. The woman understood little of politics, and Gómez needed someone to tell his troubles to. Through *Doña* Beatriz, Teresa learned much of what was transpiring in the secret meetings. On the third evening after Pérez's escape, Gómez was closeted with the assembly, and Teresa took *Doña* Beatriz her supper. Crossing the patio, she was still in the shadows of the willows when she saw the door to the Gómez quarters open a crack. She halted, wondering what it was. In a moment it was pulled wider, and Captain Uvalde stepped out. He glanced quickly around the open compound. Teresa was hidden in the blackness under the trees. He shut the door behind him and walked along the wall toward the barracks, holding his saber against his leg so it would not rattle. There was a crooked smile on his lean face.

When he was out of sight, Teresa crossed the patio and knocked on the door. *Doña* Beatriz admitted her. The woman's face was flushed, her soft eyes unnaturally bright. Teresa set the tray down.

"You should be more discreet," she said. "Captain Uvalde will do little to protect your reputation."

Teresa heard the woman's soft gasp. She turned to see that her face was dead white. The glitter was gone from her eyes, and they shone with a wild fear. Teresa smiled sympathetically.

"Do not fear. It is between us."

"*Gracias a Dios,*" breathed *Doña* Beatriz. She walked to Teresa, taking her hand. "I do not know what *Don* Augustin would do if he found out." She released Teresa's hand and turned to walk agitatedly around the room. For a moment the soft docility was gone from her face; a sullen restlessness made her lips petulant and brought a resentful glow to her eyes. "It's not that my husband is hard, or cruel. He tries to be good. But what does he know? Crops, earth, politics. What is that to a woman? He might as well be my grandfather."

She straightened quickly at a knock on the door. Both women were silent for a moment, faces pale. Then *Doña* Beatriz shook her head.

"It cannot be *Don* Augustin. He never knocks."

Teresa opened the door. John Ryker stood there, a broad and heavy shadow in the outer darkness. He wore his cinnamon bear coat winter and summer, and its pungent scent crept against her like a tainted perfume. "Gómez asked us to meet him here," he said.

Doña Beatriz's lips were parted in surprise. She looked foolish as a schoolgirl. Then she made a nervous flutter of her soft hands. "Of course. Our house is yours. Undoubtedly my husband will be here soon."

Two others followed Ryker in. Teresa knew the first one, Danny O'Brien, a trader on the Santa Fé Trail, an institution in town. He was a short, heavy-girthed man in kerseymere trousers and a broadcloth coat with black velvet lapels. His black stock and white collar flared like the ruff of a startled bird beneath a round face with cherubic eyes and a deacon's smile. But Teresa knew the mind that lay so deceptively behind that smile—shrewd, keen, sharp as a blade. He already knew both women and gave them a courtly bow.

"And this is Vic Jares," Ryker said.

Jares was obviously a trapper, six feet tall, cat-lean through the shanks, hands latticed with fresh trap scars. His eyes were as bright as beads, never still, darting from spot to spot like a hopping bird. He looked at *Doña* Beatriz, then at Teresa. He licked his lips and leered. "Looks like we'll be entertained, anyways."

Teresa flushed and did not answer. *Doña* Beatriz made a confused motion with her hands. Ryker crossed the room, watching Teresa from the corner of his eye. She saw that he still wore his pair of Ketland-McCormicks stuck nakedly through a broad black belt.

"Perhaps a drink," she said.

Before they could answer, the door was thrust open, and Gómez entered, followed by Amado. They both looked surprised at the sight of Teresa. Gómez must have been drinking steadily through the meeting, for his eyes were as heavy-lidded as a sleepy child's, his lips slack and moist.

"I ordered you not to come here," he said.

"I was merely serving *Doña* Beatriz her supper," Teresa said.

"We have no time to bicker," Amado said. He looked sycophantic, trying to placate Gómez. "Why don't we just send them into the other room? If Villapando finds Ryker here, the whole thing will be of no use."

"All right." Gómez swung his hand loosely toward the adjoining room. "Get in there. Close the door. If I find you listening, I'll have you flogged."

Like a frightened rabbit, *Doña* Beatriz scurried through the door.

Teresa sensed that this was a crisis and did not want to be left out of it. "Perhaps I can help you choose the new governor," she said. They all looked at her in surprise. She smiled wisely. "The throne is toppling. Lieutenant Pérez will take Santa Fé by force and execute the rebel leaders. You are trying to force Villapando to abdicate before that happens. You want to elect a governor and a new assembly and declare for the central government again. Then you'll welcome Pérez with open arms and save your heads."

"You've been spying," Gómez said thickly.

Ryker scowled at Teresa. "Let her finish. She seems to know more than we do."

"But Villapando is balking," Teresa said. "He won't abdicate. He has prepared a declaration that he intends to send to Texas, offering them their old boundary claim to the Río Grande if they will send a force here to aid us."

"True," Amado said. He began pacing, face shining with sweat. "Villapando is a fool. If he allows a Texas army in here, they will take us over completely."

"And if he doesn't, Pérez will have your heads," Teresa said.

Gómez walked suddenly to a spindled cabinet and withdrew a bottle of wine, pouring himself a full glass. He took a drink, then spoke thickly, slurring the words. "Villapando may be stubborn, but he's afraid. He knows what a spot he's in. It's those accursed *caciques* and Pueblo governors. They sit around him like a flock of vultures and won't let him listen to a word we say. If we could get him alone, we could convince him. One ride outside the city would convince anybody. We haven't got enough men left in camp to fight a troop of women."

Amado stopped pacing. His lips looked fat and effeminate, pouting. "It is no use. We will never find Villapando without those bodyguards."

Gómez lowered himself precariously to a rolled *colchón*. His head began to sink, then it stopped, slowly raised again, till his eyes were on Teresa. "What if we could get Villapando alone?" he asked. One by one, the others looked at her. Gómez murmured: "We know how he feels about Teresa. Like a bird with a snake. He hates her, yet he can't take his eyes from her. True, Teresa?"

She answered reluctantly. "Yes."

Gómez sat straight. "Will you do it?"

At first she was revolted by the suggestion. Amado saw it and approached her, a sly light in his eyes. "They have found *Don* Biscara," he said.

She turned sharply toward Amado. For a moment all she could think of was Villapando's threat to turn her over to Biscara. It brought a flash of panic. Then that passed. It had been but a momentary thing, a physical reaction to immediate threat. When it was gone, there was no sense of fear in her. Whatever feeling remained was bitter and deliberate, bound up with her resolve never again to become subject to any man. She saw the sly light leave Amado's face, saw it replaced with a disappointment at what little fear he had drawn from her.

But what he'd said had its desired effect. She realized that this was her right, too. She had made her decision on that basis before. If they fell, she fell. Her chin rose, light from the fire made her eyes look vividly green. "And if I get Villapando alone?"

Gómez stood, forgetting his wine. "We'll give him the true picture. We have a count on Pérez's forces, definite proof that the Escuadrón de Vera Cruz is marching north with the presidial companies from Chihuahua. Even a man as stubborn as Villapando could not fail to break under such devastating evidence. We have his declaration of abdication all made out."

"And if he still will not sign?"

"Then we will take him away by force," Amado said. "It is what we were meeting with Ryker about. Once Villapando is out of the Palace, the Pueblos will go to pieces. We can hold him at Albuquerque till we have command again. Then he will be released."

"It won't be necessary now," Gómez said. "If we can but get him alone, he'll abdicate."

They all looked at Teresa again. Her oblique cheeks

flushed with an excitement of her own. Firelight danced in her curling mass of hair as she dipped her head. "I'll do it."

The assembly was still in session, but they had ordered wine brought in. Teresa interrupted the servant in the kitchen and took the tray with bottles and glasses herself. Villapando was seated at a cumbersome oak table at the far end of the large room, surrounded by what was probably the most exotic governing body on the continent. There were a half a dozen aged *caciques*—the medicine men from the various Indian Pueblos, the real power in the tribe—dressed in their handsome Navajo serapes and Chimayo blankets, calves wrapped knee-high with the bandage-like Pueblo *bota*. Among them were *alcaldes* of the Mexican villages in shiny blue serge suits, the Pueblo governors in blue wool shirts and rawhide leggings, and the remaining officers of the presidio glittering and resplendent in their gold braid and towering shakos. They were all haggling with each other in a confusing hubbub of Spanish and Tewa and other Pueblo dialects. As Teresa approached the table, she saw Villapando through a break in the crowd. He looked desperately tired, his face drawn and haggard, his eyes squinted shut. He was shaking his massive head.

"I see no point in arguing further. The document is made. We send it to Texas at once."

Teresa circled the table and pressed through from behind, putting the tray beside Villapando. "Perhaps you would like to have your wine in private," she murmured.

He looked up in surprise. He frowned at her, red-rimmed eyes narrowing. She smiled back, a slow, lazy smile that showed her little animal teeth and the succulent ripeness of her red lower lip. The promise of it was unmistakable. Blood

114

surged up his corded neck and into his blunt-boned cheeks, making them even darker. When he spoke, his voice sounded thick.

"Perhaps you are right." He shoved the chair back, taking a bottle and a glass, announcing to his assembly: "I declare an hour recess. We must all have a little rest."

He stood and looked at her, waiting. She set the tray down. He started toward the door leading to the executive chamber. She followed.

Most of the assembly remained behind, still arguing heatedly, but a pair of the *caciques* moved to follow Villapando and four broad-shouldered Pueblos, dressed in the ragged *pantalones bombachos* of the peasant. Each of them was hung with a saber and a pair of pistols, and two of them carried smoothbore *escopetas*.

The governor's rooms were as meagerly furnished as the rest of the Palace. The only distinguishing feature was the half dozen high-back chairs of intricately carved oak. The *caciques* took their seats in these chairs, like kings upon their thrones, and the four stolid-faced bodyguards ranged themselves about the wall. Villapando poured himself a drink, watching Teresa suspiciously.

"I suppose you heard we caught *Don* Biscara."

"I don't deny it."

"And now you are afraid," he said. "And come seeking my protection."

She walked to him, past the frowning, toothless *caciques*. She stopped a few inches from Villapando. Inside she was trembling, for she knew what was at stake, but her voice held a honey of seduction. "You offered it to me once."

His turning motion brought his chest against the soft swell of her breasts for just an instant. She saw the pulse in his temple begin to throb. She settled back, and they were three inches apart. He could not pretend indifference now. Excitement rendered the earthy smell of him stronger.

"I do not trust you," he said.

"There is only one way I can prove myself."

His eyes flickered as he understood her implications. He moistened his lips. Then, with startling abruptness, he threw the glass from him, shattering it against the wall, and took her in his arms. It was a strange kiss, filled with the bruising cruelty of an animal that knew no niceties, no tenderness.

• Finally it was over. Without releasing her body, he pulled his face away. Her lips felt bruised and swollen, and she thought she would gag with nausea. His body was trembling, and a primitive excitement varnished his black eyes, and his lips were pushed back in a macabre smile of triumph. She managed to swing around till she was looking past him toward the others. He saw the direction of her gaze and said thickly: "They are my bodyguards."

"Do they sleep with you?"

He hesitated, but he was still trembling, his face hot and flushed with desire. He turned and spoke in the Pueblo tongue, quickly, gutturally. The stolid guards walked toward the door. The *caciques* got up and followed the guards out, closing the door behind them.

Breathing stentorously, Villapando released her and strode to one of the *colchónes* rolled against the wall. He jerked it open and flopped it across the floor, looking expectantly at her.

She hesitated. Where was Amado? They had promised.

An angry light filled his eyes at her hesitation, and he straightened above the mattress. "If this is another of your conspiracies, Teresa. . . ."

"Not hers, exactly, Governor," Augustin Gómez said.

Both Villapando and Teresa whirled toward the voice.

Gómez had opened the narrow door to the corner of the room and stood in it, swaying a little, still drunk. There was a big Spanish pistol in his hand, pointed at Villapando.

"Stand there," Gómez said. "Make no sound. It means your life."

He stepped into the room, and Inocente followed, scurrying to bar the door that led into the council chamber. Then Amado entered, followed by the trader O'Brien, and Ryker and Vic Jares. Villapando was trembling with rage and still was unable to believe it.

"You couldn't get in," he said. "The guards. . . ."

"They know when it is time to look the other way," Amado said, with a sly smile. "For a handful of *pesos* the sentry outside your office contrived to be off duty when Inocente crawled through one of the windows and admitted me."

A last man entered the office door, closing it softly behind him. Teresa stared blankly at him, as shocked as Villapando. It was *Don* Tomás Biscara.

The flickering candlelight drew dark shadows into his lean, goateed face. His handsome blue velvet breeches and gilt-frogged *chaqueta* were torn and dusty, and there was a fresh scar across his high-domed brow. His first sight of Teresa brought a vindictive gleam into his satanic eyes.

"It seems we are fated, *señorita*," he said sardonically.

Villapando's voice sounded squeezed from him. "Biscara, this is treason. . . ."

"On the contrary," Biscara answered, "it is escape. My good friends arranged to get me out of your dungeons. They thought I could convince you it was time to abdicate."

At Amado's nod Inocente began pulling the high-backed chairs around the heavy pine table at one side of the room.

Gómez waved his pistol at the table, smiling tipsily. "Come, *amigo*. We will have a meeting."

Villapando's hands were closed into fists. He stared at the pistol, little muscles bunching along the bony ridge of his jaw. He looked at the door. Then, with a frustrated curse, he walked to the table and took a seat at the head. The others moved to follow. Biscara bowed with mock gallantry as he passed Teresa. Amado stopped beside her a moment, muttering: "Do not fear. He is one of us now. He will not harm you."

All the men took chairs around the table, even Inocente. Ryker told Teresa to listen at the main door and warn them if she heard anything indicating trouble. She moved over to the barred oak *portal*. The Assembly was still arguing vociferously outside, making so much noise that she was sure the guards could not hear the conversation in the chamber.

Gómez unfolded a big sheet of greasy paper and laid it before Villapando. "This is a muster roll of Pérez's forces. You will see that he has three times the forces Governor Carbajal had. They are marching on Santa Fé right now."

"We will defeat him," Villapando said.

"And the Escuadrón de Vera Cruz?"

"That is only rumor. I have seen no proof that they are coming."

"Then see it," Gómez said. He looked at Biscara, and the *don* pulled another paper from his jacket pocket.

"Something your *bribónes* overlooked when they trapped me in Las Vegas," Biscara said. "As head of the remaining Centralists here, I have been in contact with Colonel Esquivel since the first signs of this uprising. This is his last communication with me . . . a promise that the Escuadrón de Vera Cruz would march north at the first word of insurrection."

Biscara shoved the order to Villapando. The governor was not literate enough to read it all, but he could make out the salient phrases, the signature of Colonel Esquivel. Teresa saw the blood slowly seep out of his face, leaving the cheeks a sallow, putty color.

Gómez shoved a third sheet of paper toward him, an imposing document covered with handwritten flourishes and bearing a handsome seal. "There is only one way to save yourself, Villapando. Sign this abdication. Choose a successor who will declare for the central government. We have gained what we wish anyway. The corruption has been swept out, a native will be governor, we will have representation in the Republic. . . ."

"No!" Villapando struck the table so hard it jumped. "We have none of that yet. The central government has given us no recognition. An alliance with Texas is our only salvation. . . ."

"It will mean the end of us," Ryker said. "They'll swallow us up."

"And rob you of every privilege you bribed Carbajal to gain," Villapando said. "I know the stake you American traders have in this. I know the fortune you stand to lose with a governor in the Palace you cannot bribe or control."

Gómez said thickly: "We offer you a chance to save your life. When the Escuadrón de Vera Cruz gets here, you will be sent to Mexico City in chains."

"They will not take this city!"

Ryker sat straight, shoving aside his cinnamon bear coat. "This is your final answer?"

"It is. I will not make deals with a bunch of traitors. I will not abdicate." Villapando turned, calling for the sentries. "¡Guardias, guardias . . . !"

The gunshot was like an explosion of thunder in the room. The very walls seemed to rock. Villapando remained on his feet for an instant, like a puppet hung in mid-air, his eyes blank with shock. Then, with the first blood pumping from the hole over his heart, he collapsed.

For a timeless second afterward, the men sat about the table, staring in surprise, in shock, in disbelief at the fallen man. All of them had at least one hand in the black shadows of their laps or underneath the table. It was impossible for Teresa to tell which one had shot. As the first shock dissipated, she realized that the hubbub of voices had ceased from behind the door. Then it started again. Someone banged on the door, calling: *"¿Gobernador, gobernador . . . ?"*

The shout galvanized the men around the table into action. Amado was the first to jump up, knocking his chair over. He looked wildly at Gómez, at Teresa. She saw that his pistol was in his belt. "This is insanity!" he shouted. "What can we do?"

As the others jammed their chairs back, jumping to their feet, all beginning to shout at once, Teresa crossed to Amado, dragging him toward the office door. She knew she had to think quickly and clearly. "Get to Pérez," she hissed. "He must be very near the city. Tell him to enter immediately."

"He'll have me shot. . . ."

"You fool, I told him you were a Centralist."

He gaped at her. "You what?"

"There's no time to explain. Simply believe. You are the hero, declaring a counter-revolution, returning at the head of your triumphant army to save your people. Pérez will accept you with open arms. Now . . . if you want to save your neck . . . go!"

He gaped at her. The door was groaning and giving beneath the battering of a dozen men. The council chamber beyond it was a riot of shouts and yells. Ryker was leading the group around the table in a rush for the back way out. Teresa and Amado had reached it first, however, and he wheeled and

120

plunged through. She slammed it shut behind him. The key was in the lock. She turned it and snatched it out and darted across the room just as Ryker reached the door. He wheeled toward her, mouth gaping.

She stood with her back against the wall, the key clenched in a sweating palm. In those first few moments she'd had no time for anything but dealing with Amado. Yet, from the first second after the shot, she had realized how this affected her, and it had filled her with a bitter, steadily growing rage that spilled out of her now.

There was blood on her hands. She had been their tool, luring Villapando into this. They had planned the murder from the beginning, if Villapando would not accede to their demands. And they had used her to bring it about.

Ryker came at her. "Don't be a fool. We'll get you out of the country. . . ."

"You'll stay!" She eluded his groping hands, darting to the other side of the room. The others started to spread out, circling to trap her. She glanced desperately at the main door. It could not stand the battering much longer. Its planks cracked under a new surge. She had to shout to be heard above the tumult. "You'll stay and face this with me. If you run, it will be murder to the world!"

Gómez stopped, swaying drunkenly. "Maybe she's right. They executed Governor Carbajal. That's all this was. We were merely instruments of the government, saving the people from the tyranny of a rebel despot."

Biscara smiled cynically at him. "Then you admit it was your pistol?"

"I admit nothing of the sort!"

"What does it matter?" shouted Ryker. He pulled one of his Ketland-McCormicks, pointing it at Teresa. "I'll give you three seconds to hand over that key."

There was another smashing blow against the door. Adobe crumbled, and the bottom hinge pulled free of the wall. The door gaped, dangling on its top hinge and its lock. One more blow would have it open. Teresa smiled bitterly at Ryker.

"You'd better save your gun for the Indians. If you can't hold them off till Pérez comes, they'll kill us all."

Chapter Eleven

 Winter was coming early to the country. In the mountains a hundred and fifty miles north of Santa Fé the rabbits were already turning from brown to white so they would be invisible in the snow—the young ducks swam in squadrons on the ponds waiting for the first storm—the dawn skies echoed to the honking wedges of geese flying southward. It was a lonesome sound. It was a lonesome country. But it was a country where a man could breathe deeply and spread his elbows and own the whole sky if he wanted. Kelly Morgan wanted. In these mountains he had discovered a kind of freedom he had never found in the river towns of the Mississippi or even the frontier vastness of Texas. He'd been hunting for something all his life, and now he'd found it, even though he couldn't put a name on it.

They trapped all through October and into November, moving north all the time. It was sometime in mid-November when they pitched their sixth camp north of Taos in a nameless valley somewhere in the Sangre de Christo Mountains. It was their custom for one to tend camp while the other two were on their traplines. That first morning in the new camp, Morgan and Saunders took their trap sacks and went into timber, separating as soon as they found water. Morgan moved upstream a mile before he found sign. It was a newly felled cottonwood. No bark had been cleared off so he allowed it had been cut for a dam instead of food. Beavers were mighty sensitive critters, and the sound of a horse stamping or its casual snort might send them packing. So Morgan tethered his roan in timber high above the stream and hiked back down with his rifle and trap sack.

A hundred feet above the felled cottonwood he found the slide. This was the path used by the beavers to ascend the bank, a muddy trough worn slick as bear grease by the fat little rumps of kit beavers sliding back down after they made their cuttings.

From his sack he got a Miles Standish trap. He cut a foot-long stake from a young willow and drove it into the sandy creekbed at the foot of the slide. Then he attached the trap by its chain and sank it beneath the surface. If a caught beaver tried to swim away, he could only go the length of the chain, and there the weight of the trap would drown him in deep water.

A woodpecker's staccato tattoo broke out somewhere on his flank, and Morgan straightened with a jerk. He stared around him at the shadowed, gurgling creek, wondering at his jumpiness.

Slung on Morgan's shoulder belt was an elkhorn phial of beaver medicine, a noxious mixture made from the musk of a male beaver and nutmeg and whisky. A man who used it couldn't wash its powerful stink off from one end of the season to the other, but it had a strong attraction for the beavers. Rubbing this bait on another peg, he drove it into the sandy shore just above the trap.

Then he moved on downstream. It took him a good part of the day to locate the rest of the sign and empty his trap sack. He planted the last trap before a dam. He was just splashing on the medicine when the single, echoing flap of a beaver tail upstream made him straighten again. The beavers were strange, gregarious creatures. They lived in clans and built bridges and lodges together and warned each other when danger was near by slapping their flat tails on the water. The noise came again, not just one slap now, but a whole volley, echoing down the timber aisles like the applause of some giant audience.

Fast as he moved, Morgan made no sound. Heedless of the man-scent he left now, he lunged up the bank and ran flat-footed for the nearest screen of brush. He was loading as he ran. With a deft flip he opened his powder horn and tilted a measure of glistening black Dupont from the charge-cup hanging to the bottom. This he dumped into the muzzle of his rifle. Without lost motion he slid open the brass trap-cover on the side of the gunstock and snatched out a greased linen patch, jamming it onto the half-ounce ball he slipped from his shot pouch. He pulled his hickory rod from its fittings beneath the gun and rammed patch and ball down the full length of the Jake Hawken barrel. By the time he was pulling out his ramrod, he was flat on his belly in a thick screen of chokeberry, ready to fire.

He lay there in the chill shadows with the forest utterly silent about him. This was a common occurrence when trapping in Indian country. If it were Cheyennes, they might be hunting, but if it were Blackfeet, they might be after scalps. He put his ear to the earth and felt the faint tremor of many hoofs. It was what had startled the beavers. It seemed to come from upstream, and he watched till finally he saw them, like shadows moving through the cottonwoods. There were three white men, dressed like trappers. Two of them were herding a dozen pack animals loaded with empty apishamores. The third was leading Kelly Morgan's roan.

Morgan waited till they were twenty feet away. Then he said: "You kin stop right there. I got you dead to rights."

They pulled up sharply, looking around in consternation. The man leading the roan put a tight rein on his fiddling horse and sang out: "Who are you?"

"The man what owns that horse," Morgan answered.

The leader relaxed in the saddle. He was tall by any standards, nervous enough to dive down a Jake Hawken barrel, dressed in a rotten shirt of antelope hide and age-yellowed buckskin britches. He had a jump-trap jaw and bead-like eyes, and, when he smiled, it made him look like a fox.

"You give me a scare," he said. "I'm Vic Jares, and we're a party o' free trappers. How about showing yourself?"

"How about lettin' go o' the roan?"

Jares glanced at the man, smiled again ruefully. "It's yours. We found it hitched up high. Didn't know if you'd lost your hair to some Injuns or what."

It didn't satisfy Morgan, but he was convinced this was all of the party and stood up, rifle pointed at them across his hip. He stepped out of the thicket without crackling a twig. Jares indicated his two companions.

"Wingy Hollister and George Quinn," he said.

Hollister was a one-armed man, seven axe handles wide, with a ruddy face, unctuous as a deacon. He wore the inevitable shoulder belt laden with the endless assortment of trapper's tools, and at the very bottom of the belt within easy reach of his swinging hand was a Mandan tomahawk. He bowed his head and addressed Morgan with a voice like a tolling bell. "My blessings, brother. May the sun always shine upon your hearth."

George Quinn was a burly Irishman, bald as an egg. He scratched habitually at the hedge of pink hair growing like a fuzz on his jowls, and his eyes twinkled secretively at Morgan from pouches of sallow fat. After the introduction, all three waited. Coldly Morgan introduced himself. Then he nodded at the empty apishamores on their pack horses.

"Aren't you startin' sort of late?"

"We're all finished," Jares said. "Ran into poachers south of Colter's Hell. Cleaned us out, traplines and camp."

"The misguided sinners even appropriated our sustenance, brother," Hollister said. "We've partaken of neither flesh nor fowl for three days. We'd appreciate it if we could join you at your camp, and perhaps beg a crumb or two."

Quinn rubbed wet lips, grinning. "And mebbe a drink."

"Venison steak and pemmican," Morgan said. "And nothing to drink but branch water."

Quinn sighed, and rolled his eyes sadly at Hollister. Jares tossed the rein of the roan to Morgan, eyes darting to his face.

"Be mighty welcome to us, Morgan. My belt buckle's gnawin' my backbone."

Morgan swung onto the roan. He had not unloaded the Jake Hawken and kept it tilted up so the ball wouldn't roll out. As they headed down the cañon, Jares asked: "Any news from Santa Fé?"

"Last we heard, they'd kicked out the old bunch and made some Taos Indian the new governor," Morgan answered.

"We got later word, then. The Indian was killed, and they set this Nicolas Amado up as governor."

Morgan shook his head. The tortuous course of Mexican politics had always baffled him. Jares filled out the story. A girl named Teresa Cavan had figured in the assassination somehow. The Assembly had broken into the governor's chambers to find her with Augustin Gómez and several others standing around Villapando's dead body. Only their drawn guns had kept the Pueblo Indians in the Assembly from tearing them apart. Word had immediately been sent to the remaining insurgents camped about the city. Infuriated, they marched upon the Palace, declaring a mob vengeance upon those responsible for Villapando's death. In the last moment, General Amado had arrived with a force of Pérez's dragoons, putting the mob to rout and saving his compatriots within the Palace.

Mention of Teresa Cavan brought her image back to Morgan—red-headed, green-eyed, soft as a cat, with claws to match. Thought of her had been with him constantly since leaving Taos.

It was black night by the time they reached camp. On a high meadow carpeted with browning grama grass a trio of half-faced shelters had been set up. Rawhide ropes had been stretched between young pines to form a corral for the horses, and rocks lay in a pair of blackened fire circles before the shelters.

The first man they saw as they rode in was Turkey Thompson. He stood at the edge of the meadow, completely naked, his stringy body white as the underside of a fish in the reflected light of the campfires. His clothes lay on an anthill a few feet away, and he was complacently watching the ants carry the lice off the garments. After the introductions, he said: "When them damn' vermin git to bitin' harder than me, I figger it's time to delouse."

Cimarrón Saunders had gotten back to camp before Morgan. He was crouched over the carcass of a fresh-killed deer, cutting steaks. The riders checked their horses beside him, and Morgan performed introductions again. Saunders grinned slyly up at Jares. He scratched at his matted red beard and licked his lips. "Vic Jares," he said. "Name's familiar."

They spitted haunches over the fire and fried steaks and roasted the head whole in a pit filled with hot ashes. They gorged themselves and sat around too full to move, swapping windies and yarning.

Saunders cleaned his *saca de tripas* on his pants, then

turned the blade over in his hands. "Ever see a knife like that?" he asked Jares. "Gets-the-guts, they call it. Got it off a Mex in Chihuahua. Got these verses etched in the blade. Bravos, they call 'em. One fer each man it'd killed, he claimed. 'With this you tickle a man's ribs a long time before he laughs.'" Saunders chuckled. "Whaddaya think o' that?"

Jares's bright eyes darted about the clearing. "I'm a Green River man, muhself."

" 'Tripe is sweet but bowels are better.' " Saunders threw back his head to emit his booming laugh. "Great scabby booshways, if that don't take the gristle off a painter's tail. . . ." He broke off as a blade flashed through the air. It struck the trunk of a pine, twenty feet away, quivering there. It was a Bowie knife.

All of them looked at Morgan. His hand was still in mid-air. He put it in his lap, belching. "I been listenin' to you brag for ten weeks. Let's see you make it good."

The blood flooded Saunder's coarse-featured face, filling his eyes till a network of little red veins tinged the corners. He looked around the circle, hefted the knife, then tossed it.

The curved blade sang past the tree, inches off its mark. Saunders let his breath out in an angry gust. The one-armed Hollister patted his bulging belly, chuckling softly.

"The bowels were full enough, brother, but the tripe was evidently not to its liking."

Saunders's thick lips twisted. "Maybe you could do better."

Somehow it took all their eyes to the tomahawk, slung so handily at Hollister's side. The man's unctuous smile caused his twinkling little eyes to disappear in their pink pouches of fat. "It is a Delaware weapon, brother, and they, too, have a saying . . . 'never put your blade to flight, unless it comes back with a scalp.' "

There was a murmur of silence. Then Saunders emitted a disgusted curse and rose to go after his knife. He came back without bringing Morgan's Bowie. Morgan rose and walked to the tree.

Thompson picked up a bull-hide bucket, as if going after water. He stopped beside the tree. "Whaddya think?"

"I don't like it," Morgan said. "They was heading north, yet they said they'd come from Colter's Hell."

"If they was in Colter's Hell, how could they hear what happened in Santa Fé before we did?" Thompson asked.

"We'll stand watch tonight," Morgan said. "I'll take it till twelve."

Near the fire were the racks made of willow withes to stretch the fresh beaver pelts and keep them from shrinking as they dried. There were a score of these pelts pegged to the racks, harvest of their last days in the fifth camp. Morgan took one off and placed it fur-side down on the graining block, a log peeled of its bark and rubbed smooth with sand. After scraping all the meat and fat from the hide, he dipped beaver brains from a trade kettle and patiently worked them into the pelt to keep it pliable. He stretched it up to dry again and took down another.

The camp grew silent, with the fire dying and the men falling asleep. After fleshing and stretching, Morgan pressed the pelts into a bale, lashing it, setting it under the buffalo robes covering the other bales. They had over five hundred pelts beneath these robes, worth six dollars apiece in Santa Fé. Turkey Thompson said that even counting out Ryker's share, such a harvest would pay them much more than a company trapper made in a whole year.

Near midnight, Cimarrón Saunders stirred in his blankets, then threw them off, and rose. He shambled to Morgan, scratching his curly red beard. He glanced at the sleeping strangers, twenty feet away.

"Can't sleep, them damn' kyeshes on my mind," he muttered. "You want I should take the dogwatch?"

"Suits me," Morgan said.

He went to his bedding and rolled in. But he remembered Saunders's first reaction to the strangers; something stuck in his craw, and he couldn't give himself up to sleep easily and deeply. After a while Saunders passed him, going over to check the corral.

He passed out of sight. Morgan heard the horses snort softly. Then he heard the soft tramp of Saunders's feet, coming back. He kept on breathing evenly, like a man asleep. The padding of moccasined feet stopped, a foot from him.

Saunders was at his head, out of sight of his slitted eyes. If he opened them, the man would see. He remained still, breathing, listening. Then he heard the rustle of clothes against a body violently put into motion.

He twisted over like a cat and saw Saunders dropping to one knee at his head, the *saca de tripas* already descending. His twisting roll to one side took him out from underneath, and the knife went hilt-deep into the earth where his chest had been an instant before.

Saunders pulled it out with a curse and wheeled toward him, lunging again. But Morgan already had his Bowie out slashing at the man. His blade slit Saunders's knife arm, wrist to elbow, as it whipped in. The man lunged backward with a howl of pain that woke the whole camp.

Lunging after Saunders, Morgan saw Turkey Thompson roll out of his blanket and come to his knees. Turkey blinked once and then scooped his loaded Jake Hawken from beneath the blanket. Before he could draw a bead, Wingy Hollister sat up in his robes twenty feet away and threw his tomahawk. The bright blade buried itself between Turkey's shoulder blades, and he squawked like a strangled chicken and fell face down across his rifle.

Rushing Saunders, Morgan blocked the man's wild thrust and drove the Bowie for his belly, but Saunders caught his wrist and lunged against his body. Grappled for that instant, Morgan had a dim sense of both Jares and Quinn rushing him. Their rifles were unloaded, and they had them clubbed over their heads.

Quinn was first, and in the last moment Morgan tore free from Saunders and threw himself backward into the sloppy little Irishman. Quinn's rifle descended in front of Morgan, missing him completely, and they both went down in a tangle.

Sprawled backward on the Irishman, Morgan had a glimpse of Jares, right on top of him, and of the man's descending rifle. He rolled away from the blow, but it caught him across the left shoulder, stunning him. Hollister was on his feet now, running in from the other side. Morgan was still rolling, and it took his face right into Hollister's kicking boot.

The world exploded. But with shocking pain came a roaring rage. It drove Morgan up, blinded, sobbing with agony, a giant rising up through the kicking, pounding mass of their bodies. He caught someone and grappled the man to him. Quinn pawed at his legs. Stamping the man back down, Morgan saw that he held Jares. The man swung a wild blow at his face. Morgan took it and wheeled him bodily around in a great arc and flung him like a sack of meal at Hollister.

Empty-handed, Morgan moved like a wild man and threw himself at Saunders's knees. It knocked the man flat. Saunders flopped over and came up on top of Morgan and drove the *saca de tripas* at him. Morgan couldn't block it, and the blade slid between his ribs. In a spasm of pain and weakness he grabbed Saunders to him before the man could pull the blade out, and their struggles flopped them over and over till they struck the steep drop-off behind the bales of pelts.

Like tenpins they rolled over and over down the rocky slope toward the streambed below. Morgan's wound robbed him of strength, and he lost Saunders. Somewhere in the descent the knife pulled out of him. He came to a stop on the sandy beach, so sick and dazed he could not move for a moment. Above him he heard them shouting as they came down the bank.

Morgan's courage went through him like a fire, seeming to burn out pain and weakness for a moment. He rolled over and came to his hands and knees. It was like new agony to face the fact that he was too weak to fight. He could hear them crashing through the underbrush above and sliding down the slick places and knew he had but a moment left.

If he stayed on the white sand, they could trail him by his blood. He crawled toward the stream. He came across a body and felt the curly beard of Cimarrón Saunders. The man must have hit his head on a rock, rolling down the slope. He was out cold.

Morgan reached the stream and slid into the icy water. He turned downstream and crawled like a sick animal, wheezing and mewing in pain. Then he heard the first one reach the beach behind him, and he bit his lip to stifle the sound till tears came from his eyes. As from a great distance—although he knew it wasn't far—came a shout. "Here's Cimarrón! He's down flat!"

A man answered, farther away, and Morgan recognized Hollister's voice "Where is our fallen brother? I fain would put the quietus on him."

Jares called then. "Hollister, you trail upstream! Me 'n' Quinn'll go down!"

Morgan knew he had to get out of the water. The stream

narrowed, and he felt thickets clawing at him. If that brush grew far up the bank, it would hide his blood in this moonless blackness. He pawed his way through the thickets, crowding up the bank opposite to the camp. He made noise at first, going as fast as he could, because he knew the sound of their running would cover it. Then he slowed down and lowered himself to his belly, moving like a snake through the bushes, biting his lip again to keep from giving voice to his pain.

He reached the top of the slope, fifty feet higher than the stream below, and lay on his belly in a carpet of pine needles. He was so dizzy he couldn't think now. If they had guessed where he left the stream and were following him, he couldn't do anything about it. He was weak as a newborn kitten. Then he heard Quinn shouting, away downstream: "He ain't here, Jares!"

"Keep on," answered Jares. "He was bleeding like a stuck pig. He knew the only way he can hide his trail is in the water."

It was like fresh agony to concentrate. Only the force of a terrible will could prevail over such pain, such weakness. He had to think about each movement a long time before he made it. For socks he wore wool wrappings. He took off his moccasins and unwrapped the strips and folded them into a compress, putting it beneath his bloody shirt and pressing it into the wound. Then, holding it there, he tried to rise.

He got only to his knees, and weakness swept through him. He must have passed out as he fell. When he came to a few seconds later, he was flat on his face. He would crawl, then. He got to his hands and knees. With one hand holding the compress tightly to the wound so there would be no dripping blood to leave a trail, he crawled. Like a three-legged dog, he crawled.

He crawled across a meadow littered with pine needles

and into dense timber. He crawled till he found some granite outcroppings near a ridge that would leave no marks, and he followed this down the ridge. Finally the croppings crossed the ridge, and he followed them over and then found some more dense brush that led him downslope. At the bottom he found another gurgling branch of the stream and crawled into it, moving toward headwaters.

The bastards wouldn't find him now. He'd get away from them if he had to crawl clear to Santa Fé, and then he'd turn right around and come back after them, and he'd get them, he'd get every god-damned one of them.

Chapter Twelve

December in Santa Fé—snow glistening like alabaster helmets on the domed peaks surrounding the town, the air so thin and brittle it almost hurt the lungs to breathe, and the shadow of the sundial in the center of the plaza turning paler and paler under the waning winter sun as it marked off the endless hours for the somnolent old town. These last months had seen a radical change in the Palace. With Amado as governor, the new regime was securely seated on the throne. Both Amado and Gómez realized they needed the Lower River if they were to survive. They had made their peace with Biscara accordingly, promising not to invoke the Expulsion Law if he would insure the support of his fellow *ricos* of Río Abajo. But Gómez had seen to it that the majority of seats in the Assembly were held by men from the Upper River, thus robbing Biscara's party of its former power.

Teresa felt that her place was now secure. She knew that *Don* Biscara had put in a claim for her as his rightful property, and that Governor Amado had flatly refused it. Even though Teresa did little of the work around the Palace herself, she was busy from dawn till dusk, managing the host of servants in the establishment.

Almost every morning, it was the shopping. Like a clucking hen with her brood, she led half a dozen servants from the main entrance about ten o'clock. The market hugged the protection of the Palace walls and ran westward for two blocks before it ended in the field where horse traders met. Squares of dirty canvas shaded the *puestos*—the stalls in which the wares were displayed. At this hour in the morning the whole market was filled with a cacophony of squealing pigs and gabbling turkeys and crying vendors.

"*Jaboncillos, señorita,* who will buy my soap? Pink like a rose, yellow for bleaching, rice powder for the shiny nose. . . ."

"*Tamales,* man, smell my *tamales,* see my *tamales,* taste my *tamales.* . . ."

Face half hidden by her *rebozo,* Teresa haggled over neat piles of firewood, fingered the silver pyramids of onions and garlic, smelled the freckled beans. But somehow this morning she could not put her heart into the bargaining; there was a restlessness in her that had been growing for days. She was bored with the constant round of marketing, of jabbering at lazy servants, of overseeing the cooking and the cleaning and the serving and the seemingly endless details attendant to the management of the Palace. This was not what she had bargained for. She had taken it only as another step in her quest for freedom. But it had put her up against a wall. She didn't quite know where to turn next. In seeking the safety of the Palace, she had trapped herself within its walls.

The plaza trembled beneath the tattoo of many hoofs, and she turned to see a party of trappers coming in off the trail from Taos. There were four men, leading a score of pack horses, their apishamores sagging with baled beaver pelts. In the lead Teresa recognized Vic Jares, the trapper who had been with Ryker the night Villapando was killed. Behind him was a bald little Irishman and a large, bland-faced man with a long tomahawk swinging from his shoulder belt. Bringing up the rear was Cimarrón Saunders.

Despite herself, she felt a stirring of excitement. As they passed by, she stepped out and caught Saunders's eyes. His broad grin suddenly brought his lips to light in the glowing brier of his heavy red beard, and he pulled his horse to a halt.

"Isn't Kelly Morgan with you?" she asked.

The grin disappeared. Saunders ran scarred fingers roughly through the curly mass of his beard, scratching his jaw. "Him and Turkey ran out on us somewhere north of the Picketwire. Said they was goin' to Colter's Hell. Never know where that hothead'll jump next."

Something poignant ran through her—a disappointment, a sense of loss so intangible she could not define it. Then her lips compressed. She was being a fool. Morgan had been nothing but a big crude beast. If she got this sentimental over him, it was better that he had not come back.

Saunders pulled his horse closer, eyes running insolently over her ripe figure. "You don't wanta worry about him anyways, honey. Why don't we slick up and tie on some foofaraw and traipse off to some *fandango* tonight?"

"Not till you wash off that beaver medicine."

"Honey, it'll take a month to git that smell out."

"You learn quick, *señor*."

Pulling her shawl over her bare shoulders, she turned and went back to the stalls. She heard Saunders's booming laugh break out behind her. Then he put heels to his horse and galloped across the plaza, lifting a thin cloud of dust that made the shopping women cover their faces with shawls and the vendors curse him. She saw him join Jares and the others as they passed through the *zaguán* gate of the new trading post Ryker had opened on Palace Avenue, just off the plaza. Before they disappeared, a squad of lancers appeared, filing past the scrawny cottonwoods in the center of the square. Pérez was in the lead, a proud and haughty figure in his handsome blue coat and glittering accoutrements. He had been north on a scout, and the strain and weariness of the long ride had planted haggard shadows in his wind-burned face. He gave an order that sent the troop clattering on toward the Palace and drew his own horse to a halt beside Teresa.

She looked at the insignia on his uniform and smiled. "I see you have your new boots on, Captain Pérez."

A prideful flush touched his sharp cheek bones. He dismounted, saber rattling, and bowed gallantly. She asked him about his scout. For a moment he was no longer the young gallant, but a mature soldier sobered by his knowledge. He told her the Pueblo Indians were still gathered at La Cañada. They were in sullen mood and seemed to be gathering new forces and arms. The uprising was by no means over. "Enough calamity howling. It seems like years that I was gone, Teresa. I thought of you constantly. I made up a million fine gallantries to say when I returned. Now it's like you tied my tongue. Why am I so stupid with you? With other women I can say the pretty words and make the handsome gestures."

Her smile softened. It was a curious relationship developing between them. At first she had been suspicious. She had met too many betrayals, had seen too much of the animal in men to believe that any relationship could be devoid of it. She knew that Pérez's attraction to her could not be completely asexual. He was a handsome, sophisticated young man with the normal appetites. He'd had more than one affair here in Santa Fé. Yet he had never showed her anything but the most impeccable chivalry. He was a veritable Galahad in his devotion.

"Sometimes I think you're being very foolish, Hilario. I think I'll hurt you."

"It wouldn't matter. A man looks for something all his life, Teresa. Maybe he can't name it even when he finds it. But when he does find it . . . he knows."

"You could have any woman in town."

"They are nothing. There's a quality about you, Teresa. I don't know what it is. I still can't say whether you are a witch or an angel."

"And if I'm a witch?"

He bowed his head. "I would still be at your mercy."

She laughed. "We sound like a couple of poets."

He moistened his lips, like a little boy getting up courage. "Would you consider celebrating my return? Perhaps at La Fonda tonight."

The thought of getting out of the Palace excited her. She smiled brilliantly. "Will you risk the jealousy of a governor?"

He answered her smile recklessly. "For you, *señorita*, I would risk the wrath of the devil himself."

With the money she had won at the monte game in Santa Cruz, Teresa had bought new clothes in the marketplace. Her snow-white *camisa* had short, embroidered sleeves and a trimming of lace; its pleated yoke was worn off one gleaming shoulder and gave tantalizing hints of swelling breasts. She brought a tint to her cheeks by prickling them with mullen leaf, wrapped her bare shoulders in an ivory shawl with a spray of roses in the center, and stepped out of the door to meet Captain Pérez at eight o'clock.

He was fresh and clean and in his dress uniform—glittering brass buttons and rich blue broadcloth and polished black leather. Together they crossed the plaza to La Fonda. This famed inn at the end of the Santa Fé Trail stood on the southeast corner of the square, a one-story building sprawled about a central patio, with a huge main gambling *sala* and a ballroom, and smaller rooms opening off the patio for private card games.

Dragoons from the barracks stood beside barefooted

farmers at the faro table, clambering to buck the tiger with their few *tostóns;* minor politicians and their mistresses mingled casually with the richest of the *gente fina* and their wives. But it was the monte games that fascinated Teresa. The layouts were permanent, painted in gaudy colors on the bright green covering of handsome walnut tables with fantastic clawed legs to support them and fancy inlay and carving at their edges.

Captain Pérez made way for her through the sweating, excited crowd. But when they had almost reached the monte table, she stopped abruptly, breath catching in her throat. Standing before a gleaming pile of silver at the table was *Don* Tomás Biscara. He had already seen her. His thin lips pulled back off his chalky teeth in a malevolent smile, and he inclined his sleek black head mockingly.

"You grow bold, *señorita*. Is this the first time you leave the Palace without the governor's protection?"

Pérez drew himself up. "The governor is not her only protector, *señor*."

Biscara turned insolently to him. "Do not let your new rank go to your head, Captain."

A black anger ran into Pérez's face, but before he could react, there was a new eddy in the crowd, and Teresa saw the manager of La Fonda pushing his way toward her. He was Alberto Maynez, a pompous little blue jay of a man with slack gray jowls and eyes blue-shadowed from a lifetime lived at night. He bowed and scraped before Teresa, rubbing his hands together and jabbering excitedly.

"My humble establishment is honored, *señorita*. The whole country thrilled to your daring gamble for the brave captain's life, *señorita*. Surely you have not come to buck the bank. Such a famous gambler can only grace the house by dealing."

Teresa knew his motive. Her gamble for Pérez's life had given her a notoriety that would benefit his tables, if she accepted his invitation. But she couldn't help feel the excitement. The play had stopped, and all the men were watching, waiting. A man clutched her arm.

"Take the cards, *señorita*. These men must learn what luck you bring."

She turned to see the swarthy, bucolic face of the farmer with whom she had won from the card shark in Santa Cruz.

"I thought you would be with the Indians, Pablo."

He flushed proudly, flattered that she remembered him. "I am Mexican, *señorita*," he said. "The proper governor is in now. We are not savages, to have a wild Indian in the Palace." He tugged at her arm again. "You will deal? You must. Your fame has spread all over Mexico. How can we lose with the cards in your hands?"

She could hesitate no longer. The sallow-faced dealer handed her the deck of forty narrow Spanish cards. She shifted her elbows to shuffle, and it pulled the shawl tightly over the taut swell of her breasts. It was a straight deck, and she planned nothing but a legitimate deal. Yet her mind slipped automatically into the agile habits to which Johnny Cavan had conditioned her. When she was finished shuffling, she knew where most of the cards in the deck lay.

Chortling like a happy baby, Pablo put seven *reales* on the queen. "Alas, the blonde queen rides toward me."

Insolently *Don* Biscara moved a whole buckskin sack of coins onto the ace of swords. Matching his insolence with her smile, Teresa handed him the deck. He bowed his head sardonically, cutting the cards. It did little good. Her mind made up the compensation, and she still knew where they lay.

"All bets are down, *señores*," the look-out announced. "No more play on the table."

Teresa began to deal. The third card out of the gate was the blonde queen. Pablo went into ecstasies.

"What did I tell you, *compadres,* with her dealing I cannot lose. She is the blonde queen herself."

It had been a straight deal, but Teresa saw what it did for Pablo. He was flushed with victory, puffed like a pouter pigeon with importance, the center of attention, a great *bravo* among his dozen barefooted companions. And she saw what it did to Biscara. His Thoroughbred nostrils were pale and pinched, his thin lips compressed. To have a *pobre* win while he lost was hard on his pride.

She began to wonder if she could do it, right under their eyes. She hadn't planned on it when she had shuffled. But she knew where the cards lay. And revenge would be sweet.

Pablo put all his money on the gold five, shouting good-naturedly to Biscara. "Follow me, *señor.* With her my luck is incredible. Bet on the gold five. Bet on the gold five. You will become rich."

But *Don* Biscara could not follow a *pobre.* Deliberately he made his bet on a trey, a pair of moneybags this time. The blood began to pound at Teresa's temples. Very well, she would accept the challenge. Her skill against Biscara's arrogance. He was angry now and would watch her hands closely. She would have to resort to the trick, then. Misdirection, Johnny Cavan had called it. An ancient device, known to magicians, necromancers, and broad pitchers.

"All bets down, gentlemen. No more play on the table."

She knew there was a queen and a jack on top. She gave them the bait, dealing the first two straight, matching none of the bets. She knew the next card was a trey, Biscara's bet. But five cards beneath there was the gold five. Now was the moment. The roof of her mouth went dry and cottony; a faint sickness ran into her stomach.

In the moment before the deal, she turned her head in a coquettish motion to the right. Her jade earrings flashed glittering prisms of light. She saw it catch their eyes, for that single fraction of a second. Misdirection.

While their attention was diverted, her sensitive fingers did their job. The gold five came out of the deck instead of the trey. Pablo went crazy. The room echoed to his howls of delight. Men were drawn from the other tables to crowd about the lay-out.

"What did I tell you?" yelled Pablo. "Four to one. It is incredible. San Augustin is with me tonight."

She knew she could not try the trick again. Biscara was white with rage and suspicion. The slightest slip might expose her. Yet, watching Pablo, it came to her how she might use this. He was from Santa Cruz, the center of the rebel forces, and would know things that never reached official ears. She leaned across the table.

"You should quit now, my friend, while you are ahead."

He looked at her, mopping sweat from his coarse face. *"Ay de mi, señorita,* why should I quit when I cannot lose?"

She looked steadily into his eyes. "San Augustin himself can lose at times. A true gambler has a feeling for the cards. It should tell him when they have gone against him."

Perhaps the fixity of her gaze conveyed the warning to him. His smile faded for a moment. Then she saw it come back again, and she sensed what was going on in his mind. A true gambler, she had said. It could elevate him even higher in the esteem and awe of his simple friends. He nodded mysteriously.

"You are right. I have the feeling. The cards are not with me now." He swept off his hat and raked the coins into it. "Come, *compadres.* The drinking is on me tonight. Everything is on me."

Whooping and yelling, they left the table in a rush. But others closed the gap. Teresa was the center of the sweating, excited mob now. Pérez stood protectively at her side, face shining with admiration. She knew she had to deal straight. Biscara bet heavily again. He won a couple of deals and regained some good humor. But luck and the percentage were with Teresa. The game went on into the small hours, and Biscara lost steadily, till he had no more cash.

Pale and stiff with the nervous tension of exhaustion, he moved back from the table. She could see what an effort he exerted to maintain his ironic air.

"You have remarkable luck, *señorita*. It is easy to be a winner when you do not have to play again."

"But she will try again," Maynez insisted. The fat little manager was at her side, cajoling, wheedling. The attraction she had constituted tonight had poured money onto his table. "I will offer you this lay-out, *señorita*. Think of how your fame will spread. The chief monte dealer at La Fonda."

She frowned, staring at him. The offer was unexpected, almost frightening. Yet she knew what a good dealer would make, on a percentage basis. It was the escape from the drudgery of the Palace that she had been looking for. Then she glanced at Biscara's haughty face. Could she risk getting even this far from Amado's immediate protection?

"I'll consider it," she said.

She shrugged her shawl up over tawny shoulders, and Pérez made way for her through the crowd. Outside, Pablo and three friends stood by the door, singing a drunken song.

"Un momento," she told Pérez. "He's an old friend from Santa Cruz."

She walked to the farmer and pulled him away from his friends. "You were wise to quit when you did," she said. "Do you like to win?"

"Like to?" He was enraptured. "*Señorita,* when a man wins like that, he is a king. For a night he owns the world."

"How would you like to win every time?" she asked. Again his eyes went blank. She smiled wisely. "It could be arranged, my friend, as it was arranged tonight."

"You mean . . . ?"

"It wasn't luck, Pablo."

He looked at her hands. "It is hard to believe."

"But true. And it could be done again. Not big winnings. Not like breaking the bank. When it's arranged, it's dangerous to win too much. But you could win enough. Every night you would be *muy bravo.* Women who never spoke before would want to share your luck. Friends would flock to you."

His eyes began to shine. "But how? Why?"

She was still smiling, but her eyes grew veiled. "You are one of the people of Río Arriba. You hear many things that could be valuable to me. You tell me those things . . . and you will win whenever you come to my monte table."

Conspiracy brought back his slyness. His pouched eyes tilted up at the tips, and he grinned, moistening his lips. "How could I refuse such a fine arrangement?"

"You won tonight."

"And will seal our bargain." He glanced around. The other men had started toward the river, still reeling and singing drunkenly. Captain Pérez waited for Teresa by the door of La Fonda, frowning confusedly. Pablo whispered in her ear. "The Pueblo *caciques* are planning to offer peace to Amado, if he will come to Santa Cruz and discuss the treaty. But bad things have come to my ears. They hear that it is a plot to kill Amado. The Indians will ambush him near Black Mesa. He should not go."

She studied his broad and sweating face. She could think

of no reason why he should lie. At last she smiled and nodded her head. "When you have more news, come to La Fonda again. This could be profitable for both of us."

She joined Pérez, and they crossed the plaza. Near the *portal* of the Palace she became aware of how intently he was looking at her, and slowed down. There was a taut look to his face.

"Teresa," he said.

She stopped by one of the pine posts supporting the *portal* roof. She looked expectantly up at him. "Yes, Hilario."

Like a snuffed candle, the light went out of his eyes. He looked down. "Nothing," he said. "I will see you inside."

Once inside, she was too busy thinking of what Pablo had told her to dwell long on Pérez's strange mood. This night had proved many things to her. It had proved that she could venture safely outside the Palace. In Pérez and Amado she had protection Biscara respected. They were as powerful as he now, and he would hesitate to cross them. She remembered her restlessness of the morning, her sense of being trapped within the Palace walls. Perhaps this was her chance to get out. Possibilities began to form, vague, tantalizing. Alberto Maynez thought her reputation could bring him more business. Why give him the business? Why not take it herself? If a man could have a gambling *sala,* why couldn't a woman?

The idea excited her. What could be more natural? She had already demonstrated her skill, had seen how the incident at Santa Cruz had spread her reputation, and tonight would only add to it. She would have the freedom, the independence she had dreamed of. She began to see how she could use Pablo's information. If true, it would save Amado's life. How much would he give in return? She smiled to herself. That depended on how important she made it seem to him. If he could see profit in it for himself, she might be able to convince him.

Instead of going to her room she crossed to the audience chamber. The door was ajar, and, as she had suspected, Amado was still up, playing cards with a pair of his officers. She pushed the door open, and they all looked up.

"What is it?" Amado asked.

"A word," she murmured.

He paused, looked at his hand, then shrugged. "Not very good this time anyway, *amigos*. Allow me to pass."

He put the cards down and came toward her. She turned and led him down the hall to be out of earshot of the others.

"What a pleasant diversion," he chuckled. "I only indulge in these games as an excuse to avoid my atrocity of a wife. And now an angel beckons me to a tryst. Where could one find so much ripeness, so much resilience, so much . . . ?"

"*¡Cabrón!*" With a curse she slapped his pinching fingers away from her buttocks. "Persist in this clowning and I'll leave the Palace. Alberto Maynez offered me a job dealing monte."

His mood changed instantaneously. His jowls grew dark with anger, and his voice rumbled. "If you wish my protection, you'll stay here."

"Very well. But you'll give me a gambling *sala* of my own. I want that house on Burro Alley that you confiscated from the Carbajal family. It will cost you nothing."

"What?"

"It will be the most famous gambling *sala* north of Mexico City. Men will flock to it from everywhere. There will be private rooms for them, special games. They'll be drunk and flushed with victory. They'll boast and brag and let things slip. I'll hear things you would never know otherwise."

"You are being fantastic. I know everything. I have already established a spy system second to none."

"Do you know about the peace treaty?"

"The what?"

"And the ambush the Pueblos plan for you when you go north to discuss it?"

Suddenly he was no longer the clowning lecher, the buffoon, the pompous governor. His eyes grew slitted and suspicious.

Before he could speak, she asked: "Did I ever advise you wrong, Nicolas?"

He considered it a moment. Some of the ugliness left his face. Finally he shook his head from side to side.

"You could test it easily enough," she said. "When the Pueblos ask you to come north to discuss the treaty, you could send an empty coach. Only you and I and the troops escorting it would know. If the Indians attack, the troops could withdraw." She moistened her lips. "And you would still have your head."

Amado settled his chin against his broad chest, eyes veiled. All the suspicion was gone from him now. He began to chuckle sibilantly. She had seen that expression on his face before, and she murmured his favorite axiom. "It is better to be thought brave, Nicolas, than really to be so."

He nodded, still chuckling. "Exactly my thought, little one. Very well. Let's consider it a test. And if it proves out, perhaps there will be a new gambling *sala* on Burro Alley next week."

Chapter Thirteen

The black coach went north, escorted by a dozen dragoons. As Pablo had predicted, in the badlands near Black Mesa the coach was attacked by a horde of Pueblos. The dragoons abandoned the coach. It was drowned in a sea of vengeful Indians, and, when they found it empty, they literally tore it apart in their rage.

Kelly Morgan heard about it. He heard about it from where he lay, feverish and pain-racked, on his dirty straw pallet in the two-room adobe hovel somewhere east of Taos. He had been there, hovering between life and death, ever since the Mexican hunter, Tico Velez, had found him, delirious and dying in the mountains north of Ratón Pass.

Morgan had no way of knowing how long he had wandered after he had escaped Vic Jares and his men. Only his towering rage and his awesome animal vitality had kept him going, had kept him alive till Velez stumbled across him. The Mexican had made a litter out of willow saplings and his serape, hitched it to his horse like an Indian travois, and carried Morgan home in it. Velez got the *curandera* from Taos, a toothless old hag smelling of wild cherry bark and romero tea and juniper juice. She made a poultice of prickly pear that sucked the putrefaction out of his wound till he thought it would take his guts, too.

When his fever finally broke and his wound began to heal,

Velez's wife took over, treating him with as much clucking solicitude as she did one of her dozen owl-eyed children. From her he learned of the happenings in Santa Fé. The Escuadrón de Vera Cruz had arrived early in 1838, and, with the combined force, Amado had marched north to do battle with the Pueblos at La Cañada. Here the Pueblo Indians met their final, crushing defeat, putting an end to their uprising.

With spring coming to the mountains, Morgan was up and around. Although most of his strength was back, he still had not regained all his weight. His eyes were sunk deeply in their sockets, and there was so little flesh on his face that his cheek bones pressed against the skin in silvery ridges. Tico offered his horse, but Morgan knew it was the only one he had, and declined.

So he started to walk south. It was a spring country he walked through. White-stemmed aspen and green grama carpeted the fields, and new silver tips were on the spruces. Kelly Morgan was a man of violent moods—shouted laughter and wild drunken sprees and soaring passions and anger so deep it could shake him to his toes. But the very violence of all his emotions excluded hate. For hate took a sustained meanness that was foreign to such a mercurial nature. Now, with the sweet perfume of the earth's rebirth swimming around him and the pure simple goodness of walking across the face of a new world uplifting him, he could not even find much anger at Ryker. He just knew his share of those pelts amounted to about seven hundred dollars. He was god-damn well going to get what was coming to him, and, if Ryker still wanted it rough, Morgan would just as soon return the old favor by leaving a knife in his ribs.

He slept two nights in hovels of the poor, and on the third evening arrived at Santa Fé. His first sight of the town came to him under a high moon—a row of flat roofs and gleaming mud walls on both sides of the river, crooked streets heading out from the plaza like spokes from a wheel, ending jam up against the shoulders of the mountains or petering out in bare fields. Before he reached the plaza, he came to a building that had once been a Spanish colonial house, a two-story building with a railed balcony supported by slender posts. In the diffused light from the windows and partly open door, Morgan saw the sign hung on the balcony: **JOHN RYKER, FURS, HARDWARE, DRY GOODS.**

Morgan stopped in the shadows at the corner of the building, but there was no Indian sign that he could see. He stepped boldly into the store. A main wall had been knocked out to combine the reception room and parlor of the old house. Oil lamps cast a soft yellow light over the seemingly endless stores of goods. Ryker had done himself right proud on another man's pelts. Morgan walked to the counter, speaking to a Mexican clerk drowsing on a stool.

"I want Ryker."

"*Señor* Ryker *es en la sala de* Teresa Cavan," the man said.

"Where's that?" Morgan asked in his cow-pen Spanish.

The man pointed vaguely. "On San Francisco Street and the Alley of the Burro."

On the counter were a dozen glittering knives. Morgan picked up a Bowie, hefted it. "How much?"

"Ten *pesos*."

"Take it off what Ryker owes me."

"*Señor.* . . ."

But Morgan was already going out the door in long strides, sticking the Bowie in his waistband. He heard the clerk scurrying around the counter and squealing. He was halfway across the square by the time the man reached the door, calling impatiently after him.

Lined for a block down San Francisco Street and

spreading out into the plaza were dozens of fine coaches; footmen and outriders and drivers stood in shadowy groups by the slender wheels or squatted between the vehicles, playing cards and smoking. A curious group of *pobres* stood around the door of the big house on Burro Alley, craning for a look inside whenever a new arrival entered.

Morgan walked to the *portal,* rapped his knuckles against the hand-carved oak. It was opened, and an astonished man-servant stared up at his towering figure. He recovered himself, sputtering: "Your invitation, *señor.*"

"I ain't got no invitation. I want to see Ryker."

"None is allowed without invitation, *señor.*"

As the man started to shut the door, Morgan threw a hand against it with all his weight. The force shoved the door open, the manservant with it, and Morgan was inside. He found himself in a reception hall with a floor of black and white tiles and walls turned white as virgin snow by countless coats of *yeso.* There were two more servants in here, Navajo slaves dressed in creamy doeskin. With the doorman, they gathered around Morgan, babbling and trying to push him out. From beyond a door at the end of the hall he heard the sound of the celebration. Contemptuously he swung the Indians away from him and strode down the hall. With one pull he opened the door.

A burst of sound swept against him. The squeak of fiddles in a bouncing *jarabe,* the high-pitched laughter of women, the nasal spiel of dealers. For an instant all his eyes would register was a confusing sea of black taffeta skirts, white bosoms swelling into low-cut bodices, glittering earrings, dragoons in dress blues, gentlemen in sober frock coats or gaudy jackets.

All this perfumed, twittering, bejeweled crowd seethed back and forth across a broad room divided by a heavy ceiling beam in the center and its supporting posts. On one side was the biggest, shiniest bar Morgan had ever seen, flanked by a bandstand, backed by a mirror of incredible size. Reflected in its glass was the opposite wall—more mirrors, narrow and regal, rising from white marble shelves to smoke-blackened rafters, windows draped with lush red velvet, monte tables before the windows, the faro games behind them, with their German silver dealing boxes, and the chuza lay-out—such a favorite with the Indians—with its three little balls that chattered and chuckled incessantly.

The Navajos were still pulling on Morgan, and the doormen squeezed past him and disappeared into the crowd, going toward the bandstand. A dragoon captain in dress blues confronted Morgan, eyes glowing with anger. Morgan recognized him as Hilario Pérez.

" 'Evenin', Captain," he grinned. "Looks like they kicked you upstairs."

"*Señor,*" Pérez said stiffly, "you have no right here. Leave at once, or I'll call my dragoons."

"I'm lookin' for Ryker. You get us together and I'll leave your shindig."

"John Ryker is a great hero. We won't have him disturbed."

Morgan put his arm across Pérez's bemedaled chest and shoved him aside. "Then I'll find him myself."

With a curse, Pérez started to draw his saber.

"Captain," a woman said, "that won't be necessary."

It stopped Pérez, and Morgan, too. It was Teresa Cavan, coming toward them through the crowd. She was a stunning change from the ragged, sullen girl he had taken out of Biscara's house less than a year before. Her red hair was massed high into a Spanish comb and half hidden beneath the delicate lace of a black *mantilla.* The bodice of a silk dress was a shimmering black sheath for her supple body. The skirt was a thing of countless ruffles, flaring out from her slender waist like a peacock's train. There was something predatory about the red-nailed hand that held the ivory fan. From above it, her green eyes looked at him, heavy-lidded, provocative. "We will welcome *Señor* Morgan as our guest," she murmured, to Captain Pérez. "He saved my life once, Hilario."

Kelly Morgan suddenly felt like a fool. It struck him for the first time how ludicrous he must look—amid all this glitter and finery—in his worn pale buckskins and his dusty moccasins and his matted yellow hair. He felt a slow flush creep up his corded neck and into his gaunt cheeks. It made him mad.

"I'm lookin' for Ryker," he said.

She put a hand on his arm. "Perhaps we can find him at one of the tables. And on the way you must toast my new *sala*."

With an astonished and confused Captain Pérez following in their wake, Teresa led Morgan through the crowd. All of her face but her eyes hidden behind the fan, she nodded this way and that. The women stared and twittered, and the men frowned in confusion, not knowing whether to acknowledge Morgan or ignore him.

Near the rear of the room he saw Governor Amado, regally dressed in a pale blue, red-collared uniform laden with immense gold epaulets and yards of braid. But they got to the bar before they reached him. Men immediately made a place for Teresa. She lowered her fan, and, from a silver box on the bar, she picked up a *tenazitas de oro*. Half a dozen men immediately offered *cigarillos,* and she allowed one to be placed in the tiny gold tongs. One of the bartenders already had a glowing coal waiting. She lit the *cigarillo,* closed her eyes as she inhaled, and let the gray smoke flow from her delicate nostrils. There was something deeply sensual about it. She opened her eyes, smiling predatorily at Morgan.

She ordered champagne, and the two drinks were brought in fancy cut glasses. They drank together.

She was looking intently at him. "You seem different. You look so pale."

"Ran into some trouble," he said. "Wouldn't be alive now if it hadn't been for a man named Tico Velez. He took care of me like I was one o' his own. I guess I never really knew you people till now. I'll never call a Mexican a greaser again."

"Not many Americans can say that," she murmured.

There was an electric impact in the woman that went right through a man, something deeper than her vibrant physical beauty. She had a nervous way of moving her hands—smoking, opening and closing her fan, turning her wrists so that the heavy silver bracelets seemed constantly to be clashing and jingling—and her uptilted green eyes had an almost greedy shine, as if drinking everything within their vision. He had caught a hint of that drive, that hunger, in her during their first meeting. But now it was clearer. He saw her, in that moment, as a vivid, beautiful animal, driven by appetites and needs that could never quite be assuaged, no matter how much they took unto themselves.

She put the drink down and picked up her fan. "Now, perhaps, you would like to buck the tiger."

Before he could answer her, something in the back-bar mirror broke the spell. The crowd had shifted at the monte table, revealing the broad, stooped shoulders of John Ryker reflected in the glass. Morgan put his drink down and started walking.

Only a portion of the people in the front part of the room had seen Morgan's entrance. There were more surprised stares now, more flustered women, as he pushed his way past the faro lay-out, across the open dance floor where a half-dozen couples were swinging to the *paso doble,* into the dense pack of men about the monte table. It brought him in behind John Ryker.

For once the man did not wear his cinnamon bear coat. He had on fawn-colored broadcloth, expensive and tailored, imported kerseymere trousers, a new flat-topped hat pulled squarely on his coal-black hair. A pile of fifty-dollar bills, American, lay on the green-topped table underneath one of his hairy, blunt-fingered hands.

"How much under your hand, Ryker?"

Morgan's soft voice in his ear made Ryker stiffen, as though in a spasm. He started to wheel, then he stopped. The point of Morgan's Bowie was pressed into his ribs. The trader Danny O'Brien stood to Ryker's left. He saw the stiffening of Ryker's body and looked at Morgan. But Morgan was so close to Ryker that the knife was not visible to O'Brien. The other players on either side were still watching the game.

"All bets down, ladies and gentlemen, no more play on the table."

"Turkey Thompson figgered we had about three thousand dollars worth of pelts," Morgan said softly. "My share would be seven hundred and fifty."

Without turning his body, Ryker twisted his head to see over his shoulder. His black eyes were smoldering with frustrated rage, and muscles bunched into little knots along his heavy jaw. "Damn you," he said. "What pelts? There's twenty dragoons in this room, Morgan. If you don't take that knife out of my back, I'll call 'em down on you."

"One squeak and I'll slip this through your ribs," Morgan said.

O'Brien finally got an idea of what was happening. A foolish look came to his round face. He tried to grab Morgan's arm. "Morgan, are you crazy?"

"Let go," Morgan said. " 'Less you want Ryker's blood on you."

O'Brien let his hand slide off, blue eyes dropping to Morgan's waist. Only part of the knife was visible between the two close bodies. Others on either side began to sense what was going on. The women spread fans before frightened faces, began jabbering at him in Spanish. The cry of a winning better rang out of the crowd. "*Dios de mi vida,* the king of cups rides toward me."

"Count out fifteen o' them fifty dollar bills," Morgan said.

"The hell with you," Ryker said. "O'Brien, get the soldiers."

Mouth popping like a fish, O'Brien eased away from the table. Morgan saw Captain Pérez pushing his way through the crowd from the bar, with Teresa Cavan behind him. They were both looking at Morgan, and he knew they'd followed him.

"Ryker," he murmured, "you have ten seconds. Turkey Thompson was my friend. I'd just as soon empty your sack right here as not."

Ryker's head was still twisted over one shoulder to look at Morgan. He saw the bleak savagery in Morgan's face and knew Morgan well enough to realize he was capable of doing just what he threatened. The breath went out of Ryker in a long gust. He began counting out the bills.

Captain Pérez was three feet away when Ryker finished. With the point of the knife, Morgan moved Ryker aside till the place in front of the bills was free. He scooped them up. Then he jabbed the knife into Ryker's ribs.

"Walk in front of me. Anybody tries to stop us, you'll get it first."

Face still and white with helpless anger, Ryker complied.

The gamblers about the monte table gave way before his broad, tramping figure.

Pérez stared at the knife in Ryker's back, gave away before the marching men. Morgan stuffed the bills in his belt to leave his left hand free. Pérez was aghast.

"Morgan, are you insane? You cannot rob a man in front of two hundred people."

Morgan did not answer. He heard a hubbub on his flanks and caught sight of blue-coated figures converging from several quarters, but he was almost to the door with Ryker. Then there was a violent eddy in the crowd; they parted on his left to reveal O'Brien and three dragoons rushing from the faro table. One was a lieutenant. Before he saw the knife at Ryker's back, he plunged at Morgan, throwing his saber. Morgan couldn't help turning part way toward the man. Ryker knew his chance had come and threw himself bodily to one side, away from the knife.

With the man out of range, all Morgan could do was save himself from the saber. He bent violently aside as the lieutenant hacked, and the blade whipped past his hip and buried itself in the pine floor.

Before Morgan could recover, Captain Pérez lunged against him, caught his arm, twisted violently. The pain made Morgan drop his knife. Face contorted, he lashed a foot out to tangle in Pérez's legs, tripping him.

As the captain fell, the other dragoons were on Morgan, kicking, pummeling, trying to snare his arms and bear him to the floor with their weight. For a moment he was a whirling tower of violence among them, like a mastiff beset by yapping curs. His flailing arm smashed one across the face, knocking the man into the crowd; his lashing foot caught another in the stomach, and the man doubled up and fell at Morgan's feet. Catching the third by his hair and his belt, Morgan saw Ryker by the bar. The man had lunged that far in his dive to escape the knife. Now he was wheeling, pulling a brass-bound Ketland-McCormick from his belt.

Morgan swung the dragoon in a great arc and released him when he was pointed at Ryker. Arms flailing, legs kicking helplessly, the trooper plunged across the room, crashed through a fringe of the crowd, and went into Ryker like a thrown sack of meal.

It knocked Ryker back against the bar with stunning force. Before he could recover, Morgan charged after the dragoon. Ryker pulled himself up, trying to swing the pistol to fire. But Morgan's charge carried him into the man too soon, and the shock of it made the gun go off at the floor.

Snarling, Ryker tried to twist free and swing the empty weapon up to strike the trapper. Morgan saw more dragoons rushing him from the crowd and knew he didn't have time to fight Ryker. He caught the upraised arm under the elbow, hooked his other hand in Ryker's belt, and heaved the man over the bar.

Ryker crashed head first into the great mirror. It shivered into a hundred pieces and then toppled forward across the bar with a deafening crash, scattering glass everywhere.

Before the dragoons could reach him, Morgan jumped on top of the bar. The leader pawed at him, and Morgan kicked him in the face, knocking him back into the others. Then the trapper ran the length of the bar, with the upturned faces of the mob gazing at him in astonishment. One of the dragoons took this chance to fire above the heads of the crowd.

The crack of the gun was deafening; the ball missed Morgan and smashed into one of the wall brackets holding an oil lamp. Morgan dropped off the end of the bar into a covey of panicky ladies. They squealed shrilly and ran from him like scared hens.

There was ten feet between him and the door, wide open. Halfway across was the Bowie he'd dropped. He scooped it up as he plunged for freedom. The noise of the fight had brought the Navajos and the doorman. They stood in the open *portal* as if to block the way. He brought the knife across the front of him in a vicious sweep. They shouted in fear and melted out of his way like wheat before a scythe. In the next second he was outside, ducking between a pair of coaches, crossing the street, plunging into the darkness of an alley. He put a hand to his waist to make sure the bills were still there.

Then the comical side of it struck him, and he let out a shouting laugh of sheer exuberance. It echoed down the alley and bounced against blank walls and came back to him like the crazy howl of a curly wolf.

Chapter Fourteen

It was early the next morning that Teresa woke and dressed and wandered through the wreckage of her *sala*. The smell of tobacco still hung rancidly in the room, and she grimaced at it, stepping within the doorway to survey the ruin of the mirror lying in a thousand glittering shards over floor and tables. She knew a return of her seething anger at Kelly Morgan.

He had made a dismal mess of her grand opening. After such violence most of the women had left in panic and half the men had gone out hunting Morgan. She pulled her shawl about her shoulders, shivering in the early chill, cursing the man under her breath. She heard scurrying footsteps in the room behind her, and in a moment her maid appeared. Pepita was a tubby woman from Acoma Pueblo, chronic perspiration making her round cheeks glow.

"*Señorita,* a man, at the alley door, the tall man with the yellow hair. . . ."

"What broke your mirror last night," finished Kelly Morgan, as he strode into the room.

Teresa whirled, unable to conceal her anger. But somehow there was more involved; she could not help feeling astonishment at his recklessness. "Are you mad?" she said. "They'll throw you in La Garita the minute they find you."

"Exactly why I came in by Burro Alley," he said. He walked over to the bar, looking down at the scattered pieces of the giant mirror. "How much was it worth?"

Her voice became venomous. "Five hundred American dollars. Had it shipped all the way from Saint Louis."

From his waist he pulled the fifty dollar bills he had taken from Ryker last night. He counted out ten of them and placed them on the bar. She tried to sustain her anger. She should be raging at him now, should have him thrown out, should call the troops. But somehow the anger would not remain. There was something too wryly ironic about the whole situation. She shook her head helplessly. "What good would stolen money do me?" she asked.

"It ain't stolen. You don't find Ryker pressing charges, do you?"

She frowned. It was true. Ryker had acted strangely about the whole affair last night, had declined Governor Amado's order to prefer official charges. She questioned Morgan, and he told her of Vic Jares, the poached furs, Turkey Thompson's murder.

"But you have no proof," Teresa said. "It would be only your word against Ryker's."

"There's enough truth in it to hurt him," Morgan said. "Cimarrón and Jares thought I was dead. They made the mistake of letting a lot of people see them bring the pelts in. Add that to what I'd tell, and Ryker'd have a helluva lot of explainin' to do. Seven hundred and fifty dollars is a cheap price for my silence."

"How can Ryker be sure of it?"

"If I'd meant to blab, would I take the money off him that way?" He grinned maliciously. "Ryker and me understand each other, honey. We made a deal last night, and he knows it."

"You mean to let the whole thing go for a few hundred dollars?" she said. "Trying to kill you . . . murdering your friend?"

His lips were still pulled back in the smile, but the humor was suddenly gone out of it. "I ain't lettin' nothin' go. What good would it do me to talk now? When I git Ryker, it won't be jist a story that'll make a stink for him. When I git Ryker, it'll be for good."

The primitive emotion behind his words crept through Teresa like a frightening excitement. She looked at the money. An emphatic smile formed on her coral-red lips. She picked up the bills. "In that case," she said, "I'll let you pay for the damage." She glanced obliquely up at him. So tall, so awesomely tall. "What will you do now?" she asked. "You can't stay in town."

She was always on the look-out for new sources of information. As yet she had no contact with any of the free trappers. This man, ranging through the vast and dangerous country north of Santa Fé, would obtain knowledge no Mexican could bring her.

"Last night," she said, "I was ready to have you drawn and quartered. Now I'll invite you to breakfast."

The humor returned to his face; his grin made creased leather of his cheeks and took the icy chill from his blue eyes. He followed her down the hall to one of the private rooms at the rear. Its walls were whitewashed with *yeso*, covered chest-high with calico print. In the dozen niches around the room were the inevitable *bultos*—the hand-carved statuettes of the saints.

They sat down at the heavy pine table, rubbed to a satiny finish with sand and left to gray with age. Pepita had come in behind them, carrying the silver box and the golden tongs. Teresa fingered a cornhusk *hoja* from the box and tapped the pale brown *picadura* into it. She placed the smoke in the golden tongs, and Pepita lit it with a candle. She closed her eyes, drawing in a lungful, and let it flow from her nostrils.

Pepita left to get the breakfast. Teresa opened her eyes part way, nodding at the box. Morgan shook his head.

"I like somethin' with bite," he said.

He was grinning widely. It made her wonder if she had lied to herself. Had she really invited him in here because she thought he might provide her with information? He had none of the striking beauty possessed by Captain Pérez. Yet there was a magnetism to him that she could not deny, the indolent, smoldering magnetism of a wild animal. It disturbed her, as it had before. She rose restlessly and walked to the narrow, barred window. "Will you be trapping in Arapaho country?" she asked.

"Likely."

"Perhaps you can find out something. The Pueblos have never forgotten Villapando's murder. There's talk that they're seeking an alliance with the Arapahoes and the Cheyennes. If that happens, we'll have a worse uprising than before."

He did not answer for so long that she turned to look at him. There was a cynical light to his chill blue eyes, and he was grinning. It became a husky chuckle.

"I don't like to be laughed at, *señor*."

"And I don't like to be included in your dirty little politics," he said. He rose from his chair and advanced toward her. She backed toward the wall, watching him narrowly, ready to call Pepita. When she had reached the wall, he stopped six inches from her, thumbs in his belt, the wide grin still on his face.

"I heard about what was goin' on down here, while I was up on the traplines. I heard about you." He waved his hand at the room. "You couldn't git all that so quick jist by sleepin' in a few beds. I guess they don't really understand it yet, but you're probably the biggest politician in the whole province.

And nobody can play politics as dirty as a woman."

"Very well," she said. "If we're being frank with each other . . . you've pitted yourself against Ryker. The only one who can give you protection from him is Governor Amado. And I have the governor's ear. If you'll agree to bring me all the information you can gather up north, I will. . . ."

"I don't want any part of it," he said.

There was something in his expression that should have warned her. His lips parted and went slack; little lights sparkled up in his eyes, half hidden by the lids that crept slowly together. His hands reached out and pulled her roughly, almost cruelly, to him. Her body went rigid with it, and both her hands started to rise to fend him off. Her hands were forced down by the embrace, and she was lifted up till she stood on her toes against him.

The kiss and the hard, bruising pressure of his chest against her breasts should have hurt, but instead a wild flood of excitement swept through her. She had no control over it. Like a flower it blossomed within her, hot, shuddering, enveloping her. It was something she had thought she could never feel again. It was like that first time with Juan. The wanting, the not wanting, one part of her struggling bitterly against it, the other greedily accepting, the world contracting and expanding and tilting on edge.

She heard herself moan, felt her body writhe spasmodically against him, seeking to get even closer. He made a hungry sound deep in his throat. One hand slid up the curve of her back to cup her head. The red hair came down from the comb and spilled through his fingers in a fiery cascade. He kissed her on the brow, the eyes, the cheeks, the neck. He was trembling against her, and she felt the palms grow damp with sweat. He reached for her *camisa*.

Perhaps that was what brought back reality—the rough

feel of his fingers in the neck of her blouse, pulling it down. With one of his hands cupping her head and the other pulling at her *camisa,* he had released her arms. She made a strangled sound and put her hands against his chest, turning away. It took him by surprise, and she tore free before he could stop her. Pulling her *camisa* back over her shoulder, breasts heaving as she panted, she wheeled across the room from him, putting her hands to the edge of the table. Her eyes were green as a cat's in the dark.

"Get out," she said.

He started toward her. His great chest rose and fell with his labored breathing, and his face was diffused with blood. He was but a foot away, and she started to swing free once more. The appearance of Pepita in the doorway stopped them both. The maid had a tray containing the breakfast. She stared at them pop-eyed, and then started to retire discreetly.

"Pepita," Teresa said, "if this man isn't out of the house in one minute, get the dragoons."

It held Morgan in check. He glanced at the maid, as if gauging his chances of stopping her. But she wheeled and ran before he could move. They could hear her voice calling the other servants, arousing the household. Slowly the ruddy hue of passion seeped out of Morgan's face. The humor of the situation reached him, and he grinned again, the broad infectious grin that spread up into his eyes and let them twinkle like diamonds in a bright sun.

"Ain't that a sack o' hell," he said.

Chapter Fifteen

By winter of 1838 the traditional power of the Lower River had been smashed and Gómez and his Upper River ruled in the capital. The leaders of the Lower River had promised their support, but they could not stand to see the gradual spread of Gómez's power. They could not fight it openly for fear Amado would invoke the Expulsion Law against Biscara. Thus the only course left was passive resistance.

They withdrew from the capital completely. They kept up a pretense of support, yet managed to withhold it in a dozen insidious ways. There was nothing Amado could pin down as evidence that Biscara was acting in bad faith. But in the spring of 1839 there were signs that the strategy was succeeding. Mexico City had become aware that the aristocrats in Santa Fé were not in support of Amado's regime. Amado began to squirm under the pressure that this brought from the capital. His treasury was empty. When he went to the Lower River for loans, all the rich ones seemed to have no liquid assets.

It came to a head in April. Teresa had just finished breakfast one morning when Pepita came to her chambers and told her that *Don* Biscara sought an audience. It was a complete surprise, since Biscara had made a point of never visiting her and not recognizing her in any way. However, she received him in the private room behind the main salon. The place had changed remarkably. Teresa had put down a floor of black and white tiles. In place of the grayed pine table that had once stood in the center was a huge marble-topped table with clawed legs of black walnut, shipped in from St. Louis. The windows were paned with opaque glass now, and there were a dozen handsome chairs, their upholstered red plush matching the heavy velvet hangings that completely covered the wall.

Teresa, too, had changed in these last months. From a ragged *moza de labranza* with a Gypsy beauty, she had become a stunning woman, poised and confident. Perhaps the clothes were part of it. She had been responsible for introducing the gown into Santa Fé. Rarely now was she seen in the traditional *camisas* and black skirts of her people. Today she wore a rich cream taffeta with a pattern of rosebuds on the bodice. It left her shoulders bare and clung tightly to the ripe curves of her hips; her red hair was worn high in an ivory comb, and diamond earrings sparkled against the golden flesh of her neck. She was sitting at the table, the inevitable *cigarrillo* held in tiny golden tongs, as Pepita ushered in *Don* Biscara. The maid closed the door softly, and Teresa was alone with him.

Neither spoke for a moment. This was the first time they had met alone since that day so long ago when she had escaped from him. She knew the power he still wielded, had an accurate gauge of the threat he constituted to her. Yet there was no trace of fear in her. She faced him across the table with a calm confidence in her own strength.

He did not try to hide the hatred smoldering in his black eyes. He stood in the center of the room, lean and haughty, typical of the Santa Fé aristocrat—contemptuous of the peasants who served him, wallowing in class privileges that approached the divine right of kings. It was his misfortune that at the time of his birth his family had been traveling in Spain. Although they had returned to their home in Santa Fé when Biscara was four, it had left the stigma upon him. He was a *gachupín*, a native-born Spaniard, and had been suffering for it ever since.

At last Teresa smiled enigmatically. "Something desperate must have happened, *Don* Tomás, to bring you here."

"Something stupid!" His tone was vicious. He was controlling wrath with obvious effort. Cords fluttered in his lean hands as they closed into fists, and he said: "Amado has asked me for a loan of thirty thousand *pesos*."

"And didn't get it . . . as usual."

"He said this was the last time. He threatened the Expulsion Law if I refused. You know none of us has that much hard cash since the revolution. What could I do? He's already ordered my arrest. The dragoons may be at my house now."

She tried to hide how it shook her. She and Gómez had jockeyed from the beginning to prevent just such a thing. She looked at the tip of her cigarette, fighting to keep her voice calm. "I find it ironic that you should come to me for help."

I come to you as a last resort, but not for help." Biscara's agitation would not allow him to remain still. He paced the room, goatee bobbing spitefully as he spoke. "If he goes through with this, you'll be ruined along with him. If you have the influence over Amado that Gómez claims, you'd better do something quick."

"It's this passive resistance of yours that has driven him to such extremes. If you'd give us the support you promised. . . ."

"I'll make no deals!"

"I'm not asking something for nothing," she said. "Let's begin with the refusal of your people to provide officer material for the dragoons. It's lowered the morale of our army dangerously. If you'll send six of your finest young men to the Colegio Militar this winter, Amado might consider giving you back a seat or two in the Assembly. . . ."

"I'll bargain no more with that pig. I've humiliated myself for the last time, Teresa."

He had halted by the window, a lean, dark-suited figure with flaming eyes. Whatever else he had, Biscara had a carriage as fine and tempered as a Toledo blade. He was a man with his back to the wall, and she saw that she could push him no further. If this situation was to be saved, it had to be done through Amado. She was about to answer when there was a loud hubbub of voices in the outer hall. The door was thrust open, and General Amado marched pompously in, shoving the protesting Pepita aside with one thick arm. He glared at Biscara, then Teresa.

"I've hunted all over for this man. Are you dealing with traitors now?"

His face was ruddy and perspiring with anger. Teresa saw the blue coats of the dragoons in the hall outside. It made her realize the true danger of the situation. When she had sought to influence Amado before, she had usually been given more time, had been able to see him alone, to set the stage. But now she saw that there would be no playing for time. Whatever she did had to be done now. He was like a child in his rages—unreasonable, blind, explosive—and, if he wasn't halted, he would pull them all down. She could not afford to stall or intrigue now. It had to be direct, jarring.

"Nicolas," she said, "*Don* Biscara has offered us a way out of our dilemma. Would you still expel him if you could get twice as much money elsewhere?"

It shocked Amado momentarily. He looked in surprise at Biscara, then in suspicion at Teresa. *Don* Gómez had moved in from the hall behind Amado. He was the Secretary of the Assembly now, resplendent in embroidered jacket, blue velvet trousers, and shiny *mitaja* leggings. He had undoubtedly been trying to restrain Amado, for his brow was beaded with perspiration, and he sent Teresa a harried, helpless glance.

"Where can I get more money?" Amado asked. "The people aren't paying half the taxes I levied."

"What about the American traders on the Santa Fé Trail?" she asked.

She saw Gómez give her a surprised glance. Teresa and he had discussed this before, but he had vetoed the move. Much of Gómez's financial strength in the Upper River came from his contacts among the American traders, and he feared they would remove their support if he antagonized them.

Amado made a disgusted sound. "They're already overtaxed."

Gómez nodded. "They wouldn't pay more. We couldn't risk losing the trade on the Trail. It's one of our biggest assets. . . ."

"*Bribón,*" swore Amado, "is not my own opinion enough?"

Gómez flushed, turned away. Teresa leaned back in her chair, grinding out the stub of her smoke. "The Trail trade is one of the quickest ways to get rich. The Americans wouldn't give it up because of a rise in custom duties. They estimate that a hundred and thirty wagons will come over the Trail this year. What would that mean if we added a *derecho* requiring five hundred dollars a wagon?"

Biscara looked at her wonderingly, quickly adding it up. "Sixty-five thousand dollars."

Gómez wheeled, a hint of panic in his face. "It will cut down the trade. Taos will be the first to suffer."

Teresa saw a way to divert Amado's anger from Biscara. "Must you always think of your selfish interests?" she asked Gómez. "There is more to this country than the Upper River."

"Keep out of this, Gómez," Amado said. "I'm tired of your drunken conspiracies."

Pouting like a child, he walked to the windows, staring out. Teresa saw Gómez look at her with a pale fury in his sagging face. He was caught between two fires. He knew the danger of expelling Biscara, yet he was unwilling to sacrifice any of his own strength to maintain the *status quo*. This was the constant problem in maintaining such a precarious balance of power. Things had happened too fast today. Somebody had to be thrown to the wolves, and Gómez was in the weakest position. Couldn't he see there was nothing else she could do?

Even though Biscara knew their weakness, Teresa hated to admit it with him in the room. Yet, with Amado now in doubt, she knew she had to lay her cards on the table. "If you expel *Don* Biscara, the whole Lower River will rise against you, Nicolas. You'll never be able to hold things together without them. When Mexico City hears that, they'll send a new governor up here with troops to back him."

Now that some of his rage had been diverted and dispelled, Amado could appreciate her logic. These were things she had tried to hammer into him before. She saw Gómez start to protest again, then check himself, fearful of turning Amado's wrath more fully on him. The governor was scowling and pulling at his lip. Teresa had used his vanity before, his ego. But he had greed, too, and now she played on that.

"This way you get twice the money you asked of Biscara . . . and save your neck in the bargain."

She saw it reach him, saw a shine come to his eyes. His massive head finally swung to Biscara. "Very well. I'll give it a try. But if it fails, there will be nothing between you and exile."

Don Biscara left before the others, by the entrance that opened into Burro Alley. In a sense he had won today. He had blocked Teresa's attempt to force a compromise, had made her reveal weaknesses he had only speculated upon before. But he took little pleasure from it, for he realized what he had missed by withdrawing so completely from the politics of Santa Fé. He had heard rumors of Teresa's growing influence. But he had never dreamed it had gone so far. The Assembly was apparently little more than a front for the conferences held in that sumptuous room.

Most of the important decisions of the new government must have been made there, guided by Teresa's complex maneuvering, her power over Amado. She had uncanny knowledge of the man. He was no dolt, he was shrewd enough in his own right, and a woman depending upon her body or her feminine wiles alone would have lost her pity on him long ago. It took a remarkable skill to maintain such a constant influence over him—a delicate gauging of his moods and tempers of the moment, an unceasing manipulation (now subtle, now obvious) of his vanities, his pride, his fears, his appetites and weaknesses.

Biscara had also not been totally unaware of the other undercurrents in the man. He knew that Gómez's veil of bored cynicism had always hidden a vague frustration that seemed to underline the man's whole life. His rise from peasant to landholder had not given him what he wanted. He had lost identity with his own people and was still not accepted by the *gente fina*. It was a subtle, insidious kind of isolation that could corrode a man. His marriage had not helped any—an old man, a young wife, a familiar story. Biscara had seen him on the street with *Doña* Beatriz and had seen the helpless look in the man's eyes. Apparently Gómez's recent rise in politics was as hollow a triumph as everything else. He was caught between Teresa and Amado, and they had bled the power from him till he was merely a figurehead, a front for their maneuvers in the Assembly. This afternoon Biscara had seen the flaring of humiliation added to the old coals of frustration. He wondered how much longer Gómez could stand it.

He waited on San Francisco Street till the man came out the front door, alone. Then he joined him, offering his copper flask of tobacco, his bundle of cornhusks. They rolled smokes together as they walked toward the place, and Biscara murmured: "When Villapando was installed as governor, it was whispered that you were the real power in the Palace. It is a pity to see a woman usurp the throne."

Gómez would not look up from his cigarette. His voice was thin and trembling. "She is a bitch."

Biscara realized he had gauged Gómez right. Teresa was not the only one who understood men. "It is sad," he said, "to see one as capable as you losing the governor's favor." He blew out smoke, looking at the ruddy Jemez Mountains rimming the town. "I have always thought that, should the people of the Upper River and the Lower River unite, they would make the strongest single faction in the department."

Gómez looked up at him, sneering. "Do you forget that you are supporting the governor now?"

Biscara smiled. "A matter of policy, *Don* Augustin. Is it not a shame to have our province ruled by an illegitimate Apache and a power-mad half-breed woman?"

Gómez licked his lips. His hands shook as he lifted the cigarette to his mouth. "I am tired of conspiracies."

"This is not a conspiracy. It is a crusade. Perhaps we are not in a position to do anything now. But sooner or later our chance will come. We should have a man on the inside then. I'm sure you could regain favor if you stopped opposing Amado and forgot your jealousy of Teresa, if you bowed and scraped and licked your chops like the servile dog Amado wishes. And when our time came, we would be standing shoulder to shoulder, you and I, leading the *gente fina* of the province back into the Palace."

Gómez's eyes lifted. "The *gente fina?*"

"Of course. I was asking *Don* Escudero only the other day why you never paid a call on any of us."

Gómez moistened his lips. "I was never invited, *señor.*"

Biscara looked surprised. "And we thought it was pride. We thought the Upper River had become so powerful in Santa Fé that you chose to ignore us."

Gómez shook his head. "You are mistaken, completely mistaken. . . ."

Biscara slapped him on the shoulder. "Then we must take steps to rectify such a tragic misunderstanding. There will be a *baile* at my *hacienda* on the Fourteenth. Some of the biggest men in Río Abajo will be there. Would you and *Doña* Beatriz do us the honor?"

A flush crept through Gómez's veined jowls and clear to the roots of his hair. The glazed frustration left his eyes, and they began to shine. He inclined his head. "It would be our greatest pleasure, *señor.*"

Biscara looked beyond him at Teresa Cavan's *sala.* He was smiling balefully to himself.

Chapter Sixteen

 In June of 1839 the wagon trains arrived from the Santa Fé Trail. It was a big event in the capital, for a great part of Santa Fé's prosperity depended upon this trade. As soon as the wagons appeared outside of town, it seemed that everyone in town began running for the plaza, shouting excitedly.

"¡Los carros . . . hay una caravana a la entrada de la ciudad!"

The first to reach the customhouse would get the choice goods brought in by the traders, and Teresa always had a hundred things she needed. She hurried down San Francisco Street, dressed in a fresh *camisa* and a bright yellow *mantón de Manila* with red roses splashed over it and a fringe that swished saucily at her bare ankles. Behind her came her body-guards, and a Navajo slave stooped under the burden of an *almuere,* the standard measure for a thousand doubloons.

The Conestogas were parked in a double line before the customhouse. They were huge wagons with wheels as high as Teresa's shoulders, yellow-spoked, iron-tired, with bright red beds that were sway-backed as a ship. The *gringos* stood awkwardly around in new suits, hands in their pockets, gawking at the unfamiliar chatter of Spanish all about them.

There was the usual crowd of inspectors and interpreters and traders before the customhouse. Experienced traders had already paid the *diligencia* and had started selling. The men new to the Trail were arguing heatedly with the sweating officials, protesting the graft and the opening of their bales and crates for inspection.

As Teresa approached the first wagon, she heard John Ryker's voice raised above the babble. "I had fifteen wagons. Valdez was cross-eyed if he counted any more."

She saw him standing in a knot of men a hundred feet beyond. Beside him was Cimarrón Saunders, towering above Ryker, scratching irritably at his louse-ridden red beard. Captain Pérez faced them, and beside him was Captain Uvalde, of the militia. Pérez's handsome sharp-featured face was flushed. He spoke in a snapping voice, making nervous gestures with his sinewy hands. "Twenty-three wagons were counted in your train at San Miguel. And Valdez said that four of them were loaded with crated Yager rifles."

Captain Uvalde smiled crookedly, trying to placate Pérez. "There must be a mistake. Maybe Valdez was drunk."

Pérez spoke to Uvalde without looking at him. "Keep out of this. The militia has no jurisdiction here." Teresa saw an ugly light leap into Uvalde's eyes. Pérez went on, speaking to Ryder: "Either you produce those guns or I'm going to search every wagon you've got."

Teresa was but ten feet from them now, yet they were all so intent on the argument they didn't see her. Ryker's elbows nudged aside the edges of his cinnamon bear coat. The butt caps of his Ketland-McCormicks winked like brass eyes in a hot sun. "Lay a hand on those wagons and you'll lose a commission, Pérez."

Pérez's face went taut. He turned to call in a corporal by the customhouse door. "*Cabo,* gather a squad. . . ."

Ryker lunged forward and grabbed Pérez's arm, trying to whirl him back. Eyes bright with anger, Pérez shoved him away and tore free. It pushed Ryker stumbling against the wagon bed. He recovered and started to pull a gun. Pérez saw his hand dip down and whipped out his saber. Cimarrón Saunders lunged at Pérez.

The captain made a half turn away from Cimarrón and thrust out his boot. The red-headed man couldn't stop himself in time, tripped over the boot, and sprawled on his face. Pérez was already whirling back toward Ryker. He had his saber out, and he didn't even have to move toward Ryker. It had all happened in an instant, and the tip of his extended sword punched Ryker in the stomach a split second before Ryker got his guns free. Ryker stopped all movement, gripping the butts of his useless pistols with their muzzles still thrust through his belt. Cimarrón Saunders picked himself off the ground, eyes tiny as a pig's with humiliation.

"Pérez," Captain Uvalde said, "you are acting like a fool."

Pérez ignored him. The corporal had already gathered half a dozen dragoons, and they were converging on the scene. *"Cabo,"* Pérez said, "put a guard on this man. Then I want these wagons searched. We're looking for crated Yager rifles. If you don't find any in the cargo, look for false bottoms in the beds. Find those guns if you have to rip every wagon to pieces!"

A pair of dragoons loaded their carbines and took their places near Ryker and the others. Pérez let his saber drop and trotted with the other dragoons to the first wagon. They clambered into the dusty beds and began throwing out bales of calico, ripping into crated hardware, prying open boxes of nails and barrels of dried fruit. Teresa saw that Ryker's face was dead white with rage.

Once Ryker saw Teresa, he started walking toward her.

"What about the wagons?" she asked.

"So I had twenty-three," he said. "I emptied eight and put the cargo in the other wagons. Every trader's doing it. This new tax of five hundred dollars a wagon will break us."

"And the guns? I want the truth, Ryker."

He moved closer, speaking in a low, vicious tone. "All right. I'll tell you the truth. Pérez's been nosing around too much. That's the truth. If you don't stop him, he's liable to uncover something that turns this whole town upside down, and you with it."

"You aren't that big," she said.

"It ain't what I'd do. It's just what will happen. The only way you can stop it is to stop Pérez . . . now."

In his coal-black eyes she saw the man's adamant refusal to explain further about the rifles. She knew he was a man who did not throw his weight about idly. There must be some truth in the danger he hinted at. If it went as deep as he implied, it went to the Palace. The truth would be easier to get from Amado. If he didn't have it, she could always come back to Ryker. In the meantime—she had woven too careful a fabric to have it ripped wide by Pérez's hotheadedness.

She gave Ryker a last glance, then walked down the line of wagons to Pérez. She called him aside. "You must stop this, Hilario. Ryker's too important a man to antagonize over a hundred dollars."

"But the rifles . . . ?"

"I have them."

His face turned blank with surprise. She smiled wisely. "Do you think something so big would be hidden from me? Pablo reported it yesterday. Ryker wanted to smuggle the rifles down the Chihuahua Trail without duty. We overtook them north of Albuquerque. He'll pay his duty."

"It goes deeper than a few smuggled rifles, Teresa. Something is going on. You can feel it at the Palace. Something is wrong."

"Why don't you come to my *sala* and tell me what you know? Captain Uvalde can take over."

She finally convinced him. Leaving Uvalde in charge, Pérez accompanied her home. They went to the familiar private room behind the *sala,* with its black and white tile floors, its red hangings. She let the *mantón* slip from her shoulders onto the table, poured him a drink. She asked him what he had found out. He said that in a skirmish with Apaches the week before he had killed three and found that they were using American Hall breechloaders. If somebody was selling guns in any quantity to the Indians, it could prove lethal.

"It's the sort of thing that fits Ryker," Pérez said. "We know he made his fortune smuggling furs."

"You have proof?"

"You told me what happened to Kelly Morgan. How else could Ryker have gotten so big? None of the other traders is half as rich. And Amado let him get away with it."

"Amado had nothing to do with it," Teresa said angrily.

"He must," Pérez said. His face grew red, and he spoke sharply. "The customs inspector at Taos claims Ryker doesn't pay duty on half the furs he ships out. Everybody knows how close he's become to Amado. . . ."

She turned her back on him, pacing spitefully across the room. She hated these clashes. No matter how much surface sophistication Pérez acquired, this part of him would always remain untouched—naïve, romantic, idealistic—making him seem forever like a little boy to her. It was his weakness, and she had used it, had used his romanticism, his rigid ideas of honor, his intense patriotism, his worship of her—all to blind him to the true state of things, had used it in self-defense, knowing that he was one of the keystones in the fortress wall she was building. His military duties kept him out of the capital much of the time, scouting the frontiers, doing duty in the outpost garrisons. But even there he could not fail to hear the rumors of discontent, of bribery and graft in Santa Fé. She had known that sooner or later the wool she pulled over his eyes would grow thin. Now she had lied to him again, about the rifles, and would have to perpetuate the lie. Her lips drooped as she turned to him, and the light went out of her eyes.

"Hilario, why do we have to quarrel? You've been gone weeks. We can't fight the minute you get back."

"It's the whole thing, Teresa. Something's changed. I used to think Amado was the right man for our country. I thought you were right to support him. Now I don't know." He shook his head helplessly. "If only you didn't have to be mixed up in it."

"You know why I do it, Hilario."

"You wouldn't have to if. . . ." He stopped, lips parted.

"If what?"

He looked at her a moment, the flesh shining on his sharp cheek bones. He was breathing heavier, and it came from him abruptly, blurted out. "If you had a husband."

She smiled. She didn't know whether to make it facetious, or to treat it seriously. For the first time, with him, she didn't know what to say. He saw it, and leaned toward her, face taut with excitement and tension. The words came from him in a rush, breathless and barely coherent.

"Been offered a transfer, Teresa . . . Mexico City. You'd never have to be afraid again. Most beautiful city in the world. Never have to play politics. A *baile* every night. My family place. A castle. Live like a queen, Teresa. You have no conception."

He broke off, breathing heavily, something almost startled in his face, as if just realizing what he'd said. Her eyes were shadowed, sober.

"I always wondered about you, Hilario."

He came to her, took her hands in his. She could feel the

tremor run through him. "It wouldn't be different as my wife. You'd have the same devotion. Only it would be a million times greater. Believe me, Teresa."

She started to cry. She freed her hands, turning from him, pacing to the table. She wanted to cry, and she wanted to laugh. It was so ironic, so bitterly ironic. What he was offering was beautiful and sincere and honest. Yet all of it was like ashes in her mouth. "I would be betraying you, Hilario. I've done that in a hundred little ways before. But I couldn't do it this way."

His steps sounded dragging as they came up behind her. His voice trembled a little. "You couldn't learn to love me?"

She looked around the room. She had created a world of her own here—no matter what the price—had found a fierce sort of individuality. She could not sacrifice that. She could not gamble with her emotions again. She remembered the last time she had married without love—the pain it had brought, the misery. And this time the pain would be Hilario's own. She could not do it to him.

"Hilario . . . I'll always think of you as the best friend I ever had. Someone so wonderful happens to a woman only once in her life."

It was a long time before he answered. His voice sounded heavy, tired. "Perhaps I knew it would be this way. Perhaps it's why I never spoke before."

His saber tinkled softly as he turned and went to the door. Without turning, she said: "I'll miss you."

He opened the door. "I'm not going to Mexico City."

She followed him out in a few moments. She reached the main *sala* in time to see his slim swordsman's figure go out the door. She walked through the gathering evening crowd. The Navajo doorman held the *portal* open for her, and she watched Pérez go down San Francisco Street toward the plaza. He passed Burro Alley. In a moment a man stepped from the dark shadows of the alley. Teresa recognized the tall, lean figure of Vic Jares. He followed Pérez toward the crowded plaza, idly cutting a chaw from his plug tobacco. A dark apprehension ran through Teresa. She realized she had not gotten Pérez's promise to stop snooping, and she remembered Ryker's warning.

Teresa walked moodily back into the gambling hall. She had come out here mainly to check things, as was her habit at the beginning of an evening. But she was too worried about Pérez to concentrate on the tables. As she walked through the thin crowd, acknowledging greetings with a nod, one of her look-outs moved in beside her.

"Escudero asks for credit again," he said.

"Give it to him."

"But he can sign nothing for it. You have the deed to his house."

"He's Biscara's man in the Assembly, isn't he?" she asked. Her green eyes turned smoky. "The deeper in debt he goes, the more power we have over him. Remember that, Pío."

He shook his head and went back to his high stool. As she passed through the room, she saw Kelly Morgan standing at the bar. He had been hidden by the crowd when she had followed Pérez out. It was the first time she'd seen him since the spring of 1838—over a year ago—when he'd come to her *sala* to take the money from Ryker at the point of a knife. She knew Morgan had spent the winter in Taos, waiting to see if Ryker would press charges in Santa Fé. This spring he'd probably been up in the mountains, working the traplines till the beaver began to molt. Most of the trappers returned to Taos or Santa Fé during the summer, waiting till fall when the furs would become prime again. Morgan leaned with his back against the bar, elbows hooked over it, an indolent grin etching a million fine lines in his mahogany-burned face.

"Maybe I can buy you a drink," he said.

For a moment she was reluctant. On the surface he seemed to be a crude and elemental man. Yet behind that grin she sensed a shrewd mind, a self-containment, an earthy wisdom that went to the very roots of life. Then her reluctance made her angry. Was she afraid if him? Taffeta hissed across her hips as she moved to the bar. His grin broadened.

"Brandy?"

"Tequila."

"Lemon?"

"Salt."

Fencing. Always fencing. A sense of walking along a very narrow wall with a dizzying drop on either side and God knows what at the bottom.

"Hitched up with a Crow squaw this spring," he said.

"Your seventh?"

He chuckled. There was a heat to him, a wild animal smell of pine smoke and sage and pungent dust blown across vast distances.

"Mighty prime Yankee gals with the wagon train."

"Buy *them* a drink."

"Ain't mean enough. I like my woman ornery."

"Thank you, *señor*."

"Green-eyed, too." He leaned toward her, till their faces almost touched. "Green as hell."

Others were watching, puzzled, smiling. They had seen this duet before. It was becoming almost a tradition in Santa Fé. In a husky voice, Morgan said: "Table's more private."

She thought of Pérez. She smiled indolently. "And more intimate."

He raised his yellow brows. Then he took up both drinks

and walked across the room to a small round table in the most distant corner. She followed. He hitched a chair around beside her and leaned forward till he was looking into her eyes again. His grin was devilish.

"Back room's even privater."

"This will do."

"I thought my time had come."

"In a hundred years, Kelly."

He leaned back, looking at her from slitted eyes. "You can't wait that long."

She picked up her glass. He picked up his. They clinked them together.

"To my experience," she said.

He laughed, emptied the tequila at a single gulp, squinted, made a sound like steam escaping.

She took a sip, murmured: "What do you think of Captain Pérez?"

"One o' the true grit."

"If he was in trouble, would you help him?"

"Quick as I'd help Tico Velez."

"He's in trouble."

His eyes opened wide, gazing at her. "What kind?"

"Ryker."

"What's Ryker got against Pérez?"

"I don't know. But Pérez needs help, Kelly."

"He can take care of himself."

"Not against men like Vic Jares, Cimarrón Saunders. He doesn't know how to fight dirty."

Morgan made a disgusted sound. He shoved his chair back and stood up. He seemed to scrape the ceiling, he looked so tall. "Thank you, Teresa. I told you I wouldn't git mixed up in your dirty politics. I meant it."

Chapter Seventeen

Kelly Morgan, standing six feet six inches in his moccasins, walked out of the *sala* and onto San Francisco Street. He was filled with his frustrated need of Teresa and with anger at himself. Why did he keep coming back when he knew how it was? Why didn't he give up? There was always a greener pasture over the hill. He spat. Hell. He couldn't help himself. When a man wanted a woman that much, he couldn't help it. So he went on making a fool of himself.

There was a crowd in the plaza, and he skirted its edge. He came in sight of La Castrenza, the military chapel on the south side of the square. Leaning against its ancient wall were Cimarrón Saunders and Wingy Hollister. They were like strange dogs with their hackles up. That was always the way of their infrequent meetings since the fight in the mountains north of Santa Fé. Finally Saunders smiled maliciously.

"Goin' trappin', Kelly?"

"For poachers," Morgan said.

Wingy Hollister smiled unctuously. "A worthy search, brother. Don't let it become an obsession."

"Not an obsession, exactly," Morgan said. His eyes dropped to the tomahawk swinging from Hollister's belt. "Jist somethin' I can't forget."

He let the drift of the crowd move him away from them toward Galisteo. Morgan was almost around the corner and into Galisteo when he saw Vic Jares join them. Cheek bulging with a chaw, the fox-faced man spoke quickly to the other pair. His bright eyes darted across the square, and he grinned toward the Palace. Hollister and Saunders looked that way. Morgan did, too.

Captain Pérez was talking to a ragged *peón* in the deep shadow of the Palace *portal*. He was nodding and asking questions and glancing off toward the Sangre de Cristo Mountains. In a moment Pérez left the man and went to his handsome black horse hitched by the customhouse. Hollister and Jares and Saunders began walking quickly toward La Fonda. There was a definite pattern to all of it that held Morgan's attention.

Pérez trotted his fretting cavalry horse past La Fonda and down the street that led to the Santa Fé Trail, not seeing Saunders and the other men in the crowd. As soon as Pérez had disappeared, the three trappers hurried to a trio of horses racked in front of La Fonda, mounting up. They held the animals there, talking among themselves, and finally followed Pérez.

Morgan remembered what he had told Teresa. But somehow this went deeper than her politics. Somehow it was part of the debt he owed Tico Velez. He got his horse from its rack in the plaza and rode after the men. It was already dark when he reached the Trail, and traffic had thinned out to nothing. It was broken, rising land now, where the cedars and piñons clustered like stunted ghosts on the benches, and the yucca stood like lonely candles in the light of a rising moon. By that same light he read sign on the Trail. He reached Apache Pass, with rocky walls towering monumentally on either side, rising through a defile so narrow and tortuous that a few men could hold back an army here. The moon was higher now, and he knew he couldn't be far behind them. He pulled off into timber, paralleling the Trail. He came to the old Pecos Trail. Here his quarry had turned off. Caution turning his face bleak, he worked his way through scrub timber. Then he heard a horse snort softly in the night ahead. He checked his animal, listening. After a while the horse snorted again, stamping. It was no farther ahead.

He hitched his mount. Rifle swinging at his side, he found brush choking a wash and used it for cover. It took him to within sight of the animals. Three horses, hitched to a dwarf cedar, with no sign of their riders.

Morgan circled them till he found the tracks of three men, heading northward. In a few hundred yards he heard another horse snort and came upon Pérez's handsome black mount, fretting nervously on its tie rope. The tracks of Cimarrón Saunders and Jares and Hollister clustered at the animal, as if they had stopped a moment, then each man had taken a different direction away from the horse. Morgan followed the deepest tracks.

Topping a brush-covered rise, he stopped abruptly. Before him, completely revealed under the high moon, was an eerie sight: two immense communal dwellings, ancient and deserted in the pale yellow light, the crumbling remains of a vanished race. He realized he had been led to the ruins of Pecos, a Pueblo village whose people had been wiped out many years ago by pestilence and war. The buildings were four stories high, laid out in a quadrangle, that left a vast courtyard in the center. Typical of the Pueblos, the upper stories were terraced back so that the rooftops of the lower level formed a balcony. Tico Velez had told Morgan that before the buildings had fallen into decay a man could make an entire circuit of the village on these balconies without setting foot on the ground.

Finally he worked his way around the buildings till he

found an approach that would not expose him. Squirming through the cover of washes and brush and broken land, he reached the adobe wall of the first great communal building. There were breaks in the age-old wall, and he climbed through one into the utter blackness of a rubble-filled chamber.

He found no doors in the walls of this lower chamber, but his hands encountered a notched cedar post leading upward. He crawled up the primitive ladder, through an open trap, and found himself on the balcony formed by the rooftop of the first level. Fifteen feet back of the edge rose the wall of the second story. A door pierced this wall, and he quickly stepped into it, feeling too exposed on the balcony.

He stood in the doorway, looking out onto the dead city, listening. He wanted to move around the quadrangle, but he didn't dare do it in the open. He finally turned and moved through the pitch-black room, seeking another door. It was then that he heard the sound. Muffled whispering, far ahead.

Sweat broke out on his palms. Passing walls till he found another opening, he stepped into the next room. Moonlight streamed through a dozen breaks in the front wall. He crossed warily, flattened himself against crumbling adobe in the darkness beyond. At last he heard the sound again. Closer this time. More distinguishable. Feet crunching rubble on the floor.

He moved down the wall to a cedar-framed door. The chamber beyond was dark again. No moonlight to show him the way. Only the sound, still muffled, intermittent, to guide him. He put his back to a rear wall and slid down it, foot by foot, feeling each time with his moccasins so they would not betray him by crunching unseen rubble. He reached a corner, stopped. This room was silent. But somewhere there was noise again. He slid down the new wall, reached another door, stopped again.

The noise was clear now, no longer muffled. It came from the room beyond. It echoed, as if in a vast, long chamber. In complete darkness, soundless as an Indian, Morgan moved through the door and put his back to the wall. He held his breath and heard the crunching, the footsteps coming, one by one.

A faint light bloomed against a distant wall. It looked to be a hundred feet away, so distant that it only illuminated the far end of the great chamber, revealing a few huge beams that held up the roof, leaving the bulk of the room still in darkness. The light became brighter, a flaring pinpoint in the velvety blackness, a sotol-stalk torch held in the hand of Captain Pérez as he moved through a doorway. The light fell on a pair of crates in a corner, long crates, with printing on their sides. Pérez exclaimed softly and walked quickly to the corner, saber clattering.

From the darkness in another side of the room came a whisper of sound. Morgan stiffened. The whisper became a sharp hiss, like an arm drawn violently back.

"Pérez!" bawled Morgan.

Pérez wheeled. The tomahawk whipped past, an inch from his chest, passing through empty air exactly where the middle of his shoulder blades would have been if he hadn't turned. It struck the sotol stalk beyond, held in Pérez's hand, and knocked it from his grip. The torch fell to the earth and snuffed out.

Morgan's shout had betrayed his position. Even as the torch fell, a gun began to boom in the huge room. Morgan heard the first bullet *whack* into the wall six inches to his right, spitting adobe all over him. He dropped his rifle and threw himself flat. As he rolled to escape the searching bullets, with the thunder of the smashing gun blotting out all other sound, Morgan felt the floor tremble beneath him with the feet of a heavy man running across the room toward Pérez. He tried to stop himself, but it was too late. The man ran right into him and spilled over his body.

He heard the elephantine grunt as the man struck the floor. He heard him roll over and scramble up. Morgan was already lunging to his knees, whipping his Bowie from his belt. The man ran hilt-deep into the knife, and his cry of agony joined the reverberating echoes of the gunshots. His great weight knocked Morgan backward and then sprawled against him. The breath left Morgan in a gasp, and he was helplessly pinned. The man wheezed and rolled off. Morgan still had his grip on the knife, and it pulled free. He heard the man gasp with pain, rise, and stagger into the darkness. Then he lay flat, motionless, soundless, till that noise died, and the shuddering reflexes of the shots faded away. The silence was eerie, aching, after so much violent sound. It seemed like he lay there for an eternity. Then there was a hiss of clothing on a moving body from Pérez's corner.

"Captain?" Morgan asked.

"Who is it?"

"Kelly Morgan."

"Are they gone?"

"I think so. If they stayed, they would've reloaded. If they'd reloaded, we would've heard 'em."

There was more movement, the flare of steel sparking flint, the bloom of fire from the sotol stalk again. Pérez was not a fool. He stood back from the torch for a few moments, looking around the room, a pistol now in his hand. Finally he said humbly: "How can a man thank you?"

"Don't bother. They pulled the same thing on me once. What's it all about?"

"Ryker's been smuggling guns to the Apaches," Pérez

said. "I've been trying to prove it. One of Teresa's spies in the plaza told me he'd seen four of Ryker's wagons turn out of the train at the cut-off to Pecos."

Morgan looked at the crates. "They've been here, all right."

Pérez said: "We're too late. They're empty."

With the light held high, they saw that there was a break in the crumbling wall, opening onto the balcony in front. They walked to the break and peered through without exposing themselves. The city lay silently, gilded with haze. Ten feet from them, sprawled near the edge of the terrace, lay the dead man, Wingy Hollister, huddled on his side, both hands still clutched over the bloody wound Morgan's knife had ripped in his paunch.

"I guess that's for Turkey Thompson," Morgan said.

Chapter Eighteen

The reverberations of the incident at Pecos took a long time to die. Jares and Saunders had disappeared from town, and no connection could be established between them and Ryker, although those in the inner circles knew that the men had long worked for him. Teresa had several meetings with Amado, but he seemed to know nothing. She could get little more out of her spies. Pablo, the farmer from Santa Cruz, was the head of her system of informers now. He had half the *peónes* in the department working for her, knowing they would get a *peso* for any item of valid information they turned in. Finally he came to her with what might be a lead.

It came from a man named Felipe Vargas. He had formerly been a servant for Juan Archuleta, one of the big landowners of the Lower River and now a member of the Assembly. In punishment for some mysterious crime, Vargas had been flogged unmercifully and had avoided death only by escaping from the Archuleta *estancia*. Ostracized and outlawed because of this defiance of his *patrón,* Vargas had turned highwayman in order to survive, and had become the scourge of the Camino Real between Albuquerque and El Pasó de Norte.

"I got word from Vargas through a rancher near Albuquerque," Pablo said. "Vargas knows something that might have a bearing on these guns, but he insists on seeing you personally. Naturally he can't show his face in town. He said he'd be at Mendoza's Inn tonight, at ten o'clock. You're to bring five hundred *pesos*."

Mendoza's Inn was a place east of Santa Fé frequented by thieves and cut-throats. Teresa knew the danger of such a rendezvous. Biscara would welcome any chance to get her out of the way. The defeat he had suffered at her hands since the revolution had made him hate her even more bitterly. If any of his men caught her at a place like Mendoza's, they could do almost anything to her without fear of being discovered or blamed. Yet this business of the guns was assuming an ever more threatening significance. Somehow she had to find out. She felt a flush of excitement touch her cheeks as she looked at Pablo.

"Whoever's mixed up with these guns knows I'm interested now."

The swarthy man nodded. "I know what you're thinking. If you're being watched, it would betray us to take the coach. Even too many guards would give you away."

Most of Teresa's intrigue had been confined to the comparative safety of her salon, and it had been a long time since she'd taken such a chance. Her voice sounded a little breathless. "Then it will be just you and me, Pablo . . . tonight."

As a decoy they let the word spread around that she would visit one of her cousins north of town, and an hour ahead of time the empty coach clattered out of the *zaguán*, followed by the half a dozen outriders who always accompanied it. At nine Teresa and Pablo let themselves into the pitch darkness of Burro Alley. She was disguised in a servant's *camisa* and heavy wool skirt, her famous red hair hidden beneath a cheap *rebozo*.

They halted at the mouth of the alley, studying the empty street beyond. There was the clatter of hoofs from the plaza, and Pablo pulled Teresa against the wall. A file of dragoons trotted onto San Francisco Street, accoutrements tinkling as they passed the alley not ten feet away. It was not any regular patrol.

"I've got a bad feeling about this," Teresa said. "Maybe the coach didn't fool them."

He grinned slyly. "You're getting soft, *señorita*. Before the revolution you weren't afraid to take things in your own hands."

Her eyes flashed angrily. "Let's go."

Tensely they crossed the street, following dingy back ways and narrow alleys to the river. They followed its sandy banks southwest, keeping to the cover of screening willows. Once near the outskirts of town they heard the tinkle of accoutrements again and stopped in the black shadows, standing, tense and breathless, while the dragoons passed them on the road above. Afterward they went on, leaving the boundaries of the town. In half an hour they reached Mendoza's, a dingy cluster of adobe buildings on the river road from Santa Fé.

Pablo led her stealthily through the dilapidated inn yard and into a rear room, lit only by the coals glowing in the cone-shaped corner fireplace. He left her there and went through a door into the taproom. She could hear the low mutter of voices, the tinkle of glasses.

She stiffened as the door opened again. Pablo led in two men. One was a tall, swaggering rogue in patched buckskins, a scraggly beard growing to a point on his chin and giving his face a devilish shape. She knew instantly that it was Felipe Vargas. He smiled mockingly and bowed with exaggerated gallantry.

"An honor I never expected, *señorita*."

The man with him was introduced as Gene Cummings. Teresa knew him by reputation—one of the numberless

Yankee renegades who had fled from some dark past east of the Mississippi. He immediately walked to the rear door and opened it a crack, head cocked like a listening hound.

Vargas walked to the table, spurs clacking, and pulled out a chair. Eyes on his face, Teresa sat down. He took another chair, watching her obliquely.

"I'll tell you my story. If it has any connection with the guns, you can pay me."

Six months ago, Vargas said, Juan Archuleta began having mysterious meetings with a pair of Texas traders in Santa Fé. During that time he sent for Vargas and ordered him to deliver a letter to Mirabeau Lamar, the president of the new Texas Republic. Archuleta said it was merely a request for certain trading concessions in San Antonio. Vargas had often acted as a courier for Archuleta and was a trusted servant. But this time he refused.

"This wasn't the ordinary way to send a commercial letter," Vargas told Teresa. "I was afraid of getting mixed up in some conspiracy with Texas. I knew it would be worth my life."

Teresa nodded. She knew that since Texas had broken away from Mexico in 1836 there were many Texans who claimed that more than half of New Mexico fell within the boundaries of their new republic. Teresa had heard rumors of a movement within Texas to make good that claim. Governor Amado had threatened death to any New Mexican aiding such a movement.

"Archuleta had put himself out on a limb by even trusting me that far," Vargas said. "He ordered me flogged for refusing his orders, but I think he meant to have them keep it up till I was dead. It was why I had to escape."

Cummings made a hissing sound by the door. Vargas jumped to his feet, hand on the pistol at his belt. For a moment they waited tensely, firelight flickering across their taut faces. Then Cummings glanced at Vargas, shrugged.

Teresa let out a relieved breath, turned to Vargas. "How do you tie this up with the guns?"

The man paced the room restlessly, eyes on the door. "If Texas lays claim to any of New Mexico, they'll have to send an invading force to take it. An invading force would need arms. Either those guns could be for Texans or for New Mexicans who mean to help them."

She saw the logic of that. "Would the proof be in that letter?"

"The arms would be one of Archuleta's big offerings. Naturally he'd be talking about them."

"Would he be sending another letter?"

"If he did, the courier would ride with the monthly patrol to El Pasó del Norte. It was the way Archuleta sent his previous messages."

Teresa glanced at Pablo. "Have you anyone capable of getting that message?"

The farmer shook his head slowly, frowning. Most of the people he relied on were farmers or townsmen. They knew what went on in the country, but they were not reckless or daring enough to attack professional soldiers. Undoubtedly the dragoons didn't know what message Archuleta's courier carried, but their job was to protect anyone traveling with them. Slowly Pablo's eyes swung toward Vargas. The highwayman sensed his thoughts, threw back his head to laugh wolfishly.

"I'm not that crazy, Pablo."

Teresa studied Vargas. He had the reputation of being a wild and reckless rogue who would do almost anything for a price.

"A *fanega* of *pesos*," she said. "Your freedom from

Archuleta, and a pardon for all your past crimes."

Cummings turned sharply from the door. Vargas's mouth dropped open. Cummings began to chuckle huskily.

"Settin' aside everything else, twelve thousand *pesos* would make me brave enough to fight the whole Mexican army."

Vargas grinned recklessly. "You won't have to do it alone, *amigo*. It's a deal, *señorita*. And if. . . ."

Cummings's sharp movement by the door cut him off. The Yankee was looking outside again. Teresa could hear it now, the *clip-clop* of horses' hoofs, the tinkle of accoutrements. The pistol leaped into Vargas's hand. His fox-sharp face was turned to Teresa, taut with angry suspicion.

She rose, cheeks flaming. "Don't be stupid. What would I gain by bringing them down on you?"

Pablo tore open a side door leading to a storeroom. Teresa saw the legs of a ladder leading upward.

"Upstairs," Pablo snapped. "You can cross the roofs to the arroyo."

With a last scowling glance at Teresa, the highwayman lunged into the storeroom, followed by Cummings. Pablo slammed the door shut on them. Then both he and Teresa started toward the door. They were halfway out when a trio of dragoons galloped into the inn yard, deploying to block them off. At the same time three more burst in from the taproom. One of them was Captain Uvalde.

A malicious light filled his dark eyes with his first sight of Teresa. Yet there seemed no surprise. He glanced around the room, then jerked his unsheathed saber toward the side door. A soldier opened it, saw the ladder, and began to climb upward. Uvalde smiled crookedly at Teresa.

"You pick strange places, *señorita*."

She stood, still and defiant, against the wall. "I might say the same for you."

The dragoon came back down the ladder, reporting nothing in sight on the roof. Teresa tried not to show her triumph. Vargas and Cummings must have dropped off into the arroyo before the soldier gained the top. A baffled light filled Uvalde's eyes.

"We had word Felipe Vargas was seen here," he told Teresa. "That would make it dangerous for you."

It was her turn to smile. "Then you can escort me back. I'd feel perfectly safe with you . . . Captain."

After Uvalde left her at her *sala,* she tried to guess his true purpose in coming to the inn. It could have been on the strength of a tip that Vargas was there. Or it could have been something more. Uvalde was one of Amado's right-hand men, doing a lot of nasty jobs for the governor. Yet he was a man who played both sides against the middle, and could be bought, if the price was right. It was possible that Archuleta had put him to watching her.

The day after her trip to Mendoza's she had a meeting with Amado and asked him to pardon Vargas. She didn't tell Amado about Archuleta but simply said she needed Vargas. Amado had come to respect the value of her spy system, and it took little persuading to make him grant the pardon. Through the next weeks she waited anxiously till the monthly patrol to El Pasó del Norte left Santa Fé. Then Pablo brought her word that a rider from Archuleta's household had accompanied the troops.

Two nights later Pablo brought Vargas and Cummings to her salon. They still showed signs of the fight. There was a livid scar on Vargas's face and Cummings had an arm in a bloody sling. With his sardonic grin, Vargas produced the oilskin packet.

"We jumped them at night below Albuquerque. I lost two

men in the fight, but we finally got the messenger away. He had the packet sewed inside his shirt."

Inside the packet was a five-page letter from Juan Archuleta to Mirabeau Lamar. Archuleta referred to previous correspondence with Lamar concerning the possibility of an invasion from Texas. Then he expressed his disgust with Amado and his impatience with the Lower River for their failure to depose him. He offered his help in an attempt of Texas to annex New Mexico, in return for a high office in the government the Texans would establish in Santa Fé. Following was a long list of his plans to undermine the present regime. It was conspiracy on a grand scale, but nowhere was there any mention of the guns.

It was a disappointment. Yet she knew the value of the letter. At first she had the impulse to tell Amado. Then she rejected that. Amado would only imprison Archuleta or execute him, and it would gain them nothing now. She knew Archuleta's conspiracy would stop as soon as he heard what had happened to his messenger. He would guess what lay back of it and would be quaking in his boots for fear of exposure. It would be better to wait till some future time when exposing Archuleta would gain them more than his downfall. In the meantime, it would be good to have such a threat against a Biscara man.

She handed Vargas his pardon. "Getting your freedom from Archuleta will take a little longer. But he won't dare touch you as soon as he realizes we have the letter. You can walk the streets like a free man. And, as a free man, how would you like to go on working for me?"

Grinning, Vargas bowed low. "At such handsome wages . . . how could we refuse?"

She told Pablo to take them out and make arrangements for a place in town. When they had gone, she sat down and closed her eyes, feeling let down, defeated. The question of the guns had not been answered. Yet she had not lost entirely. It was all a part of the endless process—an incessant balancing and counter-balancing of power, moving and checking, creating and destroying, a giant chess game that went on without end.

Vargas and Cummings proved a valuable addition to her system of spies and informers; they and their reckless gang gave it a hard core of daring it had never possessed before. More than once she used them for jobs that no one else had the courage to attempt. Through the rest of 1839 and the next year she had her fingers in almost every plot or intrigue brewing in Santa Fé. What she didn't find out from her spies came to her through the countless other channels she had developed. One of these sources of information was the trappers who came down from the wild north country where few Mexicans ventured.

They came to Taos and Santa Fé every spring, selling their harvest of furs and spending their money in drunken sprees. Kelly Morgan came with them. He showed up in Santa Fé during April of 1841 with his spring harvest of furs. He sold them to Danny O'Brien and bought himself new buckskins and a twenty-dollar beaver hat and a belt made from gold *pesos*. He found three Mexican girls at La Fonda and set about seeing how fast he could get rid of his money. By evening he'd been in three brawls, and before midnight he was thrown in La Garita, dead drunk and dead broke.

He showed up at Teresa's a few days later; it was morning, and she and the barman were the only ones in the main *sala* when Morgan came in. His beaver hat and gold belt were gone; his new buckskins were torn in a dozen places and caked with mud and straw from nights spent huddled against a wall or in a haystack. His eyes were red-rimmed and bloodshot, and a week's growth of beard covered his belligerent jaw with a blond stubble. It was a typical picture of the half a hundred trappers in town, broke, surly with hangovers, squatting against the mud walls or wandering emptily through the streets, facing a summer of starving and scrounging till fall took them back to their traplines. It was part of the price they paid for the strange, savage sort of freedom they found in the mountains. She tried not to feel sorry for Morgan, but she couldn't help it. She looked him up and down, veiling her green eyes so he couldn't see the compassion in them.

"If you want a drink," she said, "it's on the house."

He leaned against the bar, grinning indolently. "I didn't come to beg. What I got you can pay for."

She was surprised. "What's that?"

"Information."

She frowned at him. The fencing again. The antagonism. The wondering. Why should she feel this way? He should be ugly to her, with his beard, his dirty clothes, his shabbiness. "I thought you didn't like dirty politics."

"A man can change his mind," he said.

She was disappointed. She had wanted this. Yet, in a strange way, she hadn't wanted it. He had been the only one she couldn't draw into her net of intrigue, the only one she couldn't maneuver or control in some way. And it had set him apart somehow. It was odd that the pride of so simple a man could be such a shining thing. Yet it was a thing she had come to admire. And now an empty belly had humbled him.

"All right," she said thinly. "A *peso* for a tidbit. A bigger price for bigger news."

He wiped his mouth, looked around at the door. He slid toward her along the bar, voice growing confidential. "I come acrost somethin' up at Taos that's a-goin' to cause the biggest revolution in this country you'll ever see."

She remembered the guns, last year, and the questions that had never been answered. Excitement flushed her cheeks. "Revolution?"

He glanced at the bartender. "Maybe we better go somewhere. Your servants seem to pick up everything."

She hesitated, then nodded her head toward the rear. They went to the room off the patio, with its black and white tile, its wine-red velvet. Watching him narrowly, she poured him a drink. It was an old ritual in this room. He accepted it, hitching his holstered gun around to the front so he could sit down. She saw that it was not a pistol but one of the new Dragoon six-shooters that had come from the United States in the last year.

She wheeled and walked across the room, folding her arms, drumming slender fingers nervously against her elbows. "This revolution?"

"Why don't you light up a smoke? You seem to think better with one o' them cigars in your mouth."

Frowning, she opened the silver box on the table, rolled herself a *cigarrillo* swiftly, nervously. He held up the golden tongs, and she placed the *cigarrillo* in them. When she bent toward a candle to light it, he touched her hand, stopping her. He pulled a block of wood from his belt, divided into long thin strips. He tore one of the strips off, scraped it on the underside of the table. It broke into flame. Blue smoke wreathed from it, and, when he raised it, she smelled sulphur. It burned brightly. Fascinated as a child, she bent forward to light her *cigarrillo*.

"The Yankees call 'em lucifers," he said. "Wouldn't you say it was sort of revolutionary? Pretty soon nobody'll be carryin' flints and steel in Santa Fé."

She breathed the gray smoke into his face. "You deceived me."

He squinted his eyes, chuckling. "Love and war . . . ma'am."

She tried to pull away, but his hand was on her wrist, overwhelming in the force of its grip. He came up out of the chair to her. His other hand went to her bare shoulder, his callused heat sending a trembling wave of excitement through her. This was what had lain behind their constant fencing. This was the wonder and the questioning. This was the want and the hate, the scorn and the fear. Why had she toyed with the fire of it? Why had she been a fool? She was staring over the high wall now, and she could see what lay at the bottom of the dizzy drop.

"Kelly, I told you, I told you. . . ."

"I figgered it was about time to try again. You had that look in your eyes."

"Pepita!"

"She won't hear you, honey."

The golden tongs slipped from her hand in the struggle. As from a great distance she heard them tinkle against the tiles. The smell of the burning *cigarrillo* sifted up from below. "Kelly, don't be a fool." Struggling. "I can have anything done to you. I can ask Amado to kill you."

"You wouldn't kill your husband."

"Are you crazy?"

"Maybe so. I want you, Teresa. I want you all the way. This ain't no Biscara with a servant girl. This ain't no Amado pinchin' rumps. This is Kelly Morgan, honey, askin' you to be his wife!"

She stopped struggling, staring up at him in shock, in disbelief. She saw the tenderness in his face; beside the savagery, the desire, she saw the love and the wanting and the needing like she'd never seen it before. She remembered when Hilario had come to her, and she'd wanted to cry. Now it was hard to breathe. It was hard to think, it was so bad and so good all at once, so strange and so crazy.

"Then what?" she said.

He looked surprised. "You and me. You wouldn't have to fight any more, Teresa. You wouldn't have to kick and claw and cheat and lie and set one dog on another . . . ."

"I could live in a teepee," she said. "I could eat beavertail on Sunday. Sew and cook and get blind over a fire like some Crow squaw."

"It wouldn't be that bad."

"I know how it would be. I've seen the women trappers marry. Left home half the year, while you're off on your traplines, caught inside four walls somewhere. Taos, Bent's Fort, some Cheyenne camp, like a horse you put in a corral. It took me all my life to get away from that."

"God damn it, I said it won't be like that. You can have it any way you like. Jist name the rules."

"Why should I? I'm the richest, freest woman in all New Mexico. I can come and go as I please, answer to no man. . . ."

"And still you ain't got what you want." He gripped her so tightly the bones of her shoulders ground together, shaking her in his frustration. "This is what you want, Teresa, you know it is."

"The hell I do."

"The hell you don't!"

He pulled her against him, writhing, and she couldn't get free. His hand was at the back of her head, turning her face up. His face was above her, shining with sweat, cruel and tender all at the same time. The kiss. The flower of passion blossoming inside her. The world beginning to lose focus.

She knew he would have her this time. Desire was a hot,

trembling flood in her, sweeping out all will to resist. There was only a little corner of fear, of resistance, of hatred left. Only a moment remaining. One of her clawing hands felt the butt of the big Colt dragoon, holstered at his side

"Kelly," she sobbed, "don't. I killed a man once for this."

His words were muffled by the pressure of his lips against her neck, her shoulders. "He died happy."

She had the gun out, cocked, pressed against his side. It wasn't Morgan she fought now. It was herself. It was her own need, her own weakness that in another moment would make her surrender everything she had fought for, would make her subject herself to this man, would allow him to possess her, body and soul, as no other man ever had. "Kelly." She was crying openly now, the tears running down her face in silvery tracks. "Please, don't. . . ."

"You're a-goin' to be my wife, Teresa. One way or the other, you're a-goin' to be my wife."

His hands found her breasts. Her whole body shuddered, and she surged up against him with a broken sound.

The room seemed to rock as the gun went off. She was so deafened that she did not hear his cry. His great body stiffened against her, hung there a moment, then pitched back its full length onto the floor.

Chapter Nineteen

 1841 was the year of the ill-fated Texas Expedition. Since the Texas Revolution, the boundaries of the Lone Star Republic had been in dispute. Texas claimed its land ran to the Río Grande. But this river turned north at El Pasó del Norte, running up past Albuquerque and Santa Fé. The Mexicans held that this could not possibly constitute the western boundary of Texas and claimed land for several hundred miles eastward.

General Mirabeau Lamar, president of the Texas Republic, gave official sanction to the boundary claims of his people. In the spring of 1841, news reached Santa Fé that he was equipping an expeditionary force to invade New Mexico. There were all kinds of wild rumors. Gómez claimed he had letters from friends in Texas proving that the force numbered thirty thousand men and would overwhelm the New Mexicans. Ryker claimed he'd heard through his agent in San Antonio that the expedition was merely a band of traders trying to open a new trail.

Tension and threat of war had existed between the Lone Star Republic and Mexico ever since the Texas Revolution. Governor Amado was only too willing to believe that the expedition was an invading force and immediately took measures of defense. Half a dozen known Texans in Santa Fé were arrested, all foreign-born residents were forbidden to leave their hones, and Captain Emilio Uvalde was sent to patrol the eastern border beyond Las Vegas.

On September 4th, Uvalde captured three Texans supposed to be advance spies for the Texas Expedition and brought them to the capital for trial. Captain Uvalde was from Taos and had been one of Gómez's men from the first. Thus *Don* Biscara was not surprised when the two showed up together at his house on San Francisco Street. He invited them in, offered them drinks and smokes. After the traditional punctilio of the country, observed even among such close companions, Uvalde lounged on a *colchón,* surveying the bouquet of the wine. His narrow wedge of a face was still dust-grayed from the long ride, and his elongated, grasping hands were restless.

"Are they going to arrest Kelly Morgan?" Biscara asked.

Uvalde frowned into his glass. "I doubt it. Somebody remembered he was a Texan, and there was talk of arrest. But he could hardly be a spy. He's been lying in Teresa Cavan's place for months now, hovering between life and death." The militia captain shook his head. "What a woman! *I* will even fear to pass her a compliment from now on."

Gómez moved restlessly about the room, hands locked behind his back, as if coming to some decision. Finally he pursed his lips. "We have more important matters. Something came into our hands that I thought you might like to see."

He produced a document that had been found on one of the spies. It was a proclamation by General Mirabeau B. Lamar, addressed to the citizens of Santa Fé, dated April 14, 1840.

We tender you a full participation in all our blessings. The Great River of the North, which you inhabit, is the natural and convenient boundary of our territory, and we shall take great pleasure in hailing you as our fellow citizens, members of our young Republic, and co-aspirants with us for establishing a new and happy and free nation. . . .

Biscara frowned. "It says nothing here of an army."

"Does a man announce a betrayal?" Uvalde asked. "These three spies admitted there was a large force behind them, five companies of mounted infantry heavily armed, an artillery company with brass six-pounders. Does a peaceful trading party carry cannon?"

Biscara's black brows arched. "You play a dangerous game, Gómez. If the governor realized you had deliberately withheld evidence from him. . . ."

For a moment a gray tinge came to Gómez's purple-veined jowls. Then he moistened his lips, shook his head. "The men have already been condemned to death as spies. I thought you might find a way to use this."

Biscara turned it over in his mind. A vague possibility came to him. He began to nod. "Perhaps you are right. I think it may be up to you, my dear Gómez."

"Me?"

"A man who can come and go in the Palace at will . . . a man who has been the fawning sycophant, groveling his way back into their favor, waiting for this moment." Biscara's pointed beard made his smile intensely satanic. "I think our time has come, *señores.*"

On September 16th, Captain Uvalde captured five men near La Cuesta. They were in pitiable condition—ragged, exhausted, starving—but claimed to be scouts for the main body of Texans who were somewhere behind. Governor Amado was informed and left Santa Fé with the regulars, setting up headquarters at Las Vegas. The next day he encountered another larger body of Texans at Anton Chico. There were ninety-four men under a colonel and a captain. They were a gaunt, haggard, miserable lot of creatures. Many had worn their boots out marching and stood shivering in their bare feet. They were all grimed with dirt and ridden with lice, scratching bearded faces and open sores on their necks and chests. A dozen were violently ill with dysentery, unable to walk. It was an absurd travesty of an invading army.

Yet many of them carried the infamous Lamar proclamation. Hopelessly outnumbered, they surrendered their arms and suffered themselves to be marched to Las Vegas. That night, in a victory celebration, Amado had all the proclamations burned in the plaza.

The news came back, bit by bit, to the little room—the little room in Teresa Cavan's house where Kelly Morgan had lain all summer. A room so all-fired little it got him to crawling inside when he looked around at the walls.

At last he couldn't stand it. He didn't know when he decided that. Days after the capture of the Texans. Maybe weeks after. He just knew that he'd been on his back long enough, and one night for the first time he shoved the cover off.

They had put the *colchón* on a homemade bedstead, some legs and a board bottom about a foot off the floor. He swung out his feet and sat up. The world began spinning. All the blue and yellow saints in the niches around the room started dancing, and the walls tilted up. He held onto the bed till things righted themselves. He grabbed one of the niches and pulled himself upright. He swayed there, blinking his blue eyes, grinning foolishly to himself. Then he heard the scuffle of feet outside, and before he could move the door was pushed open.

Teresa stood there, eyes wide with surprise. Then, peevish

as a mother hen rounding up her brood, she crossed the room and caught his arm.

"What're you doing up? You're not strong enough yet."

"Strong, hell. I could lick my weight in . . . ."

"Pussywillows," she said, and gave a tug. It pulled him off balance, and he was too weak to fight her. She held onto him, breaking his fall as he folded up on the bed. When he tried to sit up, she put her hands on his chest and pushed him down.

"Damn it," he said, "if you don't let me get my legs back, I'll be crawlin' around on all fours the rest o' my life."

She smiled. "A little bit at a time," she said. "The American doctor told me you shouldn't get up for another two weeks at least."

She unpinned the gear holding the compress against his wound. Pepita brought in a tray with fresh cotton, and Teresa changed the dressing. He lay slack, watching her through half-closed eyes. She wore only a short-sleeved blouse, pleated around the yoke, and a skirt of heavy blue serge. She had not done up her hair yet, and it curled and massed around her head and shoulders, red as the flames of a windblown bonfire.

"Lift up now," she said. "I'll wind the bandage around."

He arched up, and she pulled the cotton strip three times around his body. The effort brought a fine beading of sweat to his brow, and he lay heavily against the bed, breathing shallowly. She pinned the bandage tightly over the compress, looking at him with troubled eyes. "So weak," she said.

He groaned. "I'd stay this way, if it brought you every morning."

She put her hands on the bed and leaned forward, her face very close above him, compassion in her dark eyes, more tenderness in the soft and pouting shape of her lips than he had ever seen before. Her breasts hung against her *camisa*, round,

212

heavy, almost touching his chest. The blood began to pound in his head, and he reached up for her. She pushed aside his hands and rose. She stood over him for a moment, lips petulant, green eyes stormy. Then, with a return of the nervousness that had come to characterize her so deeply these last years, she turned and walked to one of the windows. He put his hands beneath his head, smiling wickedly.

"It must be hell," he said, "to be so afraid of love."

She didn't answer. She looked through the narrow barred window at Palace Avenue. A *carreta* went by, wheels shrieking.

"What're you fightin' it for?" he asked. "What're you afraid I'll take from you?" He looked around the room. "This? You're trapped in four walls just the same."

She turned, goaded into answering. A brooding shadow lay on her face, and her green eyes smoldered. "They're my walls."

"Men got you under their thumb just the same. You got to play every dirty little game they bring you. Got to lie and cheat and steal and hurt somebody no matter which way you turn."

"I didn't make the rules."

"You would've spit in Biscara's face once. Now you make deals like he was your brother. Amado's your own monster. He wouldn't o' been nothin' without you. He's ten times worse'n Carbajal ever was. The people didn't know what graft was till he come in. How would you know? In this place all the time, makin' your money, spinnin' your plots. Get out jist once, Teresa. Take a look at those people starving on Galisteo. Count the beggars at your door every mornin'. I don't know nothin' about politics, but I kin see what you've done to this town."

"Kelly . . . ."

"All because you're afraid." He was on his elbows breathing heavily with the effort of such a long speech. "The whole god-damn thing you've built . . . all because you're afraid. This ain't freedom. You could have a million dollars. You could own this whole town. You'd still be trapped because you'd be afraid to trust one man in it."

"What do you know about freedom?" She was bent forward, her whole body trembling with the force of her antagonism. "Up on some mountain. Freezing in the winter, starving in the summer. Not a cent in your pocket. Living like an animal. Never knowing where your next meal comes from. Is that freedom?"

She trailed off, breathing heavily, cheeks touched with flame. It was as if they had both spent their fury. He lay back, looking up at the ceiling. "You'll know," he said softly. "When you get it, you'll know. It's like an ache inside. It's like flyin' with the eagles."

She did not answer. After a moment she started for the door. Before she reached it, someone knocked. She checked herself, then opened it. *Don* Augustin Gómez stood there, a bland smile on his gray-furred jowls. With him was Captain Pérez.

"Is the patient ready for our daily game?" Gómez asked.

Teresa regained her composure. "Just in time," she said. "The company of women bores him so."

"The captain is just back from Las Vegas with news of the Texans," Gómez said. "I thought you would like to hear."

Interest kindled in Teresa's eyes as she stepped back to let them enter. Pérez strode into the room, holding his saber against one booted leg, bowing his greeting to Teresa. His tanned face always took on a glow in her presence, and his shining eyes never left her face. Morgan had never been able to fathom what lay between these two. If a man really wanted a woman that much, how could he stand around eternally murmuring compliments and looking at her like a lost puppy?

"I hope it's good news you bring, Captain," Teresa said.

There was always something a little maternal in her attitude toward him.

He shook his head, face troubled. "Not good. I can't understand it. The Texans surrendered without battle. Would they do that if they were invaders? Yet the governor showed them no mercy. He is sending them on foot all the way to Mexico City. It's unthinkable in their condition. Hundreds of miles through the desert, without shoes, sick. It will be the worst of winter before they reach the capital. Half of them will die."

Teresa glanced at Gómez. The man raised his brows. He spoke to Pérez. "Don't misjudge the governor. If they're invaders, he has no authority to hold them here. . . ."

"Surely he has the authority to treat them like human beings," Pérez said. He paced across the room, helmet under one arm. "I don't understand it. He seems to be getting worse and worse."

"When we get word from Mexico City, you'll find he's done right."

Pérez shook his sleek black head. "Nothing can make that right. Tyranny is tyranny, under any circumstances, and that's what I saw at Las Vegas."

Teresa took his arm. "Let's go into the *sala* and talk it over while these two have their game. You've just been looking at the surface of things again, without trying to understand what goes on underneath."

She led him out, closing the door behind her. Gómez shook his head, smiling cynically. He started walking toward the spindled cupboard. Morgan put his hands behind his head.

"Why doesn't she want Pérez to see what Amado really is?"

Gómez took out the pack of cards, tilting his head to one

side quizzically. "Perhaps to avert a catastrophe, my friend. To have Pérez's loyalty now is to have the loyalty of the regular army."

"She plays a dirty game."

Gómez slid a low coffee table beside the bed, putting the cards on it. "Who is to say that we would not play the same way, under the same circumstances?"

Gómez moved a chair by the table and seated himself into it with a comfortable sigh. Morgan studied the man's dissipated face from between slitted lids. Gómez had been a faithful companion, coming in every day or so for a game of cards, a drink of wine. Despite their disparity in background, in culture, they had enough in common to establish a sort of casual bond between them. Gómez was a wit, an intellect, a charming companion with enough common clay in him to find a meeting ground with Morgan's native shrewdness and wry sense of humor. But in Gómez's relation with Teresa, Pérez, and the others, Morgan had caught vagrant glimpses of another side to the man.

"You know what toadyin' is, Gómez?" he asked.

The man frowned. "My English is not that good."

"It means lickin' somebody's boots," Morgan said.

Gómez began to shuffle.

Morgan murmured: "You ain't a boot-licker."

Gómez inclined his head ironically. "Thank you."

"Then why do you do it?"

Gómez stopped shuffling. He looked at Morgan. Then he stacked the cards and pushed them across the table. The latticework of veins seemed to grow darker in his gray jowls.

Morgan cut the cards. "Toadyin' up to Teresa. Lickin' the governor's boots. Spreadin' the honey on for Captain Pérez. That ain't you at all." Morgan lay back, looking carefully at the man. "What are you really, Gómez?"

The man smiled, picking up the cards to deal. "Someday, my friend, perhaps you will find out."

Teresa did not have dinner with Morgan that evening. After eating, he lay in the dim light, listening to the distant and muffled sounds of the gambling hall as it filled with customers. He was thinking again. During these long weeks of his recuperation he'd probably done more thinking than at any other time in his life, and most of it about Teresa. Despite his wildness, his earthiness, Morgan had a native wisdom and a shrewd judgment of people that gave him a deep insight into Teresa.

He knew it was not merely his possession of her body she feared. It was not simply the threat he constituted as a man. The thing she feared most was her own attraction to him. If she once gave way to love for him, she would be subjecting herself completely. Her very need of him was a weakness that would defeat her more than anything he could do, and it was that subjugation she fought. But she was weakening. He saw it every time she came into the room. In the little attentions she gave him, the way she watched him when she thought he was not looking. His feebleness and his pain had brought out a tenderness, a compassion he never would have been able to invoke in their previous clashes. Hers was a spirit that would not yield to force or violence alone. As long as the conquest had been all his, she had resisted. But now he was no longer the attacker. Perhaps this was the chink in her armor. Or perhaps it was the essence and the paradox of love. To conquer, one had to be conquered.

He slept, and then woke again. There was no sound from outside. That meant it was after midnight. The *sala* rarely closed till two in the morning. He lay back, motionless, wondering what had awakened him. Then he heard the scuffle of footsteps in the hall, the faint creak of the door. Senses born in the wilderness made him grow still as a dog with its hackles up.

The door opened, permitting the faintest illumination to creep in. It came from a candle in one of the wall niches outside, too far down the hall to give any real light. Against its dim glow he saw the silhouette of a woman. A woman in a clinging gown that gave distinct outlines to the flare of mature hips, the outer curve of her thighs.

He knew who it was now. She had looked in on him before like this when he was really sick, when he was delirious or sweating out a night of pain on the low bed. She seemed to stand there a long while. Then there was the hint of taffeta as she moved in, shutting the door part way so the light would not wake him. She was barely visible now, a streak of smoky movement in the textured darkness.

Then she was beside him, above him, looking down upon him. The scent of her perfume and the barely perceptible heat of her body crept over him. He should have been able to relax, now that he knew who it was. But his body was still tense beneath the cotton cover.

He could hear her breathing, like the faint rustle of silk through the fingers. What was she looking at so long? She couldn't see his face. He wanted to speak. But there was a strange spell about the moment, a sense of special import that kept him silent. Soon she would go. When she turned, he would speak. He would ask her to stay and talk to him.

Then he realized that her breathing was louder. Its warmth, its perfume was right in his face. She was bending over him. He could sense the heated softness of her body somewhere above his face. Then her lips brushed against his forehead—moist, satiny—and were gone.

But she was not gone. She was still there with him. For a

moment he lay there, held by the spell. Then he heard a little sobbing catch in the breathing, so close above him. He raised his hands and found her. His fingers closed on her bare shoulders, and he pulled her down to him and sought her lips. After the first passionate kiss she began crying.

"Kelly, " she said. "Kelly, Kelly, Kelly. . . ."

The tears covered her cheeks and her lips and gave a wild salt taste to the kisses. His feverish hands worked at her gown, pulling it off, pulling it down. Then his fingers dug into the pulsing velvet of her hips, the full roundness of her buttocks, and the nakedness of her breasts flattened against him.

In passion he found strength. The pain of his wound and the weakness faded away. She cried all the way through it. His memory of that night would always be mingled with the sound of her sobbing and the taste of her tears on his lips. Even after it was over and she lay beside him, no longer crying, he could put his face against hers and feel the tears damp on her cheeks.

There was something utterly hopeless about it, and it made him feel like a traitor. He had taken the core out of her, had smashed the very thing that had sustained her against the world. In her mind she was stripped of her armor now; she had joined the other women of this land in their slavery.

"Honey," he said, "it couldn't be any other way. Can't you see that?"

She did not answer.

"It ain't as bad as all that. I ain't taken your freedom from you. In this kind of thing you maybe lose somethin', but you git somethin', too. Maybe what you git is better, honey."

Still she did not answer. She lay limp and sodden against him. When he reached over to kiss her again, he felt a soundless shudder run through her body like a sob that was cast out into the night and went on without end.

Chapter Twenty

That same night Governor Amado arrived in the capital. He came in on the Santa Fé Trail from Las Vegas, riding his big dun mule at the head of a troop of lancers. His great weight was settled tiredly in the saddle, his cloak flopped about him like a banner, and his face was dust-grayed and haggard from the long ride.

He had left Captain Uvalde in command of the Texans, with orders to start the march to Mexico City the following day. He was still seething over the Lamar proclamation. What kind of war was this that a handful of men could make an armed march into a land and expect it to fall at their feet? It was not only a traitorous attempt to steal a country; it was an insult to the courage and the intelligence of the New Mexicans. It was unfortunate that there had been no glorious battles to communicate to the capital, but in his dispatches to Santa Anna he had made the capture of the Texans sound as dangerous and difficult as possible.

Under a dying moon the Santa Fé plaza was a dim lake of silvered earth. A black finger of shadow pointed westward from the sundial, and the shadows were even blacker beneath the *portales* fronting the Palace. Like yellow eyes peering from those shadows the narrow windows of the Assembly chamber cast out dim channels of light. The only movement in the square came from the shuttling figures of the sentries as they passed back and forth beneath the *portales*.

Crossing toward them, Amado glanced toward San Francisco Street and Teresa's house. It brought back the jealousy, the stupid, nagging jealousy that had been with him for weeks now.

How could a man be so foolish? How could he be jealous of a woman he had never possessed? It only proved what a weakness he had for her. His lecherous buffoonery had become a ritual between them, a cloak he adopted in her presence, hiding the depths of his real desire. At the back of his mind had always lain the conviction, the hope, the need that Teresa would come to him. It was inevitable. They were *simpático*. It was more than the beauty of her, curling a man's fingers with the want for ripeness. It was her spirit, her fire, going right through a man—and that yellow-headed trapper, that *bribón*, lying in her room, in her very bed, with her tending him as though she were his slave. A taste like bile came into Amado's mouth, and he spat disgustedly. If he thought for a moment, if he had the slightest suspicion. . . .

But no. He shook his head. He knew her adamant refusal to take any man as a lover. That was the very core of her. Why else had she shot Morgan? It was a joke around the capital. Even Amado could afford to be amazed by it. He certainly had no real cause for jealousy.

He pulled to a pompous halt before the sentries, receiving their salutes with a perfunctory nod. The other dragoons halted behind him, the dust of their passage settling against the night like a silver fog.

"The word you sent led us to believe you would be back early this evening, Governor," one of the sentries told him. "*Don* Gómez and several others still wait up for you."

Amado wheezed, lowering his oleaginous bulk off the mule. "What is the time?"

"Well after three o'clock."

He nodded absently, handing his reins to one of the mounted lancers, ordering them to proceed around to the *zaguán* gate. Inocente slid off his burro and accompanied Amado through the main door and into the Assembly hall. At the table a group of men had been passing the time with a game of cards—*Don* Gómez, Biscara, Captain Pérez, and a pair of lieutenants. They all rose as Amado entered. Pérez and the lieutenants slipped on coats over their rumpled, sweat-stained shirts.

"*Para siempre bendito sea Dios y le siempre, pase adelante, gobernador,*" Gómez said.

Amado grinned tiredly. "It is too late for such formality, my friend, even with the governor. Let us merely say *buenas tardes.*"

Gómez helped him off with his cloak, and Biscara poured a drink, bringing it to him. He drained it at one gulp, squinted his eyes, smacked his lips.

"A pity you were delayed," Gómez said. "A celebration had been planned in your honor."

"It can be held tomorrow," Amado said. "Last minute duty with the Texas invaders. It is over now, at any rate."

Gómez glanced at Biscara, locked his hands behind him, frowned at the floor. "Not quite over, I'm afraid, Governor. There is still one of them in our midst."

The weary affability left Amado's face. His frown dug twin vertical furrows between his brows. Gómez looked at the windows, cleared his throat.

"As you know, Teresa is harboring this Kelly Morgan. . . ."

"But he's been among us for years," Captain Pérez said. He looked surprised.

Gómez looked at him, shrugged. "Which would enable

him to spy on us with that much less possibility of suspicion."

"Spy?" Amado said. It was a trigger word for him, a lighted fuse to anger, fear, mistrust.

Gómez got something from a pocket. "I have visited his room now and then. Tonight I found this."

It was a brass button. On its face was engraved **TEXAS**. Amado felt a tremor of anger run through his body. The same buttons had been found on the other invaders.

"It does not prove he is a spy," Pérez said.

"What more do you want?" Biscara asked dryly. "I wager we would find other proof if we searched his room."

It seemed to be a culmination of Amado's jealousy over Teresa, his courage with the Texans. With his temper at the boiling point, he nodded savagely. "You're right. We'll conduct a search. If we find nothing more, the button alone would condemn him." He spoke sharply to one of the lieutenants. "Summon a squad. Follow me to the *sala* on the double."

He saw the stricken look on Pérez's face as he wheeled, followed by the others, and stalked out of the Assembly. They marched across the plaza and into San Francisco Street. By the time they had reached Burro Alley, Lieutenant Valdez and eight sleepy, grumbling dragoons had arrived. Amado went to the door on Burro Alley, pounding loudly. It took some time before a muttering, puffy-eyed Pepita unbarred and opened it. Amado let Inocente enter first, shoving the surprised Indian woman aside. They filled the hall in the next moment. Inocente snatched the candle in its tin sconce from Pepita and scurried ahead to the door of Morgan's room.

Before he reached it, the door was opened, and Teresa stepped out, blinking her eyes. "Pepita," she called testily. "What is all this?"

She broke off as she saw them. The surprise of seeing her

had stopped them all, ten feet from the door. She had nothing but a blanket pulled around her. Amado saw that she was barefooted, her legs bare—and knew that she must be naked beneath that single cover. It was like a blow to the pit of his stomach; his face turned pasty with shock, then with rage. If he had been alone, he thought, he would have beaten her. Yet he could not let the others see what this did to him. It was an immense effort to keep his voice sardonic. "Not only does our Teresa harbor traitors and spies. She amuses them in bed."

A flush ran up Teresa's satiny neck, staining her cheeks scarlet. Candlelight flickered eerily against the jade-green rage in her eyes, and the shame. She pulled the blanket tighter about her, speaking in a brittle voice. "What right have you in here at this hour?"

"*¡Punta en boca!*" Amado said. His eyes were cruel now; he waved his arm viciously toward the room. "Search it."

The lieutenant and his men swarmed around Amado. Teresa backed into the doorway, blocking it. There was something intensely savage about her. She was drawn up to her full height, her eyes flashing, her coral lips compressed. Her face was taut and bleak with defiance, its pale oval half buried against the burning flame of her cascading red hair. The lieutenant halted a foot from her, his face reflecting the fear and the awe with which the people had come to regard this woman.

"Lieutenant," Amado said, "would you like to be a private tomorrow?"

"Governor," Pérez said, "I protest this invasion. . . ."

"Lieutenant!"

Valdez reacted to Amado's shout, waving his arm at the dragoons. A pair of them caught Teresa by the arms. She fought, but they pushed her roughly out of the doorway.

"Your pardon, *señorita*," Valdez said. Saber drawn, he

stepped into the room. A pair of dragoons followed him. Amado stalked past Teresa with a savage glance, Gómez and Biscara and the other troops crowding in behind.

Kelly Morgan had swung his feet off the bed and was dragging himself up by one of the niches in the wall. "What the hell is this?" he asked. A pair of dragoons blocked him off, carbines across their chests. He swayed heavily against the wall and would have fallen without its support. The lieutenant and the other dragoons were already beginning the search. They ripped the covers off the bed, tore off the mattress, broke open the leather-bound chest in the corner, spilling out laces and taffeta gowns and jewelry. The lieutenant found Morgan's effects in the cupboard. He dumped the shoulder belt with its trapper's tools onto the floor. Then he ripped open the possibles sack. He pulled out an extra pair of beaded moccasins, a bone needle wrapped in rawhide thread.

"Damn you," Morgan said feebly. "What're you lookin' for?"

The lieutenant pulled out a rolled document, opening it. He scanned a few lines, then turned with wide eyes to Amado. "It is the proclamation of President Lamar," he said.

Amado felt the veins in his neck swell and began to pound. He turned to see Teresa in the doorway, staring at the proclamation with a shocked expression. Amado spoke in a trembling voice. "I have always admired your histrionics, Teresa. But nothing can explain the possession of this. You were harboring a spy, and I think you knew it." He hesitated a moment, not wanting to say it. Then he cursed himself for a sentimental fool. She had betrayed him, as much as their country. He gave the order to Lieutenant Valdez in a husky wheeze: "Take them to La Garita."

It was a bleak little cell. Many men had waited for death here. The name of **Granillo** was carved into the windowsill, and the date of **1694**. Other names were carved into the wood, or the crumbling walls, and other dates. It made Teresa shiver and draw her cloak more tightly about her. She walked to the barred windows, looking out upon the flat roofs of the city below. It had been three days since her arrest, and she was in a torture of anxiety. Kelly Morgan had been taken from the prison that first morning while she was still asleep. The guards told her that he had been sent south to join Uvalde and the Texans on their way to Mexico City. It had sickened her with fear. He was too weak for such a terrible march; he would surely die.

From the guards she had heard the other news. Governor Amado had taken her *sala* in the name of the government, had confiscated all of her money that he could put his hands on, had arrested all the known members of her spy ring. He was now in the process of weeding out the members she had planted in the Assembly and the other government posts. Captain Pérez had resigned his commission and been imprisoned. Amado had had him put under arrest. The sense of helpless frustration she felt over that was mingled constantly with her fears for Kelly Morgan. Yet, paradoxically, she knew a trenchant anger with herself for feeling those fears. It was a recollection of the bitter conflict that had raged within her ever since the night of the arrest. In a way, what had happened justified everything she had believed in. One moment of weakness for a man, one moment of giving in, of subjecting herself to him—and her world was smashed. In an instant she had been stripped of all the wealth, the power, the influence she had so carefully garnered through the years. In an instant she had placed herself at the mercy of all the men she had fought so long.

She was sure that Amado's jealousy was behind this revenge on her. The presence of Morgan in her room and her nakedness had been a blow his pride could not stand. If she had not been there, she was certain, he would not have imprisoned her. They would have taken Morgan, but she knew she would have convinced Amado of her innocence.

How many times had she said she was through being used by men? And yet, after all her bitter struggle for freedom, one had come along—crude, primitive, animal—and touched something within her, and she had fallen. A woman so foolish deserved to be enslaved.

She still couldn't get Kelly Morgan out of her mind. Would she still go with him, if she could? She was in love with him. She was certain of that. The passion they had known could be nothing else—and to an ordinary woman love would mean going with your man, wherever he went, whatever he did. But maybe she wasn't an ordinary woman any more. Maybe what had happened throughout her life had warped her, twisted her, embittered her to the point where she couldn't accept love so simply and easily. Otherwise why the confusion—why this bitter mingling of the fear and love for Kelly Morgan and anger and disgust with herself?

She paced the cell agitatedly, face pale, hands locked together. Holy Mother, why had she been born a woman? She heard chains rattling; the door was opened. The yellow light of the keeper's candle crawled up the wall outside, illuminating the rank of blue uniforms. The officer in charge was the lieutenant who had arrested her.

"Lieutenant Valdez," she said ironically. "The executioner now?"

"Captain Valdez," he said.

"For valor, undoubtedly."

Valdez did not answer. He looked at the keeper, and the man snuffed his candle. In utter darkness she was taken out of the infamous old Spanish prison and down the winding road to town. Like a band of ghosts they marched through the empty back streets. An uncontrollable shivering ran through her body, and she pulled the cloak tight.

Finally they reached the mouth of Burro Alley and took her up it to the side door of her *sala*. They entered and went down the hall to the familiar door of the familiar room and stopped. Captain Valdez opened the door and waved her in.

It was unchanged—the tile floor, the red drapes covering the walls, the marble-topped table. At the table, in one of the plush chairs, was Governor Amado. She heard the door close behind her and stood alone before him. Neither of them spoke. He lounged back in the chair, looking at her from beneath the pouched lids of his bloodshot eyes. He had grown heavy and soft with the dissipation of these last years. Beneath his ruffled white shirt a gross belly bulged out over his belt. The primitive heaviness of his jaw had become jowls, and, when his chin sank against his neck, it made deep creases in the unhealthy flesh.

"You do not choose to speak?" he said at last.

She studied his face, already falling into the old habits of assessing his mood, of trying to sense what he was thinking. "What do you want me to say?" she asked.

He stirred, wheezing faintly with the effort, and leaned forward, putting his elbows on the table. His brows rose, and his eyes gazed beyond her. It gave him a pained look. "A man spends his life following but one star, hoping for but one reward. All the other honors and riches and accolades that are heaped upon him mean nothing. Money is but cold metal, medals do not warm the heart, high offices are fraught with the barbs of a fickle populace. But all through his trials he can retire to this secret shrine in his heart, this little hope that someday he will be rewarded for his faithful vigil, his undying loyalty, his. . . ."

"Oh, stop it, Nicolas! The rôle of the betrayed lover doesn't become you. You have no more right to feel wounded over the one time I strayed than I have to take revenge each time you add another mistress to your harem."

The blood rushed into his face; his neck and jowls seemed to swell. With a louder wheeze he shoved the chair back and rose. His red cheeks and his distended belly made him pompous as a turkey cock. "Perhaps the rôle of the righteous governor becomes me more, then?" he said. "Would you like a priest, first?"

"I don't think you brought me here merely to tell me I was to be executed, either," she said. "Why don't we be frank with each other? If you want to be jealous, all right. But you're too shrewd a man to let jealousy wreck you. We've risen together. If one falls, the other falls. You're seeing the truth in that now."

His pose slid off like oil. He pouted, digging his chin into his neck, turning to pace across the room with an elephantine stride. "Damn you, Teresa! Why do I put up with such a witch?"

She had used the shock of truth to shake him, but she knew she could not go too far. She had him on the defensive now, and she had to palliate. She had used his vanity before. "Because you need me," she said. "I'm the only one who sees the greatness in you, Nicolas. You let these others smother it. You're a lion in a bunch of jackals. And they're trying to pull you down now."

He began to puff up like a pouter pigeon. "It's true. A lion.

Jackals. The army has deserted me. The Assembly has turned on me."

"Why did you dismiss so many Assemblymen?"

"I knew you'd planted them there. I thought . . . ."

"You didn't think at all. And Biscara had men watching to fill every vacancy. It was his plot from the beginning. He knew he couldn't pull you down without getting rid of me. Gómez planted Lamar's proclamation in Morgan's room."

He paced agitatedly, shaking his head. "They've passed this inconceivable tax. The people blame me."

"And they'll keep putting the pressure on the people till they revolt. Then Biscara will denounce you, and he'll become the new governor. Don't you see?"

"How can I see? I'm like a man in a dark room. It used to be I knew every move that was made in Santa Fé."

"You had my spies, then."

He shook his head like an angry bull. "One must pay spies. The treasury is empty."

"What did you do with all my money?"

He glanced at her, then looked away guiltily. "I paid the government's debts to Ryker and the other Americans. I thought it would give me their support."

"They're realists. They'll support the strongest man. But you can be the strongest man again. Start by reinstating Captain Pérez. It'll give you the army back."

"That pup, that traitor . . . ."

"He's not a traitor. He's maintained his loyalty when a dozen others betrayed you."

He made a grumbling sound. Petulantly he pulled at his lower lip. "Very well. But that is only the army."

"Biscara can be brought to heel. There is still the Expulsion Law."

"I invoked it. He laughed in my face. Who would enforce it for me?"

"You'll have the army again."

"There's still the Assembly. Even without Biscara, it's full of his men."

"Name them."

"Escudero, Archuleta, Echevarri, the traitor Gómez . . . ."

She pursed her lips. "Escudero owes my monte tables a hundred thousand *pesos*. It would break him, if I claimed it. Don't you think he'd resign the Assembly to escape facing financial ruin?"

Amado stood against the wall, breathing softly, the petulance beginning to recede from his face. He saw her looking at the silver box on the table. He nodded at it, and she opened the lid, fingering out a cornhusk *hoja*, swiftly tapping tobacco into it from the copper flask. The *tenazitas de oro* lay on the table, and she slid the rolled *cigarrillo* into them, lifting it to a candle. She sucked in a long lungful of smoke, eyes closed. She exhaled it on a husky breath. *"Dios,"* she said. "How can a little thing mean so much?"

"It was cruel of me," he said. "I should have had some sent up." He moistened his lips, watching her closely. "Archuleta?"

She opened her eyes. Then she smiled. "Two years ago a letter fell into my hands, from Archuleta to Mirabeau Lamar. Archuleta agreed to help the Texans in return for a high post in the government they set up here." She took another long drag. "Do you think the Assembly would let such a traitor remain in their midst?"

He tried to hold it back, but he couldn't. His eyes receded in their pouches of fat, and his jaw sank against his neck till he had three chins, and his great belly began to quiver. "Teresa, you are incredible."

There was one thing left. It had been in her mind from the beginning. The need to ask it now was like a pain. Yet she knew Amado too well. She knew his tempers and his moods, his strength and his weakness. She knew just how much she could get from him and just how far she could drive him. And she had gotten all she could possibly hope for now.

She had him half convinced that it had been but a thing of passion with Kelly Morgan, an affair of the moment. Amado could understand that. He had taken a thousand women without love. She could not flaunt it in his face now. His pride, his ego, his monstrous vanity would not take it. If she goaded him, she would be back in jail, helpless to aid Kelly Morgan. The only way she would be any good to the trapper was to gain back her own power. To ask for Kelly Morgan's pardon now would be to lose everything she had just won.

Chapter Twenty-One

 She was in her *sala* again on Burro Alley, spinning her webs, weaving her plots. Pérez was released and brought to Teresa before he saw Amado. At first, the captain was reluctant to support the governor further. But Teresa convinced him it was better than the chaos that would result if Amado were deposed. That same night she sent a rider south to catch up with Uvalde and the Texans to see what could be done for Kelly Morgan.

With the army behind him, Amado again threatened to invoke the Expulsion Law. It was stalemate, and Biscara knew it. Once more he retired sullenly to his *hacienda* south of Santa Fé. The Archuleta letters were presented at the Palace, proving without a doubt that Archuleta had been ready to betray New Mexico. The Assembly itself voted to send him to the capital for trial. It started the stampede. Seeing how thoroughly Teresa had regained her power, the rest of the Biscara faction capitulated. Gómez resigned as Secretary and left for Taos.

Within the week the rider returned from the column of prisoners. Morgan was still alive but so feeble and sick they had to carry him in a *carreta*. To arrange his escape would be dangerous, next to impossible. He was unable to sit a horse and couldn't walk six paces. Uvalde knew what a touchy subject Morgan was to Amado and would take no bribe, fearing reprisal from the governor. He had ordered his troops to shoot any prisoner attempting to escape.

Teresa's first impulse was to go to Kelly Morgan. Yet she knew how foolish that would be. Things were at the crucial stage. Her very survival here depended upon a constant manipulation of a million interlocking details. A week away and the whole precarious network would crumble, and Morgan's survival depended upon her survival.

She knew the next man she sent south would have to be more than a courier. It was going to be a long process and would take someone with daring and resourcefulness. Felipe Vargas had worked for her ever since he'd gotten the Archuleta letter. The excitement and danger had appealed to the rogue in him, she had paid him handsomely, and he had become as devoted to her as Pérez. She gave him a petition to General Santa Anna for Kelly Morgan's pardon, a message to the United States Minister in Mexico City, and money to bribe Morgan's way out if all else failed. It was not till March of 1842 that Vargas returned. She was having her morning chocolate and *buñuelos* when Pepita ushered Vargas into her chamber, sun-blackened, caked with the dust of the long journey, hollow-cheeked with exhaustion. He knew how eager she was for news and spoke without preamble.

"I did all that was humanly possible, *señorita*. Mexico is still bitter over the war with Texas. Santa Anna refused a pardon. Morgan had been out of the United States so long his citizenship was cloudy. The American minister's hands are tied. I used up all the money, trying to bribe Morgan's way out. It wasn't any good."

Her face grew pale. She locked her hands together and paced nervously across the room. "Is there nothing we can do?"

"We need more time," Vargas said. "Morgan's been transferred to Perote, at Vera Cruz. Uvalde damned Morgan at the trials with a pack of lies and half truths. We're lucky he wasn't executed."

Uvalde! She almost cursed. She knew he had done it under orders from Amado. This was Amado's jealousy of Morgan, his revenge on her. "Can't we plan an escape?"

"It would be too risky. If he were caught, he'd surely be executed. I wouldn't try it till everything else fails."

She shook her head helplessly, still pacing. "I've got to go to him now. I've got to. . . ."

"It would do no good," Vargas said. "Mexico City isn't Santa Fé. You can serve him better by staying here where you have power and influence."

She knew he was right. It was the same barricade she had met before. Her whole position here, financially and politically, depended on her constant presence in Santa Fé. A few weeks away and she'd be ruined. How could she help Morgan then?

The months that followed were an anguished, unreal time. General Sam Houston, now president of the Republic of Texas, was working unceasingly for the release of the Texas-Santa Fé Expedition. Through Texican traders on the Santa Fé Trail, Teresa got into correspondence with Houston. He promised he would do all he could, but since Morgan was not a citizen of the Republic, Houston had no official claims on him. In June of 1842 Santa Anna released most of the Expedition. The only exceptions were those classed as spies. When the list of freed prisoners reached Santa Fé, late in the year, Morgan's name was not on it.

Grimly Teresa took up the fight again, but the troubles between Texas and Mexico were still growing. There was a strong movement in the United States to annex Texas. To

Mexico, which had never recognized the independence of Texas, this would be tantamount to annexing a slice of Mexican territory. In 1843 the Mexican president, Santa Anna, warned that "the Mexican government will consider equivalent to a declaration of war . . . the passage of an act for the incorporation of Texas into the territory of the United States."

A thousand times, during those years, Teresa must have stood in the little room where Morgan had finally possessed her, remembering his hands on her body, remembering her hopeless sobbing, trying to resurrect the picture of his face. And a thousand times she wondered how that face looked now, in the castle at Perote. . . .

The viceroys of old Spain had built the prison fortress a century before. Its gray rock walls stood on a shelf in the mountains behind Vera Cruz, seven thousand feet above the sea, and the peak of Cotre de Perote towered a mile higher above it. Within its twenty-six acres was a honeycomb of cells and dungeons where countless political prisoners had languished and died. In one of these cells, deep in the earth, they had put Kelly Morgan.

He was not the same man who had left Santa Fé so long ago. An eternity spent in this dark gloom, near death from dysentery and malaria, had left marks he would never lose. The meat and muscle had been bled from his great frame till he was barely more than a skeleton. His face was a savaged, hollow-cheeked skull from which burning eyes stared, close to insanity. Behind him was an endless time of which he had only foggy memory—a time of delirium and semi-consciousness and utterly blank spaces when he must have been hovering near death. But these last months he seemed more lucid; the malaria was gone, and the dysentery had lessened, and he had enough strength to move about. Felipe Vargas had been to see him several times, bringing him gifts of food, telling him of Teresa's efforts to free him, trying to encourage him. On his last visit a month ago Morgan had asked Vargas the date, and had begun marking off the days with scratches on the wall. As near as he could tell, today was February 10, 1846.

Sometimes, when he had the strength, he paced. Sometimes he merely sat on his tattered, louse-ridden blankets, head tipped back against the wall, eyes closed. When he heard the tramp of boots in the hall outside, he thought it was merely the turnkey with his dinner and did not move or open his eyes. But when the barred door was unlocked, and he finally looked up, he saw a pair of Mexican dragoons. Crossed belts gleamed whitely against bright blue tunics, and beneath tall shakos their faces were set in a dark, professional indifference.

"I am Sergeant Antonio Barrios, señor," one of them told Morgan. His voice sounded strangely tense. "We have come to conduct you to Mexico City."

Morgan got to his feet slowly, with great effort. He was too feeble for much reaction. He had been through so many of these trials before. They were interminable affairs, accomplishing little. He would almost rather stay in the cell.

Between the dragoons he shambled into the corridor. The turnkey let them through the barred door at the end of the hall, and they started up the curving stone stairs. Somewhere water dripped endlessly, and the torches socketed against the walls cast a weird, wavering light across the dragoons' tense faces. Halfway to the next level another pair of troopers met them.

"You're to see the governor again before you leave," one of them told Barrios.

The dark-faced sergeant seemed angry. "What is it? I got my pass signed before we came down."

"Something about your papers," the soldier said.

He lowered his musket from his shoulder. It was pointing at Barrios. The sergeant frowned at his companion. Then, shrugging, he aided Morgan on up the steps. At last they reached the office of the governor of the prison. The sentry outside the door passed them in. By one of the windows was a lieutenant. Behind an ornate desk sat the governor of Perote, Colonel Rivera. He was a man in his early fifties with a sallow, bald pate and shrewd, squinted eyes.

"Your papers are hardly in order," he told Barrios.

"What more do you want?" the sergeant asked. "They're signed by General León himself."

Rivera looked toward the officer by the window. "Lieutenant Salazar has just arrived from Mexico City. His regulation is also signed by General León and contains a court decree that *Señor* Morgan is to be executed by a firing squad tomorrow."

Barrios glanced sharply at Salazar, face pale and taut. "There must be some mistake. . . ."

The governor stood, hands flat on his desk. "Indeed." He spoke crisply to the troopers who had brought them up. "Take the prisoner back to his cell. I'm holding Barrios in custody till this is settled."

The two soldiers guarding Morgan and Barrios had grounded their muskets. They had not disarmed Barrios. All he had to do was raise his musket. It took them all by surprise. His gun was covering the colonel's chest before the others could even get their musket butts off the floor.

"If you want your colonel alive," Barrios told them, "you will drop your guns and line up against the wall."

The sentry outside heard it and wheeled into the doorway, only to look down the muzzle of the musket held by the dragoon with Barrios. A pale fury replaced the stunned expression on Colonel Rivera's jaundiced face.

"Sergeant . . . are you insane?"

Barrios did not answer him. He spoke in a taut, jerky voice to his companion: "Pío, bind them with their belts, then find something for gags."

Morgan still couldn't quite comprehend what was happening. He was so weak he had to lean against the desk for support. He gaped at the sergeant. "What the hell?" he said.

"The details later, my friend," Barrios told him. "Hide a gun under your shirt. You may need it."

Pío was working swiftly and efficiently, using the belts that crossed their tunics to bind the sentry and the other soldiers. He pulled Lieutenant Salazar's pistol from its holster and tossed it to Morgan. Realizing that this was some sort of a break, Morgan stuffed the gun into his waistband and dropped his rag of a shirt over it.

Salazar and the other soldiers were tense with frustrated anger, bent forward like dogs on a leash, eyes darting from Barrios to Pío in an avid search for the slightest chance to take them off guard. But the threat of the gun on their governor held them in check. With Colonel Rivera still cursing them, Pío bound and gagged him and put him on the floor with the others. Barrios scooped his pass off the desk and took Morgan's elbow, hurrying him to the door.

"Someone's bound to go to that office soon," Barrios said. "We can only hope we get to the sallyport first."

Stumbling, tripping, growing dizzy from the effort, Morgan hurried between them down the hall. They had to slow up every time they reached a sentry post, but finally they reached the main door. They got across the courtyard and presented their pass to the corporal at the sallyport. The bored non-com had already passed Barrios in, and he only glanced at the pass, not bothering to check for a counter-signature. He nodded to the pair of sentries, and they began to open the heavy, iron-studded doors. The gates were almost open when Colonel Rivera ran from the door of the main building, still struggling to tear a knotted belt off one wrist. He was followed by half a dozen troops.

"Corporal . . . stop those men . . . they're impostors!"

The corporal tried to pull his pistol. Barrios lifted his musket and shot him through the chest. The sentries had put aside their muskets to open the gate. As they scrambled for the guns, Pío lunged against one, clubbing him across the back of the neck. Morgan was too feeble to go after the other one. Robbed of support, it was all he could do to remain erect and pull the pistol from his belt. As the second sentry scooped up his musket and wheeled, Morgan fired. It struck the man in the leg, and he went down hard.

Barrios grabbed Morgan's arm and shoved him toward the gate. The guards with Colonel Rivera were firing now, as they crossed the compound, and others were appearing from sentry boxes around the courtyard. Morgan had only gone three paces, with the bullets kicking up dirt all about them, when he stumbled and fell to a knee. But Pío was there to grab his other arm. The two men half dragged him through the gate. Just outside another pair of mounted dragoons waited with four spare horses by a black coach.

"We can't use the coach now," Barrios shouted. "Get him on a horse."

They lifted Morgan bodily into the saddle and swung aboard other mounts themselves. The coachman dropped off his seat onto the saddle of the remaining horse. Morgan got a glimpse of his face and saw that it was Felipe Vargas.

They raced away from the abandoned coach at a dead run. They had just gotten under way when the first pair of guards ran out the gate, discharging their muskets. One of the dragoons ahead of Morgan clapped hands to his face and pitched off his horse. The coachman started to pull up and veer back.

"Don't stop, Vargas!" Barrios yelled. "He was dead before he hit."

With Barrios and Pío supporting Morgan between them, the riders galloped madly down the winding mountain road. Far below, the jungle spread its misty green carpet over the land, and in the distance the tile roofs of Vera Cruz shimmered in the sun. The effort of running and of battle had drained Morgan, waves of nausea swept through him, and he would have pitched off the horse but for the support of the men on either side.

As they neared the bottom of the precarious shelving road, Vargas plunged off onto the slope, leading them in a scrambling, sliding descent down the steep pitch. At the bottom the dense mass of the jungle swallowed them. They had to slow down, picking their way carefully through the thick undergrowth. Morgan tried to straighten up. His face was sallow and drawn with nausea. Vargas dropped back, grinning at him.

"I'm sorry we had to do it this way, *amigo*. We wanted to do it legally. But only a few days ago we got word that Lieutenant Salazar had left Mexico City with orders for your execution."

"We hoped to make it ahead of him," Barrios said. "The passes were good for us in Vera Cruz yesterday, the uniforms stolen only last night."

"We have almost twenty miles to ride," Vargas said. "Can you make it?"

The sheer daring of the exploit touched something wild in Morgan. He wanted to throw his head back and howl like a curly wolf at being free. But he only had the strength to grin feebly. "I'll make it, Vargas, if I have to wiggle on the ground like a snake all the way to Santa Fé."

The man shook his narrow head. "It would be suicide to go back there. An Indiaman left Vera Cruz this morning. They agreed to stand off Los Palos till dusk. They'll take you to Corpus Christi. You'll have friends waiting there. It's all been arranged."

The world began to spin, and Morgan sagged forward on his horse. He had only a dim, agonized consciousness of the rest of that ride. He knew that it got dark and that sometime later they reached a tropical beach. The yellow moon gleamed against the reefed sails of an Indiaman out in the bay. Vargas built a signal fire, and soon a whaleboat was pulling in toward the foaming breakers. As they beached the boat, Morgan started trying to thank Vargas, but somehow the words were all jumbled up. He left them, being lifting onto the thwarts, and he was still talking when he lost consciousness completely.

It was a long trip. The sun and the sea filled Morgan with renewed vigor, and he soon began to gain in weight and strength. He was not fully recovered, however, when he was put ashore at Corpus Christi Bay in early March. The only settlement on the bay was a huddle of adobe buildings, fortified by a wall of shell-cement, called Kinney's Trading Post. They rowed Morgan ashore in a gig and held him on the beach while the bo'sun went to the post with a note Vargas had given him. Within fifteen minutes the sailor came back in a wagon driven by Bob Whitworth, a man who had fought beside Morgan at San Jacinto. Whitworth chuckled at Morgan's amazement.

"I been waiting for you almost a year," he said. "That Teresa Cavan got in touch with me through Sam Houston. She's been payin' me a reg'lar salary to wait around this bay in case they had to get you out by sea."

Morgan shook his head helplessly. Through the years, Vargas had told Morgan of Teresa's efforts to free him. Yet the scope of her operations never failed to amaze him. "I never knew a woman like her, Bob. In the whole damn' world I never knew one." He looked up as a file of blue-coated troopers passed them at a canter. "What the hell are U.S. dragoons doin' in Texas?" he asked.

"Texas ain't a Republic any more, Kelly. The U.S.A. annexed us in December, while you was on that ship."

Morgan's face darkened. He knew what annexation could mean. Despite their defeat at the hands of Sam Houston in 1836, the Mexican government had never recognized Texas as independent. They had insisted that the boundary between the United States and Mexico was still the Sabine River. The Texans and the United States claimed that the line was the Río Grande, and in between these two rivers lay the bulk of Texas. Whitworth told Morgan that President Polk, to back up the American claims, had moved General Zachary Taylor and the American Army into the disputed territory.

"Might as well declare war," Morgan said. "Santa Anna swore he'd fight if the U.S. took Texas."

Whitworth nodded darkly. "Now we hear General Ampudia's moving to Matamoras with a big Mexican army."

Morgan looked westward, his face bleak, driven. "You figure there'll be fightin' in Santa Fé?"

"That's part of Mexico, ain't it?"

Morgan's great trap-scarred hands knotted together in his lap. "I got to get to her, Bob. I got to get to her right now."

Whitworth stared at him blankly. "Don't be crazy. They'd shoot you dead the first foot you put on Mexican soil."

Morgan clenched his teeth. "There must be a way."

Whitworth clucked at his horses. "You'd be a little safer if you were in with the Army. The officers here think that, if war comes, Fort Leavenworth's the most logical jumpin' off place for Santa Fé."

"Where's that?"

"On the Missouri. Up in Kansas."

"How long would it take?"

"Kelly, don't be a fool. You got to rest. You got to get well."

"Bob, damn you, how long does it take to reach Kansas?"

Chapter Twenty-Two

In the early evening of May 17th, 1846, a rider came at a dead run into the plaza at Santa Fé. Teresa was in her *sala,* checking cash at the faro lay-out. The front door was open to admit early patrons, and Teresa could hear the sound of the running horse beat hollowly against the blank walls along San Francisco Street.

There was a frantic portent to the sound, and she could not help turning sharply toward the door. She had been on edge for weeks, waiting for some word from Mexico City. The last letter she'd received from Vargas had been dated March 9th. He'd told her that the court had decreed execution for Morgan and that, as a last resort, he was going to try to effect Morgan's escape. Since that time she had heard nothing.

As the sound of the galloping horse died abruptly, she felt her shoulders sag. None of her couriers would make such a display of their arrival anyway. Even if the escape had been successful, it was quite natural that she shouldn't hear yet. News always took weeks to arrive from Mexico City.

"You've counted that same stack three times," Antonio said.

She glanced at her faro dealer, then smiled ruefully. At the same moment there was a hubbub at the front door, and Teresa turned to see a Palace maid hurrying through the crowd. Teresa had long been garnering most of the Palace secrets via this grapevine and had a standing cash offer for any information the servants could bring her. The woman grabbed her arm and in a low, tense voice blurted out the news.

"The courier just came from Chihuahua, *señorita*. General Taylor clashed with Ampudia's army near Matamoras. Mexico has declared war with the United States."

It was no surprise. The threat of this war had been hanging over them for years. Yet for a moment she could not think of what it would mean to Santa Fé—only of what it would mean to Morgan. If he hadn't escaped yet. . . .

She shook her head savagely. It had been over two months since Vargas's letter. Morgan was out of Mexico. He had to be. In the meantime, there was so much else to do.

The following weeks in Santa Fé were hectic. None in the town had a clear picture of what the war would mean to them. Amado was in his glory, playing the part of the harried general to the hilt, storming around the Palace and making impressive, clattering rides out of town to the outposts at Taos and Las Vegas, enlisting militia and drilling them in the square. Most of their troubles had been with Texas in this last decade, and everyone looked for the attack to come from that quarter. Amado wanted to garrison all the towns along the Lower River, but there were rumors of a United States force gathering at the eastern end of the Santa Fé Trail. Amado finally came to Teresa for help.

"We haven't got enough men to protect the whole border. If I concentrate my troops on the Lower River, the United States might bring a force through Taos. But if I go north, the Texans might strike down here. A Mexican can't get beyond Bent's Fort without being discovered. No one of my agents has been able to find out what's going on at the other end of the Trail. I've got to find out where the attack will come from, Teresa."

"I'll do what I can, Nicolas," she said.

She sent for Gene Cummings, Vargas's Yankee partner who had been on her payroll ever since the Archuleta conspiracy. After the declaration of war he had fled to the mountains south of Taos to escape being jailed or confined to quarters as an enemy alien. He came to her *sala,* buckskinned, heavily bearded, jumpy as a wild animal from his primitive life of the last months. She told him what she wanted.

"If they're fixin' to come in from Missouri," he said, "I reckon I could find out. If they're buildin' any kind of army at Leavenworth, they'll be askin' for volunteers. A week on the muster rolls and I'd know everything you want."

He asked an exorbitant price for the job, but she knew the risk it involved and agreed to pay it. Through the rest of May and all of June she waited for word from him. Early in July he returned with word that Stephen Watts Kearny had been organizing the Army of the West at Fort Leavenworth. They needed men too badly to question the background of their recruits closely, and Cummings had enlisted without trouble. He had stayed with the force till it began to march along the Santa Fé Trail, then had deserted and ridden ahead. The details he gave Teresa caused Amado to take the bulk of his troops away from the Lower River, strengthening the garrison at Taos and frantically preparing defenses in the narrow defile at Apache Pass, a few leagues outside Santa Fé. It was still July when Kearny reached Bent's Fort, and the people began to flee Santa Fé.

On August 12th two emissaries of Kearny arrived in Santa Fé under a flag of truce, escorted by a dozen United States dragoons. They were closeted with Amado in the Palace. But

Teresa soon got the news that one of the emissaries was Danny O'Brien, the trader who had been with Ryker and Gómez and Teresa when Villapando was killed in the Palace. Teresa knew that he had long ago disavowed Ryker and that he represented the bulk of legitimate American merchants in town. His integrity was unquestioned, and he was trusted by both Yankees and New Mexicans alike.

In the evening O'Brien and his companion, Captain Harry Coombs of the 1st United States Dragoons, visited the house on Burro Alley. Teresa met them in the tile-floored room off the patio. Coombs was a tall, handsome man, dressed in the light blue tunic and dark blue trousers of the dragoons, his stiff shako held ceremoniously under one arm. He did little of the talking, accepting the drink Teresa offered with a polite nod of thanks, seating himself watchfully on a plush chair. O'Brien circled the table, gesturing with his hands as he talked, filling the room with his ebullient, Celtic restlessness.

"It was my mission, Teresa, to convince Governor Amado what an untenable position he is in. The only real force you have is your lancers. And we outnumber them ten to one. . . ."

"Let's say five to one," Teresa murmured. "General Kearny has fifteen hundred and fifty-eight men, and sixteen pieces of ordnance."

Captain Coombs stiffened in surprise, almost spilling his wine. O'Brien turned to him, spreading his hands helplessly, then chuckling.

"I told you, Captain," he said. He looked at Teresa , still smiling. "I should have known better, Teresa. Even so, you must admit the picture is pretty black."

"Not at all. You underestimate our militia. With them we have the superior force."

O'Brien pursed his lips, shook his round head. "Don't try to bluff, Teresa. I know your situation, and it's bad. We gave

Amado a chance for a graceful capitulation rather than a disgraceful defeat on the field of battle."

"Do you think fifty thousand dollars will be enough?" she asked.

This time Coombs stood up. O'Brien shook his head. "Is there nothing you don't know?"

"I know you were a fool to leave the money with Amado."

"He agreed to abdicate."

"He might keep his word. On the other hand, if he feels the whim, he might cut your army to pieces in Apache Pass."

O'Brien smiled. "We know the risk we took. That's why we come to you. We know the influence you have over Amado."

"You ask me to give up all I have here."

"You won't be giving up anything. You'll still have your *sala.*"

"And when you take over, you'll have to deal with the men in power, the leaders of the political factions?"

"I suppose so. We'll work with them."

"Men like Biscara?"

He knew what she meant. "It must be that way, Teresa."

"How else could it be? My alliance with the Palace is the only reason I survive now. Do you think Biscara would let me last a minute if I wasn't protected?"

He was perspiring. He ran a finger around the inside of his flaring white collar. He circled the table again, frowning. "Put it on the basis of your people, then. They are worse off than they've ever been. I know how you've fought with Amado over it, these last years, but it hasn't done any good. The whole thing is too deeply entrenched, too rotten at the core. Kearny plans to set up a decent civil government. No graft, no making *diligencia,* no *ricos* feasting while the rabble starves. We know it can't be done overnight, but it's the concept that counts. You have it in your power to change things, Teresa."

Long years at the monte table had schooled her to an expressionless face. She looked at the floor, as if coming to a decision, but the decision had already been made. How could she betray her people and sacrifice herself as well? O'Brien's assurances were hollow. How did she know what kind of a government the Americans would set up here? If men like Ryker were in power, it would be as bad as Amado. And yet, if the Americans really believed Amado was abdicating, and marched into Apache Pass. . . . She took a deep breath. "I suppose you're right. Resistance would be hopeless." She looked him full in the eyes. "I'll work on Amado."

Time was running out now. Teresa had a meeting with Amado the day after O'Brien left. It did not take her long to see that his pompous production of the 8th and his hectic military activities had been, as usual, a convenient pose. The old caution had taken precedence over his love of pomp and power. He smelled defeat in the air and was preparing a back way out. The fifty thousand dollars O'Brien had bribed him with were probably what had opened the door.

His weak point was the militia. She told him that Captain Uvalde had the muster rolls over two thousand now. Amado sighed disgustedly.

"Armed with pikes and lances and a few old *escopetas*. . . ."

"What if they had decent guns, and ambushed the Americans in Apache Pass?"

She saw the excited glow come to his eyes for a moment at the thought of it. And she knew it was the key that would hold him here. After he left, she put the wheels in motion, and within the hour a hundred men were at work between Taos and Albuquerque, trying to uncover the necessary arms. She put up a standing offer of a hundred dollars for any decent gun handed in. The results were bitterly discouraging. Dozens of ancient flintlocks and smoothbore *escopetas* in execrable condition were presented to the quartermaster in the hopes of obtaining the reward. Only a few Jake Hawkens and one or two Hall breechloaders showed up in the whole lot.

On the 14th she got a request to visit John Ryker at his store. Amado had ordered all foreigners confined to their homes, and Ryker could not visit the *sala*. He was in the back room, smelling of musty beaver pelts and blackstrap molasses. A single candle dripped on the round deal table, and in the shadows outside its circle of light Teresa saw Cimarrón Saunders and Vic Jares seated on baled pelts. She took the seat Ryker offered, with her pair of Navajo bodyguards standing at her back. Ryker peered at her closely, from under his black brows.

"I hear you're offerin' a hundred dollars for a decent gun."

"That's right."

"How about five hundred Yager rifles?"

At first she didn't comprehend. Then she remembered the attack on Pérez at Pecos, and the guns that had never come to light. As the true purpose of those guns came to her, she felt a little sick. No wonder Ryker had been willing to kill Pérez to keep him from finding the weapons. This was Ryker's big deal. All his other operations were puny beside it. He had been planning it for years, and the scope of it was staggering. He saw the wonder in her face and grinned maliciously.

"That's right, honey. The Indians never got those Yagers. I saw this coming a long way off. Either Texas or the United States, I didn't know which, but I knew it would come sooner or later. And I knew Amado couldn't do anything without guns for his militia. That shipment in Eighteen Forty was only one batch. We got Hall breechloaders and Jake Hawkens and enough powder and lead to blow Kearny out of Apache Pass. I want to know exactly what it would mean to me."

She realized what he faced. This was a desperate game he played. Even if Amado won, the Americans would sooner or later find out who had betrayed them. They would hang a man like that if they caught him. Yet she saw what was driving him. He would lose everything by annexation. All he had built was based on the graft and corruption of Amado's regime. With Amado's favor gone and a new order in he would be wiped out. An excitement began to pound at her as she realized this was the key she had been searching for.

"You would probably have anything you asked," she said.

Sweat greased the broad grooves of his broad face. "How about a monopoly on the fur trade in the department of New Mexico?"

She smiled enigmatically. "You have big dreams, Ryker."

"Amado can do it."

She nodded. "And he will . . . for something like this. He's inspecting Apache Pass now. I'll meet with him as soon as he comes back. In the meantime, you can get the guns."

He moved closer. His voice lowered to a husky rumble. "Don't cross me up, Teresa." His eyes dropped to his hands, his corded, hairy hands. "I think I'd kill you myself if you crossed me."

Chapter Twenty-Three

On August 15th at eight o'clock in the morning the Army of the West reached Las Vegas, eighty miles east of Santa Fé. General Kearny and his staff accompanied the *alcalde* of the town to the roof of an one-story building overlooking the plaza. The people pressed in on all sides to hear what Kearny had to say. He held out his hands and in a loud clear voice began to recite his proclamation.

"Mister Alcalde and people of New Mexico, I have come amongst you by the orders of my government, to take possession of your country and extend over it the laws of the United States. We consider it, and have done so for some time, a part of the territory of the United States. We come amongst you as friends, not as enemies, as protectors, not as conquerors. . . ."

The speech went on, outlining Kearny's plans for a civilian government. One of those who listened, standing quietly among the staff members in the plaza, was Kelly Morgan. He had recovered fully now, had regained most of his weight, his old look of restless, animal vitality. But there were marks of his imprisonment that would never die. The twinkle was gone from his eyes, and there were lines around his mouth, deep and compressed, robbing it of the earthy humor that had lurked about the edges even when his face was in repose.

Despite his burning desire to join the Army of the West in

Kansas, he had been forced to rest at Whitworth's home in San Antonio for several weeks after the landing at Corpus Christi. Strong enough to travel at last, he had made the long overland journey to the Missouri. Arriving at Fort Leavenworth in June he had signed on as a scout for the First Dragoons.

The march to Santa Fé had followed, a cruel trek through the scorching summer desert and the mountains around Bent's Fort. But there had been no action up to now. The few small towns they had passed through surrendered without battle.

As General Kearny was concluding his speech, Morgan saw Danny O'Brien ride into the plaza with an escort of dragoons. The trader gasped at Morgan, then forced his horse through the crowd, frowning deeply.

"Man," O'Brien said vehemently, "how did you get here?" Morgan told him briefly, and O'Brien shook his head. "I wish I'd seen you yesterday. Not knowing about you has been like a knife in Teresa's back."

The thought of Teresa went poignantly through Morgan. "She'll know soon," he said grimly.

O'Brien frowned, obviously thinking deeply about something. Finally he glanced up at General Kearny, then muttered: "Will you come with me?"

Wonderingly Morgan trailed the horse to the building. Kearny and his staff descended after he finished speaking. O'Brien dismounted and spoke to the general for a few moments, glancing several times at Morgan. Then he beckoned Morgan to follow, and they entered the door. It was a store, smelling of dried apricots and musty dry goods, a dim place of whitewashed walls and narrow windows. Kearny put his back to the counter, studying Morgan with shrewd eyes. Then he said: "I sent Mister O'Brien on a confidential mission to Santa Fé to meet with Governor Amado and assess the situation there. Officially, the picture hasn't changed. But in Mister O'Brien's opinion Amado might . . . under certain circumstances . . . be willing to capitulate. According to O'Brien there's only one person left capable of holding things together and stopping us."

Morgan knew whom they meant. He moistened his lips. "Teresa Cavan?"

O'Brien nodded. He twirled his watch chain, watching the bright links flash in the dim light. "You know Teresa's been the one who kept the balance of power in Santa Fé for years. Part of her strength lies in the army. Anyone who has Colonel Pérez has the troops. And Teresa's the only one he's loyal to."

"This spy system's another dangerous weapon," Kearny said. "Apparently she knows more about the Army of the West than I do myself."

Morgan knew. They didn't have to go down the list. What about the Assembly? Her influence there was as important as control of the army. With Gómez in exile and Biscara out of the capital she had the rest under her thumb. She'd given half the Assembly their seats and had enough against the other half to hang them if they didn't jump through the hoop.

"All of which leads us to her power over Amado," O'Brien said. "He wouldn't be governor if it wasn't for her, and he knows it. I think she can make him believe almost anything she tells him. But he's ready to abdicate. Kelly, I saw him yesterday, and I'm convinced of it. Teresa's the only one capable of changing his mind."

"Will she?"

"We aren't sure. The one thing we do know is that if she isn't there to hold Amado . . . he'll capitulate."

"The minute that happens the fight for power begins,"

Kearny said. "Everything she's held together will come apart. It will be Biscara and his Lower River against Pérez and the army. It will split the whole town wide open. By the time we get there, we won't have anybody to fight." The general paused, then said: "We've got to be blunt, Morgan. O'Brien tells us this woman is in love with you. Is that right?"

Morgan looked slowly around the circle of their faces. Then he said: "Damn' right."

"Then, if you reached Santa Fé, say, a day ahead of our army, could you get her out of there?"

Morgan did not answer. His blunt cheek bones seemed to push against the prairie-burnt skin of his cheeks till they shone like a drumhead. The only sound in the room was the husky rasp of his breathing. Then O'Brien began to twist his watch chain again.

"In other words, Teresa Cavan holds the key to Santa Fé." The Irishman smiled at Morgan. "And you hold the key to Teresa Cavan."

On the evening of August 17th Governor Amado was due back from Apache Pass. Later that afternoon Pepita informed Teresa that *Don* Augustin Gómez requested an audience. She told Pepita to take him to the now famous room off the patio. He was seated in Amado's great leather chair by the table when Teresa went in, savoring the bouquet of the governor's private brandy. He rose, assayed a courtly bow. He was heavier, his hair almost white, the veins a purple latticework in his doughy jowls. She closed the door softly, smiling, watchful.

"A truce talk, Augustin?"

He sighed. "I am getting too old to carry the burdens of battle, Teresa. How can a man be so astute in some ways and so stupid in others?"

"Perhaps when he wants something very much, Augustin, he becomes blind."

"I suppose that was it. I was naïve as a child. But at last I have seen the sneer behind their smile. The *gente fina* still think me a pig. I know now they are merely using me."

"So now, having gained their trust, you betray it."

Some of the old cynicism returned to his faded eyes. "You and I always understood each other. I am getting too old to ask much. Merely that you find some minor post for me, perhaps customs inspector at Taos, with which I can regain the dignity and respect an old man should have."

"And in return?"

"What I have is of utmost importance to you."

She studied his unhealthy, parchment face, his lips graying with senility. Was she really dealing with an old man too tired to fight any longer? Or was he setting another trap? It didn't matter. She could lose nothing by talk.

"It's a deal."

His eyes squinted with strain. He rose, hands locked together. His gray lips trembled as he told her. O'Brien's true mission had not been completely hidden, Gómez said. Runners were already circulating that Amado had accepted a bribe from the United States to capitulate. Whatever Biscara's politics, he had a hatred of the *gringos* and would do anything to keep them out. But the Army of the West was too close, and things would be in too chaotic a condition for him to do any good if he waited any longer for Amado to step down. The whole thing was a culmination of Biscara's long struggle for power.

Biscara had such a great fear of Teresa's spy system that he knew he could not trust any hired assassins, or even any of his own people. It had all been done within the inner circle of his trusted companions. Gómez had not yet shown Biscara any of his resentment or disillusionment; with his old Machiavellian tendencies he had convinced Biscara of his allegiance, waiting for the moment when something would be put into his hands that he could turn to his own gain. So he was one of the four in the plot, along with Biscara, Captain Uvalde, and Valdez. They were each dead shots, and each stationed in a building at one of the four corners of the plaza. When Amado returned from Apache Pass, he could not fail to pass one of them. His death was certain. As soon as he died, the machinery of the Lower River would go into action, putting Biscara in his place, and he would hold the town against the Yankees he hated.

As soon as Gómez finished, she grasped his wrist tight. "Augustin, if you are telling the truth, you will stay here till it's all over."

He nodded, hands trembling. She pulled her shawl about her bare shoulders and hurried out. She told one of her Navajos to watch Gómez and stop him if he tried to go out. Then she went into the *sala* to get Gato. Before she could tell him what was happening, there was a clatter of accoutrements outside, and the doorman ushered in Colonel Pérez. His blue coat and *mitaja* leggings were filmed with dust, his face haggard and tired-looking.

"Hilario," she called sharply, "you aren't with the governor?"

He rubbed red-rimmed eyes. "He sent me ahead to clear the plaza and make things safe. He's about a mile behind."

She hurried to him. There was no time for privacy. In a tense mutter she told him of the plot. "You've got to get to them," she said. "Uvalde has rented one of the private gambling rooms at La Fonda. Biscara's supposedly making a friendly visit to the Arballos. Their sitting room window looks out right onto the plaza."

He shook his head. "I almost think it would be best to let them go through with it. You should have seen him this morning. A pig, a pompous pig. He is crazy with power. He had Crespin Vigil sent to La Garita for neglecting a salute. He knows nothing of engineering. The defense he plans will get us wiped out. I think he should cheerfully suffer that if it meant more fame for him."

She shook his arm. "It's not him you'll be saving, Hilario. It's your people, your country. If Amado is killed, everything will go to pieces. The Americans will conquer us without a shot. Biscara could never pull things together. We have to save Amado. Between us we can control him, we can make something decent out of this town. . . ."

"You've told me that so many times before. It's just gotten worse. What can we win, if he capitulates, anyway?"

"He won't. I've found the guns for the militia. You'll have an army that will overwhelm the Americans."

She saw it reach the military man in him. His eyes took on a shine, and a fine sweat broke through the film of dust on his cheeks.

"There's no time to explain. Just believe me. We've got to save Amado," she said. He hesitated, then wheeled toward the front door. She caught his arm. "The Palace Avenue door. You'll be under Biscara's gun on San Francisco."

He turned back, and she ran with him through the countless rooms and halls to Palace Avenue. They hurried down the avenue to the square. This was the only safe corner of the plaza, for it had been Gómez's post. The dozen dragoons that had come with Pérez were spread around the square, pushing the crowds back against the walls, clearing the way for the governor. A horse holder stood with the two sentries at the Palace door, tending Pérez's handsome black mount.

The colonel ran across the square toward the black,

calling to a corporal: "Lopez, gather your men here . . . !"

Then—like a pull of smoke staining the sky above the flat roofs on the south side of the plaza—Teresa saw the dust: Amado, coming in off the Trail.

She called sharply to Pérez, but her voice was lost in the clatter of accoutrements and the tramp of horses as the dragoons crossed the plaza from every side to form in front of Pérez. He hadn't heard Teresa, and he hadn't seen the dust. By the time she reached Pérez, the governor would be in the plaza. She was the only one who could stop Amado in time.

Picking up her skirts, she ran across the plaza toward the south side, coughing in the dust raised by the dragoons, shuddering through the knots of confused people, hoping against hope that Biscara or Uvalde would not see her in the general confusion. She passed the cottonwoods, the sundial in the center, and recognized the yellow walls of La Fonda ahead. She saw Amado's mountainous figure on his great mule as he galloped down the street toward the plaza.

"Nicolas," she called. "Stop, turn back . . . !"

Ten feet from the square, he started reining in his mule. Skirts held high, stumbling and gasping, she reached the corner. Uvalde's room in La Fonda was directly across from her now. He must have seen her, must know what it meant. Still running, she saw shadowy movement in the open window. She knew she had but an instant left. As the mule ran past her, skidding to a clumsy halt, she reached up and grabbed Amado's belt. She threw all her weight against it. The governor's mouth popped open in surprise, and he toppled from the saddle. As he fell, three shots cracked out in the plaza.

One of the bullets struck the mule, and the beast screamed and reared. At the same time Amado hit the ground beside Teresa, his weight making the earth tremble. Hand still caught in his belt, she was pulled to one knee.

The wounded mule was running wild through the plaza. Pérez's dragoons had split into four squads, each squad charging toward a corner of the plaza, lances down. The sight must have panicked Captain Uvalde. With an abrupt shout he jumped from his window and tried to run for it. Two lancers caught up with him and spitted him from behind like a pig, lifting his body up, kicking and squalling, before they dropped it into the road and loosed their bloody blades.

Crouched by the governor, with the dust settling about her, Teresa saw that Pérez led the squad charging Biscara's post on the corner of San Francisco. The colonel waved his saber as a signal to his men, his shout cutting through the other babble. "A pair of you down Gallisteo to the Alameda. I'll take the front."

As they split up, Amado heaved his bulk to a sitting position. He was wheezing, stunned. He looked about him, the glazed look receding from his eyes. He glanced at La Fonda, then at the wall of the house behind him. There was a bullet hole in the wall, about the height of a mounted man's chest. He drew a shaky breath, trying to grin.

"*Gracias, chiquita.* Had you not pulled, that bullet would be in me instead of the wall."

She hardly heard him. She rose from her knees, watching Pérez as he swung off his horse before the Arballo house. The door opened before his rush, and he disappeared inside. The two dragoons following ran in after him. Another dragoon came at a gallop through the crowd.

"Valdez has escaped by the Alameda. Corporal Ortiz took a detail after him. . . ."

"Join them," Amado squealed. "Follow him down. Kill him!" He pulled and wheezed, trying to get to one knee. "Teresa, help me up."

She paid him no heed. Wondering why there was no fear in her, she started toward the Arballo house. Pérez and his two men had left their horses at the door, and a crowd was gathering around the stamping animals. Teresa was halfway to the corner when the muffled shots came from inside the building.

A moment later a man staggered from the door. He had a smoking pistol in one hand. The crowd spread from him in fright. Looking over his shoulder at the house, he stumbled three steps into the street, then fell forward on his face. It was *Don* Biscara.

Before Teresa reached him, one of the dragoons ran from the door. He went to Biscara and turned him over. The man was dead.

The dragoon straightened, saw Teresa. "We came in from the back," he said. "Drove him toward the front of the house. The colonel met him in the dining room. . . ." He hesitated, lips pale. "You had better come."

Colonel Pérez lay on the dining-room floor. His blood made a spreading stain on the black and white *jerga* beneath him. He had both hands clenched against the bullet holes in his chest, and his handsome face was pale and drawn with pain. She knelt beside him. He heard the rustle of her skirts and opened his eyes. His voice was feeble and shaken.

"Have they sent for the priest?"

"He's coming, Hilario."

"Teresa," he whispered. "Where are you?"

He reached up, pawing frantically for her. She caught his hand and held it against her bosom. Then, with a sob, she bent to him and took him in her arms and put her face against his and began to cry softly and hopelessly while the daylight faded from the window and the darkness crept in.

Chapter Twenty-Four

 It was the night of August 17th. The plaza was empty, a yellow lake bordered by the broken black shadows of the surrounding buildings. The streets were empty, spreading out from the square like the crooked spokes of a wheel, losing identity as they twisted and turned into the blank mud walls of the houses. The people had been told that the Army of the West had passed Las Vegas and was marching on the capital. The people had also been told that the Americans would brand them on the cheek like cattle, rape their women, kill their babies, turn their men into slavery, and those who had not fled to the mountains huddled in their darkened hovels, shivering and saying their Ave Marias and waiting to hear whether they were conquerors or the conquered.

Kelly Morgan moved like a shadow through the willows of the river. Only his long years in the wilderness had enabled him to get past the countless Mexican patrols in the mountains rimming Santa Fé. Kearny had known what was involved. He'd made it plain that the choice was completely up to Morgan. He'd said a man had maybe a fifty-fifty chance of getting through. That was stretching it. But it didn't matter. Morgan knew what was involved, too. A hundred to one chance—he'd still have come. After what O'Brien said about Teresa, they couldn't have stopped him.

Morgan had hoped she would see the light on this one, had

hoped she would realize she wasn't big enough to stop the whole damned U.S.A. But apparently she was still trying to juggle everything on her head. Only this time it was too big for her. The thing was going to blow up in her face, and it wouldn't come when the Army of the West marched into Santa Fé. It would come a long time before that, according to O'Brien, and Teresa would be caught right in the middle of the whole explosion.

Morgan thought of Biscara and Ryker and Gómez and Amado and Uvalde and a dozen others she had used and twisted and dangled on a string all these years—any one of them capable of killing her if she made a single false step in this big tight rope walk. And he prayed to a God he'd never known that he wouldn't be too late.

Moving like a rat against the walls, he made his way to San Francisco Street. At the corner of the Arballo house he stopped, looking down toward the plaza. It was empty save for the shadowy movement of sentries under the *portal* of the Palace.

At last he took the chance and crossed San Francisco, ducking into the blackness of Burro Alley. He ran down to the familiar door, knocking on it. Anticipation was an ache in him now. He wanted the sight of her so badly it hurt.

The door was opened a crack; there was a gasp, and it was pulled wider, to reveal Pepita, one fat hand to her gaping mouth in shock.

"I want to see Teresa."

Pepita gulped, blinked, shook her head wildly. "*Señor* Morgan, we think you're dead. . . ."

"Teresa!"

"*Señor* . . . she is at the Palace." Fear contorted her face. She clutched his arm. "Something bad is happening. Get her out of it, *señor*, please."

He couldn't move for a moment. Then he turned and

started to run. It had begun already. He knew it as sure as he knew his name. This was her last big gate card, and she'd started to turn it already—God damn him to an eternal hell if he was too late.

The guards at the Palace door were expecting Teresa, and they passed her through without comment. The Assembly chamber was ominously dark and quiet, but she saw that there was a light in the governor's quarters. Inocente admitted her, fawning and grinning like a jackanapes.

"The crows fly before the wind, *señorita*. The short man and the fool are seen from afar."

She did not answer him tonight. Her mind was too filled with bitter thoughts about Pérez's death. Inocente frowned, rubbed a thumb over his bulbous nose, and led her to Amado. The governor had already sent his wife to Albuquerque and was alone in the bedchamber. Here was the bed Santa Anna had sent him, a thing of glittering brass whorls and embossed brass posts upholding a complicated canopy crowned with an elaborate brass floral piece. It was a thing of blinding elegance in the mud-walled room, almost overwhelming the governor himself. He had been pacing, but he stopped when he saw her look at the bed. He made a feeble attempt at a chuckle.

"What displeasure it would give my wife to know you were in this room tonight."

She made no attempt to answer. Her eyes swung across the ornate wardrobe, the claw-legged table, the red plush sofa—all trying so pompously to be regal and splendid, and achieving nothing but tawdriness. She looked at Amado. An oily sweat gleamed at the folds of his multiple chins and dampened his shirt till it clung like paste to the gross bulge of his belly. His lips were slack now, petulant as a child's; his little eyes were barely visible behind the veined dissolution of their pouched lids. It was as if she saw him for the first time. Why hadn't she seen him like this before, as a man, instead of a mere tool to gain her ends? She had used his selfishness, his ego, his cruelty, his greed, all for her own purposes, without really knowing what they were, what they meant, beyond what they could do for her.

"What is it?" He was staring at her.

She shook her head. "Nothing."

He frowned, breathing in shallow puffs. "I suppose it's this afternoon. Pérez's death hit us both hard, Teresa. He was the finest. *Pues*"—he shrugged—"he died with a gun in his hand. What soldier asks more? And you . . . I owe a million thanks. Running across the plaza under their very guns. Risking your life for me."

"For you?"

He rose, locked his hands behind him, and paced ponderously across the room. The movement made him wheeze softly. "We have to decide tonight, Teresa. The Americans will be at Apache Pass tomorrow." He stopped near the foot of the bed, toeing a heavy black satchel. "I suppose you know how much O'Brien offered me to capitulate. I don't know whether it came from the traders here in town or the American government. Either way, it is a tempting offer."

This ain't freedom. Morgan's voice came, out of the past, almost as if he were in this room, beside Teresa, speaking. She looked at her hands. An hour ago they had been dark with Pérez's blood. He had represented everything that was fine and loyal and honorable in her people. And her hands had been dark with his blood.

"Fifty thousand dollars would give a man a fine start somewhere else," Amado continued. "Chihuahua, Vera Cruz, any of the departments could use a governor with my talents . . . and that kind of fortune. On the other hand, I could cut the Americans to pieces in the pass if my militia were armed." He glanced at the satchel again, chuckling slyly. "It would be even better to be governor here . . . with fifty thousand dollars."

This ain't freedom. You could have a million dollars. You could own this whole town. You'd still be trapped because you'd be afraid to trust one man in it.

"Were you able to get any guns?"

Morgan had been right. She had struggled to escape one subjection only to become enslaved by another— the subjection of lies and cheating, conspiracy and plot. And fear. Her fear had perpetuated Amado. And to perpetuate him she had killed Villapando, and Pérez. If only she had gone with Morgan when he had first asked, if she had refused to hire Villapando for them, if she hadn't asked Pérez to save Amado from Biscara. . . .

"Teresa!"

"What?"

"I said could you find any guns?"

In that moment all the last years seemed to sweep against her, gagging her with the knowledge of what would happen if she stopped fighting now. Then she looked at her hands again. What a travesty that it should take Pérez's death to make her see the truth. It was like a debt that she had to pay, to Pérez, to Villapando, to Morgan, to all those who had ever suffered by her fear. "No," she said. "There are no guns."

Amado's sensual lips compressed, and his chin sank against his neck, creating half a dozen fat furrows. He was but a foot from her now, watching her closely. "And if I capitulate," he wondered. "What of you?"

In his face she could see some of the sly lechery that had always seemed to characterize their relationship. But now there

267

was something more, a shine to his eyes, a beaded moisture on his upper lip, hinting at the real needs he had always hidden behind that mask. She had sensed those needs before, had felt that the lechery and the buffoonery were merely a defense. As long as he made a sly joke of it, her rejection couldn't hurt him. But underneath it wasn't a joke. And now she had to use it.

She lowered her eyes. "I suppose I'll be finished, Nicolas."

"You don't have to be." He moved closer. "Instead of the end, Teresa, it could be the beginning. You always said it. We rose together. We could do it again. The governor of Chihuahua is in dishonor with Mexico City. The army is disaffected. A *grito*, a *pronunciamiento*, and we could be in again."

She bit her lip. This would be the hardest part. This last act, this last lie.

He clutched her arms, breathing heavily. "More than just partners, Teresa. You know how little my wife and I have left. You know how I've always wanted it, with you. If I thought you would go with me, that way, I would abdicate tonight."

Her lower lip began to tremble. She didn't try to stop it. She looked up into his face, and she felt a feverish flush run into her cheeks. It made a convincing picture. "Nicolas," she breathed. "Why did I fight you so long?"

"¡Alma de mi vida!"

With a gusty sound he took her in his arms. She permitted it. He smelled of sweat and perfume and sour chili and *pincho de aperitivo*, and being held against the perspiring blubber of his belly was like being pressed into the softness of a hog, an eunuch. She let him kiss her, and she cursed him and began to cry because this was the last rôle she had to play, this thing of disgust and revulsion and strange pity for a man who was at once ridiculous and frightening, a buffoon and a tyrant, a giant and a little boy, a man she had sometimes admired, sometimes feared, and often hated. He thought the curse was passion, and the crying for him.

"Teresa, I never guessed . . . you always seemed against me . . . how could you hide so much feeling for me?"

A hysterical little laugh ran through her sobbing. "Because it's over now, Nicolas. I can show you what I really feel, no more hiding, no more being afraid, no more acting, just what I really feel. I'm thinking of a man I hated and loved all at once, a man I never really understood, a man who told me many things I didn't believe, but now I know, now I know. . . ."

"Of course you do. We'll go south together. You and I. . . ."

He tried to kiss her again, but she pushed him away, her face all twisted and wet with tears. "You've got to go now, while there is still time."

"But you . . . ?"

"Someone has to stay behind to make explanations. If they find out you're going, there are some who might follow. You know Gómez is still alive."

He held her by the arms, frowning. But lust blotted out suspicion. He wanted to believe; for years he had wanted to believe. And now, at last, he had broken her resistance. She had come to him. His ego would support no other answer. She could see it all in his face. He had read passion for him in her hysteria. He accepted it as entirely as a schoolboy, flushed and trembling with the victory of first conquest.

"I'll tell the dragoons you've gone ahead to Apache Pass," she said. "You'll have a whole night's head start. I'll meet you at Lemitar tomorrow."

"You're right," he said. "Always right. What would I do without you? Inocente!"

His call brought the half-wit, scurrying from the other room. Together they threw clothes into a bag, took the satchel with the money. Teresa followed to a rear door. Here Amado took her in his arms again. She began to cry. The shock of Pérez's death and the intense strain of this grotesque sham had left her little control over her emotions. He covered her wet face with kisses.

"It's all right, *querida*. We won't be parted for long. A few hours, a day, and then the world."

"Go on, Nicolas. Please. You haven't a moment to lose."

She sagged against the door frame, watching them scurry through the empty courtyard. A coach had been waiting at the stables, and all Amado had to do was climb in. The sentry at the *zaguán* did not challenge. He undoubtedly thought the governor was going to Apache Pass.

She stood emptily in the open door, the storm of emotion gone. It was all over now. They were all gone. Pérez, Biscara, Amado—all the men who could have held the town together. There was no one left strong enough to meet the Americans. They would have Santa Fé tomorrow.

She knew what she had lost. The whole intricate structure she had built would topple, and she with it. But perhaps, in her loss, the town gained. Perhaps all the greed and the misrule and the corruption that had fed on her conspiracies would be gone, too. On their wreckage the Americans could build something better for the people.

Then something new crept through her. A sort of giddiness. And she knew what it was. Whatever lay ahead, she had cut her last bonds. There was no fear in her. She was surprised at that. No fear of the future, of men, of anything. Maybe later it would be different. Maybe the fear would come again, the bitterness, the regret. But now she knew Kelly Morgan had been right, right about everything. That's what he had meant, when you were really free—like flying with the eagles.

Chapter Twenty-Five

 Kelly Morgan stood in the black shadows under the *portal* of the Arballo house, on the corner of the plaza. He had stood there for precious moments, waiting for the break that would allow him to cross the square to the wall surrounding the Palace. But he was stalemated by the sentries pacing in front of the Palace. He knew what it would mean, an American, to be seen by them, in this town tonight. He had thought of circling back through the streets to the Arroyo Mascaras and coming on the Palace from behind. But that would take too long. The pattern of things was like a pressure against him, building up till he thought it would burst.

There was a creak of the *zaguán* gate in the wall surrounding the compound at the rear of the Palace. The gate swung open, and a black coach clattered out, pulled by four snorting bays. The horses broke into a gallop toward the square, the coach rocking and tilting. Morgan saw his chance. The coach would hide him momentarily from the Palace. As it entered the plaza, drawing the attention of the sentries, he darted down the wall on the west side of the square. Rattling, roaring, pitching, the coach passed in front of him, hiding him from the sentries. Then it was gone, leaving a silvery cloud of dust that didn't settle between Morgan and the sentries till he had reached the corner of the Palace. He flattened himself against the wall around the corner from the soldiers, panting.

As the coach disappeared southward, down Galisteo, a line of wagons rolled slowly into the square from Palace Avenue. There were a dozen of them, with barefooted Indian drivers pacing beside the mules. Two mounted men were in the lead. Morgan recognized John Ryker and Cimarrón Saunders. Ryker halted his horse by the Palace *portal*, dismounted, and said something to the sentries.

Morgan didn't have time to wait in order to piece it together. Still driven by the fear he had seen in Pepita's face, he moved like a rat down the wall, passing the zaguán. He knew the place where woodsheds backed up against the wall, at the rear. He found it and clawed his way onto the roof; from here he reached the top of the wall, bellying over, dropping down inside.

Most of the troops were at Apache Pass, but a few dragoons still guarded the Palace. He slipped through the dark maze of servants' quarters, officers' houses, stables, and barracks. He huddled against the well as a woman crossed the patio, carrying washing; he dodged from there to an alley between two adobes as an officer stepped from his door to light a pipe, looked at the moon, and moved back inside. There was only twenty feet of open compound between Morgan and the Palace. Heart thudding, he started across it.

Teresa had remained at Amado's bedroom door long enough to make sure he left the compound. She had heard the call of the sentry at the *zaguán* gate, the rattle of the coach as it passed out. Now she seemed drained of emotion, of will. She walked listlessly through the room with its brazen bed, through the outer chamber, to the Assembly chamber door. It was completely dark in the room, save for the feeble stripes of moonlight that came through the narrow windows. She was one step into the long room when the door at the opposite end of the hall opened. Candlelight bloomed across the floor. She saw that it was a sentry carrying a tin sconce in one hand, a carbine in the other. Behind him came John Ryker and Cimarrón Saunders.

The dragoon crossed the room, peering at her. "*Señor* Ryker seeks audience with the governor."

Ryker came toward her. She tried to block his way. The strained look in her face made him suspicious, and he caught her arms, swinging her out of the way, stepping into the open door of the executive chamber. He crossed that to look into the bedroom. Teresa glanced after him, then started toward the entrance of the Assembly chamber. Saunders blocked her way.

"I've got to get back to my *sala*," she said.

He pulled a pistol. "You'll wait here."

Ryker came back, frowning. "Where is he?"

She shook her head. "I don't know. I came here. He was gone."

His swarthy cheeks glowed with rising anger. "You're lying. You'd know if he was in. You wouldn't come away unless he was here. Where is Amado, Teresa?"

"I don't know."

He grabbed her by the shoulders. "You do know!"

The pain of his grip made her cry out.

The dragoon started to lower his rifle, stepping toward Ryker. "*Señor* . . . ." He passed in front of Saunders, and the red-bearded man whipped his pistol up and brought it viciously against the back of the dragoon's head. The man fell forward on his face, unconscious.

Ryker was shouting in his rage, shaking Teresa. "Tell me the truth! I told you what would happen if you crossed me! I did it to Villapando right here in this room, and by God, I can do it to you. . . ."

"Villapando?" Face pale with pain, she stared blankly at him. "You?"

"Don't play dumb," he snarled. "You knew who fired that shot."

"I didn't, I didn't. . . ."

"Well, now you do, damn you! You'll tell me where Amado is, you bitch, you'll tell me where he is!"

There was the sound of running feet in a corridor outside. Someone called her name. Saunders whirled, then ran for the door. Ryker was too enraged to notice. He was still shaking her and shouting at her.

"All right!" she panted. The pain brought on a rage of her own. She didn't care any longer; she wasn't afraid, and she didn't care. "Amada's gone." She was through lying, through cheating, through conspiring with cut-throats and traitors. "He's abdicating." She shouted it at him, addressing him the way she'd wanted to talk to Biscara and Gómez and Uvalde and a hundred others through the years. "You can't have anything, Ryker. You've made your last deal. The Americans are coming, and they'll find out and they'll hang you for it. . . ."

With an inarticulate curse he flung her from him. She stumbled backward, tripped, and fell in a heap against the wall. She saw his face contorted with rage, saw him pull one of his Ketland-McCormicks. "I think I'd kill you myself if you've crossed me."

Kelly Morgan ran down the corridor outside the Assembly chamber, Walker Colt in one hand, the echo of Teresa's husky cries still running hollowly through the darkened rooms of the old Palace. He called her name again, wildly, and at the same instant Cimarrón Saunders lunged into the hall, and they both fired together.

Saunders's ball passed Morgan so closely it took a piece

out of his buckskin shirt. Morgan's slug caught Saunders squarely in the belly. The huge man coughed and doubled over. Morgan was running too hard to stop himself and went right into Saunders as the man fell. The heavy body tore the gun from Morgan's hand and spun him around, throwing him heavily against the wall.

He caught himself, as Saunders slid down his legs, and wheeled so that he was looking through the door. He saw Teresa, pulling herself up against the wall. He saw Ryker, a brass-bound pistol in one hand, turned toward him. He saw the complete and terrified surprise in their faces, as moonlight revealed who he was. Then Ryker shouted: "Kelly!" He aimed his pistol to fire.

With a crazed sound, Teresa threw herself at the man. Her whole body lunged against Ryker's arm, knocking it aside. The gun went off at the floor, and the detonation of the shot seemed to rock the Palace. Ryker cursed savagely and flung Teresa aside, pulling his other Ketland-McCormick.

But it had given Morgan time to get his Bowie out. He threw it with such savage force that it struck Ryker in a giant blow, sinking to its hilt in his chest and knocking him backward half a dozen paces till he came up against the wall. He slid down the wall, glassy eyes rolling upward in his face, dead before he reached the floor.

Morgan was already halfway to Teresa. She came into his arms, face taut, dazed. The words came from her in a hysterical, barely coherent stream.

"Kelly . . . what happened? How did you get here? Kelly . . . I don't know. . . ."

He pulled her to him, hard, and she buried her face against his chest, still uncomprehending, yet content for that moment to be held in his arms. Her body was trembling in reaction now. He heard shouts outside, the running of other sentries who had heard the shots. He started to drag her toward the door. It was too late. A pair of dragoons burst in, guns leveled. They stopped, gaping at Ryker's body, at Morgan.

"Ryker tried to kill me," Teresa said. "This man saved my life."

One of the troopers recognized Morgan. "But he's a Texan."

She nodded. "And in my custody."

"The governor will have to confirm it, *señorita*."

Morgan saw a little muscle twitch in her cheek. She was fighting for composure, still struggling against the shock of seeing him here. But she carried it off like a queen. "Amado has left for Apache Cañon. In the meantime, you'll take my orders. There's a wagon train outside. Bring the wagons into the courtyard. No one is to touch them till Amado returns."

The men hesitated. For years this woman's word had been law in the town; they had been subject to her dictates, directly or indirectly, for almost a decade, and it hardly occurred to them to question now.

Teresa looked at Ryker. "Take care of his body, and the one in the hall. I'm taking Morgan to my *sala*."

The soldiers stepped aside. Teresa took Morgan's arm. Her hand squeezed tightly, and he could feel her still trembling. Chin high, lips compressed, she walked out of the room at his side.

The Army of the West arrived in Santa Fé at six o'clock in the evening of August 18th, 1846. They had met no resistance in Apache Pass. News of Amado's capitulation had broken the morale of the dragoons. With no one to lead them, they had deserted the fortifications of the Pass, a great portion of them following Amado south to Albuquerque. The militia, deserted and disorganized, had not even attempted to distribute the arms Ryker had brought.

Kearny and his staff were received at the Palace by the aging lieutenant governor. With sunset turning the clouds to ragged, blood-red banners over the Jemez Mountains, the American flag was run up over the ancient building and Kearny's cannon fired a salute of thirteen guns from the eminence above the town. The detonations shattered glass in the Palace windows and echoed like thunder into the cañons of the Sangre de Cristo Mountains.

Teresa Cavan and Kelly Morgan were a part of the crowd that watched the ceremony. They stood apart, at the edge of the plaza. Morgan had already made his report to Kearny, and this American knew how much was due Teresa for this peaceful occupation of Santa Fé. As Morgan and Teresa walked back to her *sala*, he saw the brooding look on her face.

"It won't be so bad," he said. "We're together now. We can leave any time you want."

She turned sharply to him. "Leave?"

He was surprised. "It's what you want, isn't it? You said you were free now. You weren't afraid any more."

"Free for what?" Her eyes blazed. "To live like a trapper? An animal? Didn't we go through this before . . . ?"

"Who's going to live like a trapper?" he asked hotly. "Don't you think I can do anything but trap beaver? Don't you think I had enough time to figure it out down there in Peroto? A man's got to offer a woman more than a trap sack and a . . . ." He broke off because he could see that she was starting to laugh at him.

"Kelly," she said helplessly, "are we always going to fight?"

He couldn't stay mad. He began to chuckle. "I guess we are," he said. She came into his arms, and he held her. "I wouldn't want it any other way. Red-headed, green-eyed, soft as a cat . . . with claws to match."

THE BLOODY QUARTER

LES SAVAGE, JR.

Paul Hagar has always had hard luck. He's drifted through the Southwest, trying his hand at a few different things, but always with no success. Then it looks like his luck has changed. He has a chance to file for land in the most important quarter section in all of Converse County, Wyoming. Known as the Bloody Quarter, the strip serves as a gateway for the surrounding ranchers to summer graze their herds in the high country. But it is called the Bloody Quarter for a reason—some pretty ruthless ranchers are willing to do just about anything to control it. Even commit murder. Paul Hagar's luck might have changed, all right . . . but for the worse.

___4863-9 $4.50 US/$5.50 CAN

THE SHADOW IN RENEGADE BASIN

LES SAVAGE, JR.

The novels and stories of Les Savage, Jr., have always been famous for their excitement, style, and historical accuracy. But this accuracy frequently ran afoul of editors in the 1950s. Only now is Savage's work finally being restored and presented in all its original glory. Finally, the realism, the humanity, and the honesty of his classic tales are allowed to shine through. This volume collects three of Savage's greatest tales, including the title novella, a brilliant account of a cursed basin where the mineral deposits look like blood, and where treachery has wiped out all the residents . . . except one.

___4896-5 $4.50 US/$5.50 CAN

FIRE DANCE AT SPIDER ROCK

LES SAVAGE, JR.

Rim Fannin will do just about anything to prove that John Romaine, the owner of White Mountain Freight, is the traitor responsible for his father's death. So when he gets word in the sooty blackness of a Tucson alley that twenty heavily guarded White Mountain wagons are traveling by night toward Tubac, Rim signs on as a mule skinner. He isn't very good with a mule whip but he manages . . . until his train is attacked by Indians and he is captured. Rim knows escape is hopeless when his captors take him to Canyon de Chelly. And late one night when the Bear Clan holds a fire dance in the shadow of Spider Rock, he realizes why he has been taken alive. . . .

___4696-2 $4.50 US/$5.50 CAN

Dorchester Publishing Co., Inc.
P.O. Box 6640
Wayne, PA 19087-8640

Please add $1.75 for shipping and handling for the first book and $.50 for each book thereafter. NY, NYC, and PA residents, please add appropriate sales tax. No cash, stamps, or C.O.D.s. All orders shipped within 6 weeks via postal service book rate. Canadian orders require $2.00 extra postage and must be paid in U.S. dollars through a U.S. banking facility.

Name_____
Address_____
City_____State_____Zip_____
I have enclosed $_____ in payment for the checked book(s).
Payment <u>must</u> accompany all orders. ❏ Please send a free catalog.

COFFIN GAP
LES SAVAGE, JR.

When Alan Craig's father was shot years ago, there was no doctor in Coffin Gap to help him. Now Alan returns with his medical degree to what has become a thriving town. But Jada MacQueen's hydraulic mining has polluted the lowland waterways and killed part of the range, and Alan has his hands full trying to head off a possible typhoid epidemic—which means cleaning up the mine. And MacQueen's not the only one against Alan—there's also Bowie French. French used to be Alan's best friend, but now he's the biggest rancher in the area, and he doesn't like the way Alan's interfering with his plans either. Between the two of them, MacQueen and French aim to show Alan just how dangerous it can be to come home again.

___4632-6 $4.50 US/$5.50 CAN

THE
SMOKY YEARS

Alan LeMay

The cattle barons. They were tough, weathered men like Dusty King and Lew Gordon, who had sweated and worked along the great cattle trails to form a partnership whose brand was burned on herds beyond measure. they had fought hard for what they had. . . and they would fight even harder to keep it. And they know a fight is coming. It is as thick in the wind as trail dust. Newcomers like Ben Thorpe are moving in, desperate to get their hands on the miles and miles of grazing land— land that King and Gordon want, and that Thorpe needs to survive. No one knows how the war will end, but one thing is certain—only one empire can survive.

ALAN LeMAY

SPANISH CROSSING

The stories in this classic collection, in paperback for the first time, include "The Wolf Hunter," a gripping tale of a loner who makes his living hunting wolves for bounty and the crafty coyote who torments him. Old Man Coffee, one of LeMay's most memorable characters, finds himself in the midst of a murder mystery in "The Biscuit Shooter." In "Delayed Action," Old Man Coffee's challenge is to vindicate a lawman who's been falsely accused. These and many other fine stories display the talent and skill of one of the West's greatest storytellers.

MAN ON A RED HORSE

FRED GROVE

Jesse Wilder is a man who has seen more than his share of violence. A former captain in the Army of Tennessee, he is inducted into the Union army as a "galvanized Yankee" after the Battle of Shiloh. After the war he heads to Mexico to fight with the Juaristas against Emperor Maximilian. That costs him the life of his wife and his unborn child. All he wants then is peace. But instead he is offered a position as a scout on a highly secret mission into Mexico, where bandits are holding the Sonora governor's daughter for ransom. The rescue attempt is virtually a suicide mission; the small group is vastly outnumbered and is made up of men serving time in the garrison jail. Jesse has every reason to walk away from the offer—but he can't. Not when one of his wife's murderers is second in command to the Sonoran bandit chief.

__4771-3 $4.50 US/$5.50 CAN

THE LEGEND
OF THE
MOUNTAIN

Will Henry

Everything Will Henry wrote was infused with historical accuracy, filled with adventure, and peopled with human, believable characters. In this collection of novellas, Will Henry turns his storyteller's gaze toward the American Indian. "The Rescue of Chuana" follows the dangerous attempt by the Apache Kid to rescue his beloved from the Indian School in New Mexico Territory. "The Friendship of Red Fox" is the tale of a small band of Oglala Sioux who have escaped from the Pine Ridge Reservation to join up with Sitting Bull. And in "The Legend of Sotoju Mountain" an old woman and a young brave must find and defeat the giant black grizzly known to their people as Mato Sapa.

Man From Wolf River

John D. Nesbitt

Owen Felver is just passing through. He is on his way from the Wolf River down to the Laramie Mountains for some summer wages. He makes his camp outside of Cameron, Wyoming, and rides in for a quick beer. But it isn't quick enough. While he is there he sees pretty, young Jenny—and the puffed-up gent trying to get rude with her. What else can he do but step in and defend her? Right after that some pretty tough thugs start to make it clear Felver isn't all too welcome around town. Trouble is, the more they tell him to move on—and the more he sees of Jenny—the more he wants to stay. He knows they have something to hide, but he has no idea just how awful it is—or how far they will go to keep it hidden.

___4871-X $4.50 US/$5.50 CAN

Dorchester Publishing Co., Inc.
P.O. Box 6640
Wayne, PA 19087-8640

John D. Nesbitt

Travis Quinn doesn't have much luck picking his friends. He is fired from the last ranch he works on when a friend of his gets blacklisted for going behind the owner's back. Guilt by association sends Quinn looking for another job, too. He makes his way down the Powder River country until he runs into Miles Newman, who puts in a good word for him and gets him a job at the Lockhart Ranch. But Quinn doesn't know too much about Newman, and the more he learns, the less he likes. Pretty soon it starts to look like Quinn has picked the wrong friend again. And if the rumors about Newman are true, this friend might just get him killed.

___4671-7 $4.50 US/$5.50 CAN